Wolves & Blades

by

Amanda Kaye

To hear about the next exciting release from Amanda Kaye
sign up for her newsletter at
www.amandakayebooks.com/subscribe-now/

1

"Lisette, don't you dare!"

I ignore my sister's shriek as my horse flies across the meadow. The stone wall beckons, daring me. The rhythmic pounding of hooves fills the air. I narrow my brown eyes as we approach the barrier. *Steady, steady ... now!*

The mare gathers her strength, and with one powerful push we're airborne. Wind and silence wrap around us. A whoop rises in my throat as we soar over the wall. A bone-jarring jolt, then we're on the ground. I throw back my head and crow. The mare tosses her mane in agreement, prancing, eager to resume our run.

My sister calls out to me. I look longingly at the open meadows, briefly imagining my victorious escape, before squaring my shoulders with a groan. *Those annoying lordlings will be at the palace soon. I can't abandon Maddie to those two throne-chasers.* Reluctantly, I tug the reins to turn the mare back. She resists, twitching her head, but finally acknowledges my signal.

Maddie's blue eyes are huge as she trots up on her horse.

"Lys, are you all right?" She fans herself. "My heart stopped when you took that jump. It's a good thing Mother and Father didn't see you, especially after the last time."

I wrinkle my nose and grin as I pull the ribbon out of my tumbling hair. "We don't talk about that."

She chuckles. "Of course not. Or the time before that, or the time before that." She leans away as I swat her arm.

"Point taken. Did Mother task you with making sure I act respectable in public?"

"She knows better than to ask me to do something so futile."

"Thank the heavens. You're proper enough for the both of us." I make a face as I tie my blond curls back. "I don't know why she approved of Von Something-or-Other's and What's-His-Name's visit. Being a princess comes with enough duties without being bored to death by uppity lordlings. And why does every noble look alike? They should write their names on their foreheads when they visit, so I can tell them apart."

Maddie's lips twitch. "Lord Von Lagerfeld and Lord Schneider."

"That's what I said, Von Something-or-Other and What's-His-Name. Not that it matters, they're all interchangeable and obnoxious." I deepen my voice and leer at her. "You look stunning today, Princess Maddalyn. May I call you Maddalyn?" I grab her hand and smother it with kisses as she dissolves into giggles.

"They're not that bad." At my raised eyebrow, she relents. "Fine, they are. But it's because they're nervous. I think it's sweet."

"Better you than me." Poor Maddie gets the worst of it. As heir, she has to fend off every relatively suitable—and a lot of completely unsuitable—nobles. *Thank the heavens they won't start sniffing around me until she's off the marriage mart. From what I've seen, the prospects are slim if I want to have an actual conversation.* "We should come up with a code word in case you need to be rescued from them. I can pretend to choke on a scone, or spill my tea in their lap. Ooh, wait, I know! I'll fake a faint. That way, I don't have to talk to them while you go for help."

"I don't think it'll come to that, but I appreciate the offer." She shields her eyes and checks the sun. "We better start back now or we'll be late. We don't want to keep our guests waiting."

I barely keep from rolling my eyes as I nudge my horse toward the palace stables. "Yes, let's hurry back. It would be a shame to miss tea." I shake my head. "Cook's tarts and pastries will almost make it worth being trapped in a room with those halfwits for an hour. If only Oma was back from her trip. She always has fun stories. It would be almost tolerable if she was here."

My sister's gaze drifts past me, a frown on her lips as our horses walk across the field. I try to see what's capturing her attention, but nothing seems worth noting. Just another ordinary day in Lorria. The rolling meadows around the palace scattered with late-summer blooms should be enough to capture my heart, but I can't help feeling restless. My feet want to wander, to see what's over the next hill, around the next mountain. Oma Emera's the only one that's ever understood me. I picture my grandmother tossing her wavy white hair over her shoulder and giving me a wink as she says, "When the road calls your feet, you must go. And you, my darling, my soul's twin—never doubt where your feet take you."

I sigh, fixing my eyes on the horizon. "I hope Oma comes home today. Do you think she actually made it to Slevan this time, or are you betting she got distracted by another adventure? I hope she went because I want to hear everything about it. They're supposed to have an entire palace made of ice, and colors that appear in the night sky. Can you imagine? I'll bet it's even more amazing than I dream."

Her grip on the reins tightens. "Mayhap Mother and Father will let you take a trip there next summer. You'd have so much fun."

"Now who's dreaming? Besides, if they ever let me go on one of Oma's trips, you need to come too. There's a whole world out there waiting to be explored. Don't you want to see some of it before you have to deal with boring kingdom business every day? Father and Mother won't say no if we both ask. We could make a grand tour of it. Oma's been everywhere, knows everyone. She can take us to Travenia, and Rus, and Floren, and …" My breath catches as she chokes out a sob.

My stomach twists. I grab her mare's reins, pulling our horses to a stop, my pulse speeding up. "Out with it, Maddie. What's going on? "

She bites her lower lip, her eyes shimmering with tears. "It's Grandmother. She's been kidnapped."

I burst into the council chamber. "We have to save her! "

My father and his advisors look up from the papers spread across the table. The tall windows lining the room bathe them in a harsh light, creating silhouettes and picking up the light wood tones in the room. The advisors squawk and shuffle their feet at the interruption, but Father stills, his brown eyes tracking me.

He slowly straightens, his blue-and-scarlet tunic a bright spot even in the crowd of yellows and greens, naturally drawing the eye to his royal presence. "We'll discuss this when you're calmer, Lisette." The sunlight glints off the gold crown resting on his brow.

His calm fuels my anger into an inferno. *He's just standing here, doing nothing. Grandmother's been kidnapped and he doesn't care.* "You have to help Oma. The Kingdom of the Wolves are barbarians." My heart thunders in my chest and I can't catch my breath. "You can't just leave her there. They could be torturing her, or—"

"Lisette." His hands grip the edge of the table and he fixes me with a stern look. "Not. Now."

The senior advisor standing closest to me runs a hand across his shiny head, his bushy moustache twitching. "My dear, we all care about the Dowager Queen and want to see her safely returned."

"Then what is there to discuss? Pay the ransom. We have plenty of money."

"They haven't asked for anything."

The surprise snuffs out my anger, and I blink. "Then what do they want then? Why take her?"

"We're trying to find out." He steps closer to me and lowers his voice—not that it matters, since the room is silent. "King Stefan loves you and your grandmother very much. We'll do everything within our power to bring her home." Sympathy shines from his eyes as he pats my blond curls.

I press my lips together. *The curse of being short: people constantly treating you like you're still a child.* I push past the men to Father's side. "Please, Father. There must be something we can do. Offer to pay them anything they want. Give them" —*what do bloodthirsty savages care about?*— "weapons, or jewels, or whatever they ask for. We have to get Oma back." I swallow hard around the lump in my throat.

My father wraps his arm around my shoulders. "I give you my word, we'll bring her home. But as Advisor Odolff said, it's not as simple as paying a ransom. They want us to know they have her, but we don't know why. There's increased activity along the border. The Wolf King might plan to use her as a hostage if he invades Lorria. Or this could be a diversion for something bigger. We just don't know yet." His face softens as he looks down at me. "You can help by keeping this to yourself and not scaring our people. Act normal and go about your day. We need to keep Oma's disappearance quiet for as long as possible, so the people don't panic."

Heaviness settles into my muscles. "There must be something else I can do …"

He shakes his head, smothering my last hope. "We'll determine the best way to deal with the Kingdom of the Wolves. They think they've wounded us, but we're stronger than they know. We'll show the Wolves and the other kingdoms we bow to no one."

I bite my tongue. *Is pride all that he cares about? That won't help Oma.* "It doesn't matter what the other kingdoms think as long as Grandmother comes home. Beg if you have to." I ignore the gasps and mutterings from the counselors, keeping my eyes locked on him.

His mouth settles into firm lines as he glares at the

papers on the table. "We can't show any weakness, not when the Wolves have already humiliated us. We'd never negotiate a reasonable treaty again. We'll get her back, but it will be on our terms."

Fear crushes my heart. "What if she gets hurt? They could kill her."

Father's features are etched in stone. "I have to think of the kingdom. She'd understand."

I clench my fists, my frustration spiraling until I want to kick something. *The Wolf King isn't afraid of us. We've let his kingdom get away with stealing and raiding our border towns for too long. Now the council wants to do what it always does—endless debates and squabbling.* I spin on my heel, stalking out of the room. The door slams closed behind me. My cheeks burn as the guards stationed in the hallway carefully keep their eyes over my head. I brush past them and nearly barrel into Mother coming around a corner.

"Lisette." She grabs my shoulders. "What are you doing? Did you disrupt the council meeting?"

I wrench away from her. "How could you not tell me about Oma?"

"Let's talk about this privately." Her hands are tight as she steers me down the hallway and through the closest door. She closes her eyes and presses a hand to her forehead. "Are you trying to start a riot?"

"Not yet." I pace the room, bumping into furniture and knocking it aside. "The Kingdom of the Wolves has Oma. They hate us. And we're just sitting here."

"Your father is working on it."

"Is he? All I saw was people talking and doing a whole lot of nothing." I kick the table leg. "All he cares about is his reputation and power and—and keeping up appearances."

Mother folds her hands in front of her, her face blank except for the tightness around her eyes. "We can't show any weakness, otherwise we'll end up in another war."

"If they want a fight, we'll give them one. Oma is more important than anything. We need to get her back."

"And we will. We just need more time."

More time. I whirl around, eyes narrowed. "How long have you known?"

Her gaze doesn't waver. "Three days."

Three days! I twist my fists into my skirt and kick the table leg again.

Mother takes my shoulders, more gently this time, and guides me to a chair. She kneels in front of me and takes my hands between hers. "I promise you we'll get Oma Emera back. But you have to trust us. These things are bigger than any one person. We have to think about the kingdom, too."

I grind my teeth and stare down at our hands. *For the good of the kingdom. How many times has that been thrown at me? Everything is for the good of the kingdom. If I hear about the good of the kingdom one more time, I'll scream. What about Oma? What's good for her?*

Mother tucks a finger under my chin and brings my face to meet hers, her periwinkle eyes searching my brown ones. "Can you understand that?" There's a strain around her mouth I hadn't noticed before and new lines at the corners of her eyes.

And if Father and the counselors think getting Oma back isn't the best thing for the kingdom? A chill spreads to my fingers despite the stuffy air and sunshine pouring through the windows. *Oma is the only person who understands me. I can't lose her.* The lump in my throat grows until it's suffocating me. I press my lips together and give her the nod she's waiting for as my stomach clenches.

"Your father and the council are coming up with a plan, you'll see. Give them a few more days."

Oma can't wait that long. It's a long journey to the Wolf Palace, no matter what decision they make. They've already had three days. Are they going to leave Oma in our enemy's hands, suffering the heavens know what, while they waste more time?

Mother continues, "The important thing is not to panic. Everyone thinks Oma is extending her trip. That'll buy us enough time to get her home without anyone realizing something's amiss."

I squeeze her hand to avoid responding. *So that's the story they're spreading. They can keep stalling indefinitely because they know how Oma gets distracted on her trips. How long do they expect to leave her in the Kingdom of the Wolves?*

Mother holds my eyes a moment longer, then stands and smooths her skirt. "I was on my way to the council meeting. I'll speak with your father after. You'll see, we'll have your grandmother home soon. I know it's hard, but you need to be patient and trust us. Everything will be all right. In the meantime, go join your sister and your guests for tea." Mother kisses me on the cheek, then turns and leaves, closing the door with a soft click.

As if I can make polite chitchat while Oma is in danger. I jump up from the chair and resume pacing, my mind starting to race. *Everyone keeps promising Oma will come home safe, but they won't say how or when. We can't leave her in the Kingdom of the Wolves. She's is the strongest person I know, but the Wolves are ruthless killers. Father doesn't want to look weak, but allowing the Kingdom of the*

Wolves to murder—I shake my head, bumping against a chair. *No, I won't even think about it. Why doesn't anyone care about Oma? Don't they love her?*

Stop it, Lisette. I swipe at the tears clinging to my cheeks, then plop down on the seat with a sigh, guilt settling into my stomach. *They love her as much as I do. I know they do. Father's probably just as frantic as I am, but he can't show it because he's the king. If he panics, everyone will panic. And ... I shouldn't have barged into his meeting. No wonder he treats me like a five-year-old. Like he always says, respect is earned with actions, not words. Mother and Father said they're going to rescue Oma. I need to trust them. She's family. They wouldn't leave her in the hands of our worst enemy. Mother will be back any moment to tell me what they're going to do.*

My slipper beats out a silent rhythm on the silver-blue carpet as I snatch glances at the door every few minutes. *Oma must be so scared. She's the bravest, most adventurous person in the world, but being kidnapped ... She knows we'll save her no matter what.* My tapping speeds up. My stomach squirms, knotting as an image of a terrified Oma flashes through my mind. *Father won't let anything happen to her.*

The nervous energy makes it impossible to sit still any longer. I beeline for the window. At the edge of the earth, the tips of mountains rise above the impossibly thick tree line, marking the home of the Kingdom of the Wolves. Appropriate that such a bloodthirsty and deceitful kingdom would live in something called the Black Forest. Even their name, *Kingdom of the Wolves*, is sinister.

Despite being neighbors, our two kingdoms couldn't be more different. Lorria thrives on technology and education, creating wonderful libraries and schools. The Wolf King keeps everyone uneducated and on the edge of poverty so he can control them. Over the years, I've asked Father why he doesn't take over their kingdom so they can share in all the wonderful things we have in Lorria. Usually, I get shushed for being impertinent. As if wanting to help people is something shameful.

Now I wish Father had burned the Black Forest to ash.

Mother and Father say they'll do what's best. So will I. One day. If they don't have a plan to save Oma by then, I'll do it myself. Burn the consequences, Oma's counting on me. The Wolves had no idea what they were starting when they took Oma, but I'm going to make them sorry they ever dared to challenge Lorria.

If they want an enemy, they've got one.

Time's up. Now it's my turn.

The crickets greet me as I lead the pack horse down the moonlit road. I pause next to the tumbled cairn marking the edge of the field, listening for anyone following me or an alarm announcing my absence was discovered. The night is silent except for the nocturnal rustlings of its inhabitants.

The mare bumps her cheek against mine, and I reach up to rub her nose. "Sorry to wake you, sweetheart, but I have a long journey ahead of me and I need you for the first part." I swing up in the saddle and take a last look at the golden palace shining on the hilltop. "Don't worry, you'll be home soon. As much as I'd like company for the trip, my business is going to take me to some unfriendly places."

I fix my eyes on the road ahead and nudge the mare into

a walk. *Hold on, Oma, I'm coming. I'll make the Wolves pay for what they've done.*

This is it?

I clutch the pack to my chest and check the sign again. The man at the coach stop warned me the next inn was small, but the snug, two-story structure tucked in between a few shops and open stalls is barely large enough to be called a house. A thatched roof instead of slate, with oiled paper in the windows instead of glass. The wooden slats are weathered and stained. *Guess I'm roughing it tonight.* At least I won't be here long.

With a deep breath, I duck through the door. I weave through the scattered tables and benches to the innkeeper standing behind a bar, wrinkling my nose as the sour smell grows stronger.

The man mops his face with a brown handkerchief and gives me a friendly smile. "Hello, little lady. How can I help you?"

I arrange lodging for the night, pleased to find they serve dinner in the common room in the evening. *One less thing to worry about.* After the man points me to the stairs, I add,

"I'm also looking for Herr Bannan."

"Egh? What might you need him for?" The innkeeper peers more closely at me.

"He was recommended as a guide. My family sent me to collect plants that grow on the edge of the Black Forest used to make some of our dyes. Our normal supplier fell ill, and the others didn't have enough in stock." The practiced lie falls easily from my lips.

His brow wrinkles. "I've never heard of any special plants out that way."

"It's a bit of a hike, which is why I need Herr Bannan. Do you know where I can find him?" I give my most winning smile.

He frowns. "If you need a guide, there's plenty I can recommend. Lots of the lads know every inch of the land between here and the Black Forest."

"Thank you, but Herr Bannan is the one I need. He knows exactly what I'm looking for."

The man mops his forehead again, his frown deepening. "He's here most evenings." The innkeeper seems to struggle with something, then shrugs. "Be careful with that one."

I thank him, uneasiness creeping over my skin. Then I shake it off. It's not surprising my intended guide has a bit of a reputation. Most people have the good sense to avoid the Black Forest. Few can venture into it and come out alive. If I want to be one of them, I need someone who knows what they're doing and I can't afford to be picky. Herr Bannan was the only name given when I made a few cautious inquiries at the inns along the way.

After a quick wash in my room to rid myself of the road dust, my stomach grumbles, reminding me that the bread and cheese from this morning was hours ago. The innkeeper has disappeared from the common room, so I pick a random direction and set out.

I'd expected the largest town along the Black Forest to be like the one near the palace, but Eelan is small enough to fit in the palace gardens. The shops on either side of the inn carry an odd assortment of clothing and household items. The few food stalls have vegetables and some questionable lumps that may be meat … or leather. It certainly smells like a burnt shoe.

Not willing to push my luck, I continue past them, reveling in my anonymity. My drab brown dress blends in perfectly. I miss my bright skirts and dresses that remind me of the wildflowers around my home, but grays and browns are the common fashion for ordinary citizens. Even the buildings are tans and bland beiges. No colorful doors or window boxes full of flowers. Everyone seems determined to blend into one dull landscape.

My stomach growls again. No signs to indicate a tavern or food stalls in sight. I finally approach an older woman carrying a basket. She kindly points me to a wizened woman standing next to a few stacked crates. Despite my misgivings, a few minutes later and a few coins lighter, I walk away happily munching on a pear and hunk of cheese, two wrapped sticky buns in my pocket for later.

The edge of town is only a few minutes down the road, the buildings giving way to long stretches of fields with homes dotting the landscape. Most of the harvest was collected, but a few farms are still heavy with crops waiting to be gathered. I let my eyes wander down the countryside, ignoring the growing menace at my back. My shoulders twitch as I watch a lamb frolic through the grass, rolling around the field. The chirping birds are muffled, as though an invisible hand is reaching out to smother them. The hair on the back of my neck rises.

Reluctantly, I turn and get my first close look at the Black Forest.

The grass covers the land for a short distance, ending abruptly at the thick line of trees. It's easy to see where the forest got its name: everything under the trees is shadowed; even the sun refuses to touch that part of the world. The border lies about a mile inside, but it's only a technicality. Everyone knows the Black Forest belongs to the Kingdom of the Wolves.

A shiver runs down my spine. *I'm going to enter enemy territory soon.* The darkness seems to grow, its shadowed tendrils reaching out to grasp me. The temperature drops. I rub my arms against the goosebumps breaking out on my skin.

Don't be ridiculous. It's just a forest. Oma's in there somewhere. She needs me. I'm not going to let a bunch of trees scare me.

I straighten up and march into the forest. It's noticeably cooler, even a few scant feet from the open grass. The trees tower overhead, growing larger, blocking out the sun. I force my shaking legs to carry me deeper into the darkness. My pulse races. A chill crawls down my neck. No light makes it through the interwoven branches overhead. Thick grey-brown trunks stab skyward, with barely an arm's length between them. Roots break through the dirt. Patches of slippery moss cover the ground. There's no easy path forward. It's an untamed wildness, so different from the gentle meadows around the palace. Not being able to see more than a few feet in any direction gives me a closed-in feeling. My breath comes faster.

I clench my fists and glare into the darkness, shouting, "I'm not scared of you. You'll be sorry."

"I wouldn't taunt them. They might take it personally."

A shriek rips from my throat. I whirl around, heart pounding.

A gigantic man with an axe looms over me.

All I can see is leather, fur, and the sharp blade glinting
wickedly overhead. Roaring fills my ears. I back away,
holding my arms out in front of me.

And crash to the ground.

I scramble back, hands and feet slipping on the slick
bark and moss.

The man follows me, his bulk blocking everything else.
"Whoa, girl. Are you hurt? "

Images of the axe flying at my head flash through my
mind. "Stay where you are!" I shriek. "Don't come closer." I
hold my breath, my heart racing in my chest. *Do you want to
die on the ground? Get ahold of yourself.* I struggle to my
feet, keeping an eye on the stranger, forcing my brain to
focus on what's in front of me.

My first impression of danger wasn't unfounded. The
man is a beast. Everything about him reminds me of a bear,
from his dark hair and towering height to his broad shoulders
and huge hands. Most of the lower part of his face is hidden
behind several days' growth of beard, but his dark brown

eyes shine through. Even his rumbling, deep voice could belong to one of the creatures. The axe strapped to his back would look like a toy in his hands. Instead of a dull tunic, he's dressed in leathers dyed a deep rusty red, and carrying an oversized pack on his back.

"All right, all right." He retreats a few paces, giving me some breathing room. "Fur and fangs, you startle easily."

His annoyed tone snaps me out of my panic. *He doesn't get to be irritated. He snuck up on me.* "At least I don't go around spying on people. Didn't your mother teach you any manners? "

"Yah, she warned me about girls who yell at trees."

Har, har. He's younger than I thought, probably close to my age. I put my hands on my hips and glower at him. "Well, my mother warned me about men who like to poke their noses into other people's business."

"If I see someone like that, I'll warn you." He crosses his arms. "I was on my way home when I heard someone yelling her head off. If I'd known the big emergency was you scolding a bunch of trees, I would've kept on walking."

"Next time, see that you do." I narrow my eyes. "What are you doing out here anyway?"

He rocks back on his heels, a smirk visible beneath the beard. "I should ask you the same thing. What did the trees do to you? Drop an acorn on your head?"

"Hilarious." I wipe my hands off on my skirt, wincing at the cuts on my palms. "It's not the trees, it's the kingdom. I'm not fond of Wolves."

"Most people around here aren't, but they know better than to provoke them." He pulls the pack off his back and rummages through its contents. "Let me see your hands."

I take a half-step back, thrusting my hands behind my

back. "I'm fine."

"You need to clean those scrapes if you don't want an infection." He inspects a small jar, then shoves it back in his pack.

The cuts throb. "I'll wash up when I get back to the inn."

He shakes his head, holding out a small bundle of leaves. "Here. Chew them up, then spread the paste on the cuts and leave it on for ten minutes."

Chewed up leaves? Ew. "No, thank you." I take another step back.

He snaps, "I don't bite. You don't have to be so afraid. I'm trying to help you."

I cringe, then snap back, "I'm not. Afraid of you." *Am I? No—I refuse to be. If one man can scare me, how am I going to face the Kingdom of the Wolves?* "You surprised me, is all. I didn't expect to find anyone else out here."

"Neither did I. What are you doing here? You never said."

I tilt my chin up. "You first."

He breaks out into a wide grin. "I guess you aren't scared. Obviously, you don't have any common sense, besides being crazy."

"So it would seem." Something about his smile puts me at ease, even as I fight it. It's one thing not to be afraid of the giant, it's another to feel friendly toward him. "You wouldn't happen to be Herr Bannan?"

The friendly mood vanishes and his eyes narrow to slits. "Why are you looking for him?"

I blink at the sudden change, reeling at the waves of hostility coming off him. Everything about him seems designed to keep me off balance. I pull out the practiced lie. "My family sent me to collect plants that grow on the edge of the Black Forest. We need them for our dyes and he was recommended as a guide. Our normal supplier—"

He snorts. "Nobody goes into the Black Forest."

I bristle. "You are."

"That's different."

"How?"

"Never you mind."

What an arrogant, annoying beast. "Are you Herr Bannan, or aren't you?" *Please don't be him, please don't be him, please don't be him. If I have to trust this man to take me through the Black Forest, I might as well turn around now.*

"Not, thank the goddess. And you'll stay away from him if you know what's good for you. He can't be trusted."

I don't have a choice. I stiffen my spine and look up at him with every ounce of dignity I can muster. "I'll decide who I keep company with. Good day, sir."

Before he can respond, I brush past him. He gives a quiet curse. A massive hand falls on my shoulder, spinning me around.

I shove his hand away and kick his shin. "Stay back." *Fists up. Feet planted.* I try to remember what else Johan said about brawling. *Uhhhh ... show no fear. What was the other thing?*

"Oi, what did you do that for?" The man glares as he rubs his bruised leg.

"I'm not scared of you." *Was it run away? Or never run away? Burn it, burn it, burn it.*

"We've established that." He mutters under his breath and thrusts the leaves into my hands. "Use them, or not. It's none of my concern." He stomps, grumbling, into the forest. For such a large person, he's remarkably quiet as he disappears into the trees.

I snap my mouth shut. *What a strange man. He thinks he can order me around and I'll just blindly obey him.* I shove the leaves in my pocket. *I never asked his name. Someone in town must know him. There can't be too many men resembling a bear around here. Not that I need to know who he is. If he isn't Herr Bannan, I shouldn't concern myself with him. Still, it would only be polite to thank him for his help. Although I didn't ask him for it. Mother would never approve of how I treated him, no matter how rude he was. She'd demand I make amends.*

But Mother isn't here, and I have more important things on my mind. I'll forget about him and find Herr Bannan. It's important to keep my priorities straight, and the man isn't a priority.

"A bear-man, you say?" The innkeeper gives me the side-eye as he wipes down a mug.

"He only looks like a bear. Dark hair and eyes. Very tall, broad shoulders." I hold out my arms for emphasis.

"Lots of men like that around here. None of them are bears, though."

"He's not a bear." *The heavens grant me patience.* "He went into the forest. And he gave me some healing plants." The leaves worked like magic. I couldn't bring myself to chew them, but grinding them with water created a paste that instantly took the pain away. The cuts closed within an hour, leaving shiny pink skin behind. I've never heard of anything like them.

The innkeeper's face darkens. "You mean Markus."

The disgust on his face surprises me. Yes, the man was a bit rude, but not enough to elicit such a powerful reaction. *What did Markus do to deserve such loathing?*

He picks up another glass, giving it a vicious swipe. "Don't go near that one. He's one of them Wolves."

A chill runs down my spine. *He's from the Kingdom of the Wolves? Nobody leaves there alive.* "What? How?"

"Nobody knows for sure. Just showed up one day. Came stumbling out from the trees must be, oh, six or seven years ago. He must've committed a terrible crime for them to cast him out like that. Those people are clannish. They never let go of their own." He puts the glass down with a thump. "Like I said, best stay away."

I press my lips together. *If he's so terrible, why did he help me?* "Mayhap he left on his own."

"You ever hear of that?" He stares pointedly until I shake my head. "Neither have I. And I've lived here my whole life, and my father before me, going on five generations. Nobody comes out of the forest. The Wolf Guards don't leave any survivors, just bones."

I gulp. "What are the Wolf Guards?"

"Wolves. Real wolves. Monsters they train to patrol the borders. Keeps them in, and us out." His face relaxes. "But don't worry, little miss. You're safe as long as you stay out of the trees."

Except I plan on going into the Black Forest tomorrow. Thank the heavens Herr Bannan will know what to do about them. I rub my arms. Markus must know a way past the Wolf Guards, too. Or mayhap the wolves don't come close to the border. *Wait, if it was seven years ago ...* "Markus must've been young when he came here."

"Yah. A big lad, even then. Burning up with fever and clothes in rags. It took three men to pin him down. He was ranting and raving about fires and witches. Kept attacking anyone who came close, so we finally left his fate up to the heavens. For some cursed reason, they let him survive." He makes a warding sign.

What heartless people, to abandon a sick child. It's a battle to keep the distaste off my face as I grind my teeth, but my curiosity pushes me on. "Why doesn't he leave?" I can't imagine staying some place that treated me like that. I'd run away as fast as I could to somewhere else, anywhere else.

"It's the forest. It's in his blood. Can't leave it behind, more's the pity. Be best for everyone if he did. The Kingdom of Wolves causes nothing but trouble. Raiding our supplies and taking livestock. Nothing good can come from there." The innkeeper spits on the floor. "The King should've burned the forest to the ground years ago."

I murmur my thanks and wander back to my room, turning over the new information. *Markus.* If he's actually from the Kingdom of the Wolves, he's exactly what I need. Herr Bannan's reputation is for knowing how to get past the border, but Markus will know everything. Customs. Shortcuts. He might even know how to get into the Wolf Palace. He's the perfect guide.

But he's a Wolf, which means I can't trust him. They're notoriously treacherous. All of them are bandits and thieves. No honor among them. He'd slit my throat the moment I turn my back.

But he gave me the leaves for my injuries. Why would he do that? A moment of weakness? Trying to earn my trust for some future purpose?

I shake my head. If he wanted to attack me, he could've

knocked me down with a flick of his wrist. He was surly, but he didn't seem wicked like all the stories I've heard about Wolves. Mayhap they kicked him out of their kingdom for not being cruel enough. Or his time in Lorria taught him some manners. Whatever the reason, it can't hurt to approach him about taking me to the Wolf Palace. I can always hire Herr Bannan if I decide Markus isn't trustworthy.

How long will he be in the forest? I grab my cloak as I hurry out the door, determined to talk to him. My excitement grows with every step. For thc first time, there's a sliver of hope that I can actually pull this off. I make a best guess about where I entered the forest earlier, slipping back among the grey-brown trees. It's tempting to search for Markus, but the shadowy threat of Wolf Guards keeps me close to the tree line.

I pace back and forth, scanning for any movement. *Why do the trees have to grow so burning close together?* The chill creeps into my skin and I look longingly back at the sunshine a few feet away. *Why would anyone choose to live in here? It's so depressing.* I shake my head and focus on Markus.

If all the townspeople share the innkeeper's feelings about him, it must be a lonely existence. His size and his reputation work against him before he opens his mouth. *No wonder he was annoyed when I shrieked at him. He must get that reaction all the time, no matter what he does. I misjudged him. Or mayhap he really is some sort of crazed criminal and my luck is about to run out.*

Markus was so young when he left the Wolves, he couldn't have done anything too terrible. He must've run away. But why stay here? Why not go back, or leave all together? I get more questions than answers the more I think about him.

My legs finally tire. The days of coach rides have done nothing for my endurance, and I've always preferred horseback to going anywhere on foot. There aren't any rocks or fallen trees to sit on, so I settle for a mossy root with a sigh, tucking the edges of my cloak under me.

"What do you want now?" Markus watches me warily from a few feet away.

I jump up. "How do you do that?"

"What?"

"Move so quietly. I didn't hear you." I bounce on my toes, looking him over. He's even bigger than I remembered. It's the height and shoulders. He's not overweight, just more muscular than the men I see at the palace and around town.

His eyebrows come together. "Practice. What do you want?"

I barely keep my eyes from rolling. *And here I thought little fairy sprites carried him everywhere.* I hold my hand out. "My name's Lisette."

He looks down at my outstretched fingers, then slowly reaches out, my smaller hand disappearing in his oversized grip. His palm is rough with callouses, his skin hot to my icy touch.

"Sorry." I wince and pull my hand away, quickly rubbing my fingers together. "I got chilled sitting here." I grab his hand again and give it a hearty shake. Something zings between us, surprising me with a light zap. *This is not going well. But as Mother says, all beginnings are hard. This one is just harder than most.*

"Markus. But I'm guessing you know that." He slides his hand away from mine, rubbing his fingers against his palm.

"The innkeeper told me." *Ugh, I probably shouldn't have said that since he's not exactly one of Markus's biggest supporters.* "I wanted to thank you. For the plants. They're amazing." I wave my hands in the air, grinning like an idiot. "Wherever did you find them?" *I sound like a halfwit. Get it together, Lys!*

His eyes shift away from me. "They grow around here."

"Yes, well. Thank you." I rock back on my heels, then take a deep breath. "I wanted to ask you something."

"No."

I bite my tongue against the flash of annoyance, giving him a bright smile. "You don't know what I'm going to ask."

Markus crosses his arms. "You want me to take you into the Black Forest. The answer is no."

How did he— "You haven't heard my offer."

Markus shakes his head. "Forget whatever you're planning and go home. The Black Forest is no place for a lady." He adjusts the pack back on his shoulders and turns away. "Stay out of the forest."

"No, wait." I jump in front of him. "I can give you money. Lots of it. Enough to start a new life somewhere else."

He walks around me. "No."

I hurry to keep up with him. "How about a business? All yours for the taking. Commission on a ship? A knighthood?"

Markus laughs. "What makes you think I'd want a knighthood?"

Be polite, you need him. I keep my teeth clenched in a smile as I grind out, "Doesn't everyone? You get a yearly allowance, and honor, and fame. People would respect you."

He snorts. "People can burn for all I care." Anger flows

heavy under the words.

Aha, a sore spot. The knot in my stomach loosens now that I've found his weakness. "You'd have the crown's backing. Nobody would dare insult you if you were a knight."

"They don't mess with me now. And respect is earned, not given."

I puff as I keep up with his long stride. "But you would earn it." *What will convince him to change his mind? Mayhap I can appeal to his altruistic side.* "You'd be helping the crown with something very important. A matter of life and death."

"Life and death, you say." He stops at the last tree. The sunlight teases out blue-black highlights in his thick, wavy hair. Markus folds his arms and stares down at me, his eyebrow lifting. "What's got you all fired up? What's so important that you'd court death with open arms?"

"That's my concern, not yours."

"If you want me to take you through the Black Forest, you're making it my business."

He's probably humoring me. But if there's a chance it'll convince him ... "They have something of mine and I want it back."

"That's highly unlikely since nobody and nothing crosses the border."

"Except you." *Haha, point for me.*

His lips twitch. "I never said I go into the Kingdom of the Wolves." He leans against a tree. "You said it was a matter of life and death. Did a Wolf steal your favorite hair ribbon? No wait, I know. They insulted your favorite pony and you're going to demand an apology."

Don't kick him, don't kick him, don't kick him. "All you

need to know is I'm willing to pay you handsomely for your help. So what will it be? A knighthood or coin?"

He raises an eyebrow. "You're offering some very grand things. Things a normal person can't provide. How do I know you're not lying to get your way?"

Burn it. I can't tell him my identity. I cross my arms and stare him straight in the eye. "You don't. You'll just have to trust me."

He snorts. "Never trust a Lorrian."

"I would never lie. Everything I promised, I can deliver."

"Just because your parents spoil you doesn't mean they can give you anything you ask for. A less scrupulous man would make you sorry for such outlandish lies."

That conceited, egotistical, arrogant hypocrite. How dare a Wolf call me a liar. Heat crawls up my neck as I clench my fists. "Everyone knows the Wolves are the untrustworthy ones. I don't know why I even tried talking to you. This was a waste of time."

Markus throws his hands in the air. "Finally, we agree on something."

Why did I bother? Wolves are all criminals. I'm better off with Herr Bannan. I should walk away. Go back to the inn. But ... Markus is still my best chance of rescuing Oma. If saving her means putting up with this oaf, I'll do it. For her. "Name your price."

"You haven't given me a reason to believe you can pay it. And we've established we don't trust each other, so you'll have to do better than your word."

I can't tell him I'm the princess. He's a Wolf. He'd betray me in a minute. Try to trade me to the Wolf King for permission to come home. Nobody knows I'm here. The innkeeper knew I was asking about Markus, but that's it. Why did I come out to the woods instead of waiting for him to come back to town? He doesn't live in the forest. Stupid, stupid, stupid.

He scratches his beard, then yawns.

I can't lie now. Can I say my parents are nobles? That isn't technically a lie ... but I said a knighthood. Burn it, why did I spout off about that so many times? Could my parents be powerful nobles that have sway with the king and queen? Burn it, burn it, burn it. I can—

"That's what I thought." He smirks and turns away.

I grab his arm. "I'm Princess Lisette. My parents are the king and queen of Lorria." I lift my chin. *That should shut him up.*

Markus stares blankly for a moment, then guffaws. "A princess? You?" He slaps his knee as his shoulders shake with laughter. "A princess. Princess Lisette. What a coincidence. I'm Prince Markus Von Dien." He gives me an elaborate bow, his smile wide and mocking. "Since we're both royalty, perhaps I should ask for your hand in marriage. Or your sister's. Which one will get me the throne?"

It takes all my willpower not to kick him in the shin as heat blazes on my cheeks. "That would be Maddalyn. I can introduce you if you'd like." *Not that I would ever let Maddie marry someone so rude and scheming.*

He gasps between laughs. "What, no promises of marriage?"

I grind out, "We don't have arranged marriages, which you should know by now. So it's up to you to woo my sister with your ... charms." I wrinkle my nose. *Not burning likely. This guy couldn't get someone to give him a cold.*

He wipes the tears of laughter from his eyes. "No,

thanks. I like my life simple.”

My best chance to rescue Oma is slipping away. “There must be something that you want. Everyone needs something.”

“Do you really think you know what I want?” Markus shakes his head. “Go back to your palace. Herr Bannan can’t help you. Nobody can.”

“I’m going into the Black Forest.” I poke him in the chest. “Are you going to help me or not?”

“Not.”

Markus stalks off, leaving me in the shadows.

The inn’s common room fills after nightfall. The innkeeper points out Herr Bannan with a shrug and a frown, then goes back to serving customers. Herr Bannan is deep in conversation with an older woman with a white braid, so I take the time to study him without his notice.

It’s hard to make out much through the haze of pipe smoke hanging in the room, but Herr Bannan is a surprise. So average as to be nondescript, the type of person you wouldn’t remember seeing even if you passed him every day for a month. Light brown hair and eyes, a pleasant enough face, but nothing to call attention to it. I’d expect someone with a tarnished reputation and dangerous profession to be a bit more interesting.

The conversation at the next table distracts me from my examination.

“… Wolves set fire to field on the Dunst property during that last big storm. Snuck away before we could catch them." The skinny man gives his friend a knowing look.

"Yah, that was after they sickened Becker's flock. Had to destroy them so it wouldn't spread to the rest of the livestock." The friend takes a swig from his tankard. "I'd like to teach all those savages a lesson. Show them Lorria shouldn't be trifled with. The King needs to send troops in there and attack 'em on their land for once." He thumps his meaty fist on the table, his face flushed.

My lips press together and I drum my fingers on the tabletop as the men continue to trade stories of mischief from the Wolves. *It's worse than we thought. Father needs to hear about this. If he knew what was happening at the border, he wouldn't hesitate to send soldiers.* I toy with waiting to tell him until after I triumphantly return with Oma, then decide to post a letter before I leave for the Kingdom of Wolves. *As much as I'd love to gloat, the news can't wait. People are in danger.*

The woman speaking with Herr Bannan gets up and shakes his hand, then limps to a table where a young couple sits. The girl is close to my age, with black hair and incredible bright blue eyes that would make the court ladies die from envy. I can't make out much about her companion aside from dark hair, since his back is to me. The woman with the white hair shakes her head as she sits down, and her friend looks disappointed.

Seizing the opening, I make my way to Herr Bannan's table and slide into the empty seat.

He tilts his head. "Hello, little miss. Is there something I can help you with?"

I fold my hands on the table and lean forward. "I've been told you're a man who guides people to ... hard-to-get-to places."

He leans back in his chair, an eyebrow raised. "Who told you that?"

"Someone I met on my travels. I need a guide."

He gestures to a server, and they plop a tankard in front of him.

I tap my foot until the server leaves, glancing around to ensure nobody is eavesdropping. The people are chatting amongst themselves, but a few too many pairs of eyes flick our way. I lean in closer and lower my voice. "I need to go to the Kingdom of the Wolves. Their palace."

The other eyebrow goes up at my declaration. "What business do you have there?"

"I'm escorting someone back here." *After I rescue her.* "Can you do it?"

He clasps his hands behind his head and looks at the ceiling. "I don't normally go that far into the kingdom. It'll take at least two weeks each way, maybe longer depending on the weather. We'll need more supplies since we can't count on the villages to supply us."

Herr Bannan names an amount that makes me wince. But Oma's life is worth any price. I'll have just enough to get us home if we're careful.

I shift in my seat. "That covers everything? The supplies, lodging, horses once we're inside the border?"

Herr Bannan's smile widens. "Of course. This is a full service."

"And you'll take me to the palace? And make sure we get back to Lorria safely?"

"Yah, my dear. Herr Bannan always keeps his word." His eyes flash in the firelight.

My stomach squirms. I can't tell if my uneasiness is because I'm about to do something incredibly dangerous, or something else. How much can I trust a referral from strangers? Markus flashes through my mind and it's hard not to compare his bluntness to Herr Bannan's smooth dealing and lavish promises.

I'm stalling. Something keeps my lips closed when I should seal the deal. He's offering me everything I wanted. He's my only hope of rescuing Oma since Markus turned me down, and yet … *Say yes. Oma needs you.*

A silence falls over the room.

Markus stands in the doorway, a frown evident under the beard. He surveys the room, his head almost brushing the ceiling. As his eyes meet mine, Markus gives a small nod. His frown deepens when he spots my companion. He shakes his head, then takes the empty chair at the table with the woman with the white braid and her two younger companions. The silence holds a moment longer, then chatter slowly starts up again.

"That one always brings trouble." Herr Bannan takes a long drink.

A flash of annoyance makes me sit up. "He looks pretty harmless to me."

"You're the only one. But enough about him." Herr Bannan gives me a smile that puts me on edge. "Do we have a deal?"

A prickle on my neck makes me look over my shoulder in time to catch Markus looking away. *Even after rejecting me and all of my offers, he can't leave it alone.* His scornful laughter from earlier echoes in my ears.

I square my shoulders and hold out my hand. "Deal."

"Liar!"

I kick the cold logs in the fire pit, scattering ashes across the ground. "Cheating, no good, lying, burning, aaaarrrggghhhhh." I press my fists tight against my head. "He abandoned me in the middle of the forest. Took my money, took the supplies, and just—just left. Arrrrrrghhhh." I kick another branch. "I'm an idiot. How could I be so stupid?"

Markus steps around a tree and into the small campsite. "I tried to warn you. Herr Bannan is a thief."

Of course, he's here to witness my humiliation. "Don't you start." I march over to him and poke his chest. "This is all your fault."

"I told you not to trust Herr—"

"You told me no." I emphasize each word with another jab to his chest. "You wouldn't help me. I didn't have any choice. I have to save her."

"Save who?"

"All you did was laugh at me. Laugh." I poke him again.

"Like I was ridiculous. But I have to. Father won't help her. All he cares about is 'the good of the kingdom.' Like saving Oma is a bad thing."

Markus rubs his chest as I stomp over to a tree and kick the trunk.

"They took her. They took her and who knows what's happening to her. I can't leave her with those—those barbarians. I have to save her. But nobody will help me, and I don't know what to do, and I can't do it all by myself. I was raised to know which fork to use at supper, not infiltrate an enemy kingdom." I swipe angrily at my eyes. "And I hate crying."

Markus watches me, his eyebrows crinkled together. "Is it safe for me to talk now?"

"No." I drop to the ground and blow out a breath. "Yes. But be nice, I'm upset right now."

"Really? I couldn't tell." He settles next to me and hands me a pear from one of his packs.

"I'm not hungry."

"Eat it anyway."

I stare at the fruit, turning it over and over in my hands. "What are you doing here?"

"I came to take you back to the village."

"How did you know ..." My hands still. "This isn't the first time Herr Bannan has pulled this trick."

Markus doesn't say anything.

Heat creeps up my neck as my pulse speeds up. "You knew he was going to do this. You knew he was going to take my money and dump me in the woods, and you didn't warn me."

He runs a hand across his bearded chin. "Would you have listened?"

"Yes! No. I don't know. But it might have made me think twice about going with him. It doesn't matter. What's important is that you didn't tell me. You intentionally didn't say anything, even when you knew you should."

Markus grimaces as he looks at the trees overhead. "You're right."

Surprise replaces the anger. "Could you repeat that?"

The corner of his mouth twitches. "No."

"That's all right, I heard you the first time." The first bite of the pear awakens my appetite, and I attack the fruit with gusto. The sweet juice washes away the bitter betrayal of the morning. "Now you're going to say you're sorry for laughing at me."

He smirks. "Let's not get carried away."

I catch myself smiling and quickly smother it. *He's a Wolf. Keep your guard up.*

Markus leans back on his hands. "So. Tell me. Why do you need to cross the border and who are you saving?"

I arch my eyebrow. "Are you going to help me?"

"No. I'm just curious why a pampered little princess is desperately trying to get herself killed on a fool's errand."

"Oh, of course I'll tell you all about it, since you're obviously so sympathetic and understanding about my dilemma." I glare at him.

He runs a hand across his mouth. "Perhaps your tale of woe will change my mind. So, let's try this again. Why are you crossing the border and who needs saving?"

What do I have to lose? I swallow hard to dislodge the piece of fruit stuck in my throat. "Actually, I need to go to the Wolf Palace."

His dark eyes widen. "Have you lost your mind?" He springs to his feet, deceptively fast for a man of his size.

"The palace is at the heart of the kingdom. Traveling through the mountains is death this time of year. It'll take weeks to get there. Not to mention you'll be killed if anyone figures out who you are. It's impossible."

"Um, that's not all." I bite my thumbnail, then take a deep breath. *I've dipped my toe into the water, now time to jump in.* "The King kidnapped my grandmother. I'm going there to rescue her."

He takes a step back. "No. That's not possible. He wouldn't kidnap anyone."

"Well, he did. He didn't even ask for a ransom. He took Oma and then taunted us about it."

Markus makes a slashing motion through the air. "It doesn't make sense. There's something wrong. He wouldn't do that." He paces in front of me, shaking his head. "We don't go around kidnapping people. It's not our way."

I press my lips together. "There are not a lot of ways to interpret this. Kingdoms don't usually kidnap the Dowager Queen to start trade negotiations." My chest tightens as a dull ache settles there.

"It could have been one of our enemies. Another kingdom trying to start a war between ours. It wasn't the Wolf King. It's impossible."

"How would you know? Are you close friends with him?" I snap. "He did it because he could. He's just trying to make us look weak, or he wants to invade Lorria, or—or—or I don't know what, but it's what happened. He's going to kill Oma." I rub my chest, trying to ease the knot buried there. "I'm going to the Kingdom of the Wolves, with or without you. Are you going to help me?"

I hold my breath as he paces the small campsite, muttering to himself, too quiet for me to catch.

After an eternity, he faces me. "Do you have money?"

Not much now. "How much do you want?" I mentally cross my fingers I have enough left.

"We'll have to go back to Eelan to buy supplies. I didn't come out here planning on an extended trip." He frowns as he looks me over.

I sit up, giving him a hopeful look. "You'll help me?" A warmth chases away the chill I've felt since I woke up.

He runs a hand across the back of his neck. "If the King really kidnapped your grandmother, or is thinking about invading Lorria, then he's abandoned everything we value and he's putting our kingdom in danger. There's no reason for me to stay. If you'll pay me enough so I can start over somewhere far from here, I'll help you." He names a sum more than five times Herr Bannan's fee.

A smile breaks out on my face and I clamp my hands on my legs so I won't run over and hug him. "Thank you. You don't know—I mean—Oma means everything to me. Thank you."

"Thank me after we make it back alive. If we manage to make it to the palace—which I wouldn't bet on—once we have your grandmother, they'll be after us with everything they've got. We'll be lucky if we make it five minutes before they catch us." He mutters, "Why do I do this to myself?" Then louder, "Let's go get the supplies."

I bounce in place, rubbing my hands together. "And strangle that lying thief, Herr Bannan."

"Grab your pack. We'll need to get everything and head back out as quickly as possible."

Guilt prompts me to confess, "I don't have enough money to pay for the supplies and pay you. That lying rat took most of it."

Markus frowns, staring in the direction of the Kingdom of the Wolves. "Fine. You can leave a promissory note with the blacksmith."

Trust only goes so far, I see. I shove the annoyance away. *It's not like I trust him either. Look what happened with Herr Bannan. I won't make that mistake again.*

As we start the walk back to town, something about our conversation keeps nagging me, telling me to be careful. At first, I attribute it to the rawness of Herr Bannan's betrayal, but there's more to it. Something bigger than yet another guide who could abandon me in the woods and run off. It's like a stone in my shoe, poking me every time I think I've wiggled it out. The twinge refuses to be ignored, but doesn't provide any clues.

The nagging finally comes up with an answer. *Markus said 'we' when talking about the Kingdom of the Wolves. He thinks of himself as a Wolf, not a Lorrian. If it comes down to a choice, he'll pick them over me. I'll have to watch my back. He could betray me at any moment.*

It's going to be a long trip.

Markus sets a ground-eating pace, forcing me to trot to keep up with him. Despite resembling a bear in stature, his movements are easy and graceful. Every step he makes is sure. He moves as silently as a shadow among the trees, while I manage to find every twig and dry leaf within reach.

My steps falter as the reality suddenly hits me. *I'm going into the woods with a man I know nothing about except he's been exiled from the most barbaric kingdom in the world and my kingdom's sworn enemy. I'm going to be spending weeks with him. Alone. This is not smart. But it's not like I thought waltzing into the Kingdom of the Wolves would be easy. All right, to be fair, I didn't think about it at all. I just know I have to save Oma.* Which means not only do I need to watch out for any sign of betrayal, I need to find a way to take care of myself as much as possible and not rely on him. He's my guide, not my bodyguard or even my friend.

Self-sufficient ... I can do that. I'll learn as we go. Watch him. Observe every movement. Study him until—hey, where did he go?

I hurry forward, peering around the trees. "Markus?" Silence. "Where are you? Markus?" *He can't have abandoned me already. I haven't even paid him yet.*

He steps around a tree. "Yah. Did you get lost already?"

Of all the— "No. I wanted to ask you" *—think, think, think—* "what supplies we need."

"I'll take care of it." He starts walking again.

I bristle, huffing as I catch up. "It's my money. I don't want you to waste it."

"I won't. You can wait at the inn and I'll collect you when I'm done."

"I should go with you. We can buy things twice as fast." *And get a better deal.* Markus hasn't proven to be much of a negotiator so far. Although I did agree to pay him an astronomical sum without a second thought, so perhaps I shouldn't brag about my own skills.

He gives me a skeptical look. "Do you know much things cost?"

I smirk. "You're talking to a champion negotiator. Shop owners wail in fear when they see me coming. As for prices." I shrug. "You can tell me what they cost here, and I'll take it from there."

Markus raises his eyebrows, his lips pressed into a thin line. "Hmm. We'll see."

"Prepare to be dazzled." I chuckle to myself, giving an extra spring to my step. *He has no idea what he's in for. I'll have that shopkeeper begging for mercy before I'm through. And after, I won't even gloat about my superior skills ... much. Ha!*

Gnats buzz around my head no matter how much I swat them. Markus walks along like he doesn't have a care in the world. *It's the beard. It makes it easy to hide his expression.*

I clear my throat, trying to get rid of the dry patch. My foot slips on a root, sending me stumbling.

I swipe a damp curl out of my face. "Could you slow down? My legs are half as long as yours."

"What?" He glances over at me, then scratches his beard. "Fine." He slows to a crawl.

I roll my eyes. "I'm not that short."

"Yah, you are." He speeds up to a slow walk for him and normal pace for me.

Breathing a little easier, I walk alongside him, tugging on the pack straps. *If we walk back to town and then back out again, we won't get far today. A whole day wasted because of that lying, thieving jerk. Herr Bannan is lucky I have more important things to deal with than tracking him down. After Oma's rescued, he is going to pay for this.*

The gnats are swarming in force. I bounce on my toes, tugging on my dress. The forest sounds … odd. No people talking, or carriages wheels squeaking, or a thousand other sounds of civilization. The silence echoes, broken only by my pounding footsteps and jangling pack. I rub my palms against my skirt. My skin crawls, the feeling of being watched creeping in. Everywhere I look is the same eerie nothingness of trees. I tuck a strand of hair behind my ear. "So. Markus. Where did you learn about those healing plants?"

He grunts.

"What did you say?"

"Around."

"Around where?"

"Here and there."

"Your mother? A friend?" *A troll that lives under a bridge?*

"My grandmother."

"That's nice you're close with your Oma. I'm close with mine, too. She loves to travel. Oma always brings back the most interesting stories and trinkets from the places she visits. I'm going go with her as soon as Father and Mother let me. There are so many places I want to see. Where have you been? Besides your kingdom and here, I mean."

He swipes his hand against his brow. "Nowhere."

"Well, soon you can go anywhere you want to. Where are you going first?"

"Do you ever stop talking?"

I hop over a root. "No. I've heard Floren is nice and it's not too far. The Florens are coming to visit the palace soon. Then there's Rus, that's practically the other end of the world. Mayhap you should go there after we've rescued Oma. You can see lots of places along the way. There're rumors the women in the Ye'Let tribe can perform magic. I've always wanted to learn magic. Of course, there's no such thing. My friend, Evie, used to try and brew love potions, but they never worked. Whatever the apothecary gave her packed a wallop though. She accidentally put it in our tea one afternoon." I giggle. "Maddie kept falling over every time she stood up, and I ended up splashing around in the fountain in my nightgown until one of the footmen fished me out. Mother kept trying to get a robe on me, but I insisted I was a mermaid and didn't need clothes. Then I—" I snap my mouth shut.

He looks away, the tips of his ears turning bright red.

My cheeks fill with heat. *Quick. Change the subject.* "Gaul is supposed to be beautiful. It's not as far as Rus, but it's unlikely you'd meet anyone you know there. I wish I could see it, but I'm not allowed to go there because Mother said their dresses are sheer, and they don't wear undergarments so you can see everything, and it would be too scandalous."

Markus makes a strangled sound.

"Oma told me about these hot springs where men and women bathe together nak—err, uhhhh—I mean—uhhhh." *The heavens strike me down. Death can't be any worse than this.*

He heaves a loud sigh. "Thank the goddess, we're back."

I send a silent thanks up to the heavens before I do a double take, blinking at the meadow. "How can we be here already? That stinking, lying rat and I walked for hours before we made camp last night."

"Herr Bannan likely led you around in circles for a bit. Didn't want to get to close to the border in case he ran into the Wolf Guards."

I gulp. "Those are real?" I was really hoping they were a myth parents told to keep their children out of the forest.

"Yah. And nothing you want to mess with."

Picturing a salivating pack of wolves sends a chill down my back. I look around nervously. "Let's avoid them too."

As Markus steps out of the forest, he transforms into a different person. The confident ease drains out of his body and tension rushes in. He slouches, his eyes darting from side to side. There's a subtle edge to his movements, as though he's ready to attack at the slightest provocation. After seeing how quickly he can move, I feel sorry for anybody who thinks they can challenge him.

I realize my fists are clenched and I force my fingers to loosen.

"Come on, we don't have much time." His voice is gruff. He stalks off across the grass without looking back.

I trail behind, puzzling at the change in him. *The forest really is his home.* No wonder it's hard for him to leave. *I wonder if he'll find a new forest to call home.*

Markus pauses at the edge of town. I reluctantly pass over most of my money, knowing we need the supplies, but flashbacks of Herr Bannan's treachery makes me keep a small amount back for myself. *Just in case.*

As we pass the food vendor from yesterday, my mouth waters. "We should stop for breakfast."

"You already had it."

If he means the pear, we're going to need to have a serious discussion about what constitutes a meal. I shake my head. *He's huge. There's no way he considers one piece of fruit breakfast. He just doesn't want to stay in town a minute longer than he has to.*

A man in a bright green tunic catches my eye. He's wearing a large pack on his back, another in his hands. There's a thick, ropey scar that starts at the jawline and disappears under the collar of his shirt. He passes a couple of coins to the man he's speaking with, then moves to the woman a few feet away and starts up a conversation. Nothing about him seems unusual and it takes a moment to place why he stands out: the color of his tunic. I haven't seen anything like it in weeks. Everyone around him is in grays and browns and tans, making him the only spot of color in a sea of drabness.

He's from the palace. My heart leaps into my throat. *He's looking for me. We have to hide.* There's a gap between two buildings big enough for us. I grab Markus's arm and yank.

He doesn't move.

Markus looks down, frowning. "What are you doing?"

I dig my heels into the dirt, trying to budge his bulk. "That man. He's hunting for me." *He's going to drag me back to the palace and then Oma will be trapped at the Wolf Palace and why won't he move.* "Movemovemovemove."

Markus glances over at the man, then stiffens. Before I can blink, he's dragging me behind the building. "We need to leave. Now." He doesn't stop until we've reached a small alley behind the structures. "Wait for me in the forest. Stay out of sight."

He takes off running, disappearing around the corner before I can protest.

I look down both sides of the alley. Empty. No point in stalling; the man could walk by and spot me at any moment. I bend my head so my blond hair falls forward across my face and scurry down the narrow passage, keeping close to the backs of the buildings. My heart races as I reach the end of town and risk a glance back. The man's closer than I'd like, but I'll have to risk it.

I run across the field, my feet flying through the grass. Once I hit the forest's edge, I don't stop, weaving between the trunks until I'm lost among the trees. I hide behind one of the trunks, curling up as small as I can. The bark presses into my palms as I clutch the tree, darting looks around the side. I keep my lips pressed together, afraid the slightest noise will give away my hiding spot.

The forest is silent, not even wildlife disturbing the stillness. It feels like there are a thousand eyes on me. *Where is Markus? I shouldn't have listened to him. We should've stuck together. This is a terrible plan.* Thoughts fly around my head faster and faster. *What if the man follows us into the forest? Who is he? Wait—what if Markus turns me in for a reward? He wouldn't do that ... would he? He has my money. What if he wanted to scare me away and he's left me here just like Herr Bannan?*

Just when I've made up my mind to go back, Markus trots through the trees, his arms loaded with bags. He's traded out his wood axe for two hand axes and has a small dagger strapped to his belt.

"You made it." All the suspicions fly out of my head as I run over and grab his sleeve, my knees weak. "Did he see you?"

He drops everything and wipes his forehead with the back of his arm. "I don't think so. Let's pack up quickly and get moving. He won't be able to follow us once we're in the forest."

"We're in the forest. See? Trees, roots, other nature stuff." I wave my hand around.

He snorts and crouches down. "If that's what you think, you're in for a rude surprise when we reach the Black Forest."

He must be joking. A forest is a forest. Just because the Black Forest sounds sinister, doesn't mean it's going to be any different from this place. I chew on my thumbnail, looking around. *He's joking. He is. The Black Forest will be like this ... with Wolf Guards. No, he's just trying to scare me. Everything will be fine. He's teasing me.*

Markus divides up the supplies between my pack and his. I shift from foot to foot as each item disappears inside my bag. *How heavy is that?*

He sets my pack closer to me, then stands and swings the other onto his back. "That's it."

I try to copy his easy movements, but the weight sends me staggering to the side. "Whoaaaa!"

"Hey there." Markus grabs the bag before I tip over and

lifts it up to my height. "Sorry, I forgot you're not used to this."

My cheeks burn. "I'll figure it out." *I have to.*

He helps me slip on the pack, the weight settling heavy on my hips. Markus eyes me, then adjusts a few of the straps and shows me the long belt to fasten around my waist. "Don't forget to untie that one before you take it off unless you want to fall over again."

"Right. Thanks." *I'm doing this for Oma.* Picturing her laughing, wrinkled face chases the fear away. "What are you waiting for? Lead the way."

Three hours later, I'm questioning my life choices and ready to kill Markus. The gear doubles in weight with every step. My muscles feel like water and the pack threatens to tip me over at any moment. My mouth is sticky with dryness and sweat pours down my back. My sense of time and distance are wobbly. Stuck in a perpetual twilight under the thick tree canopy, and with miles of identical forest surrounding us, it's hard to believe we're making progress and not trapped in some endless loop of torment.

"I think that's far enough." Markus stops ahead of me and looks around the trees. "This is a good spot to make camp for the night."

"Wonderful." My legs collapse and I drop to the ground with a thud. It looks exactly the same as the rest of the forest we've passed through, but I bless whatever mysterious trait made Markus decide to stop here.

Markus stretches his arms out and rolls his neck. "Our bedrolls should be warm enough that we can forgo a tent tonight. We'll get an early start in the morning."

"Uh-huh." I lean back on the pack, feeling like an overturned turtle. Overhead is a dizzying mosaic of interwoven branches layered upon each other. I wince at a sharp pain in my side, then shift and nudge a rock away. *Even the ground is trying to hurt me.*

"Tomorrow's going to be a long day."

"Longer than today?" I slip my arms out of the pack's straps and struggle to sit up, remembering too late the band around my middle. My fingers are clumsy and I can't remember how the knots work. *Burn it.* I lay down and wiggle out of the contraption as Markus watches with barely concealed amusement.

Go ahead and laugh. If this was a civilized kingdom, it'd have inns and roads and carriages instead of all this dirt and trees. My head throbs in rhythm with my heartbeat. I take a pull on my waterskin, grimacing at the musty water that does little to alleviate the parched landscape of my mouth.

He bends over my pack and works on the knots. "I'll get supper going while you gather firewood."

Markus has the same patient, vaguely patronizing tone my mother uses when she thinks I'm being unreasonable. "I'm doing my best," I tell him crossly.

"I didn't say you weren't." He sets my untied pack next to me. "It takes time and practice to learn how to live out here."

I really hate that tone. "How much firewood do you need?"

"As much as you can carry." He pulls a small tin pot from his pack. "I'll find water. Shout if you get lost."

I push to my feet and stomp out of earshot, biting my lip as my legs threaten to collapse. "Get lost. Why would I get lost? Just because everything looks exactly the same. He thinks I'm useless. I can do lots of things he can't do. It's not like the only thing I can do out here is pick up firewood. He thinks I'm some helpless princess. I'll show him."

Arms full, I turn around … and I can't see the campsite. *Burn it. I'm not going to give Markus another thing to laugh about.* I set off in the direction of my best guess, breathing a sigh of relief when I finally spot our packs off to the right. The firewood makes a satisfying thump when I drop it on the ground. My pride forces my tired feet to carry me back out for more wood. This time I'm careful to move straight out and back as I collect the fallen branches.

After my third trip, Markus returns and gives my woodpile an appreciative nod. I consider going out a fourth time just to prove a point, but my feet win the argument with my pride. I settle on the ground and shake out my arms.

He tosses me a couple of bars that look like squished oatmeal. "Crumble those into the water while I dig the fire pit."

I follow his instructions, taking careful note of how he sets up camp, knowing I might have to do this on my own one day. Soon there's a bubbling pot of stew on the fire, and he adds a second pot of water for tea. While the food cooks, Markus takes me to the small spring to clean up and refill our waterskins. It's a wide pool spilling out into a trickling stream that disappears among the trees. The basin is lined with mossy rocks and a few dark green plants grow around the edges.

It's strange washing with a man next to me. Despite my being fully clothed, it's a forced kind of intimacy. I keep one eye on him as I dab water on my arms and neck, then use a scrap of cloth to dry. The bear similarity comes back in full force as Markus splashes in the tiny pool. He ends his wash by dunking his whole head under, then tossing back his head, sending a sheet of water behind him.

He grins, his dark hair plastered to his head. "Nothing will wake you up faster than that."

I resist the urge to smile back. *He's not my friend, he's a Wolf.* I flick a bead of water off my hand. "I'd rather have kaffee. Or a cup of spiced chocolate."

"Unfortunately, there isn't a tea shop nearby, Your Highness. But if we run across one in the middle of the forest, I'll buy you whatever you want." He gives his hair one more shake, flinging a spray of droplets through the air. "Supper should be ready."

I ignore his offered hand and stand, inwardly groaning. My muscles are getting stiffer by the second. *If I hurt this badly now, I don't even want to think about tomorrow.*

The silence grows as we walk the short distance back to our campsite. Markus navigates the terrain easily, seemingly picking out invisible markers on some mental map. The dim lighting and gray trees make me long for the sunlit meadows bursting with wildflowers around my home. At least there are bits of green from the moss here and there. Without it, I'd worry all the color's been sucked out of the world. The never-changing scenery makes me fear we've stepped out of the real world and through the veil, never to be heard from again. Markus's footsteps are soundless, the only noise my shallow breaths. *Shouldn't there be birds, or insects, or something?*

I scratch my arm. Tug on a sleeve. Squint, trying to make out the firelight from our camp sight. Scratch my arm again. "What's your real name?"

He smirks. "I told you. I'm Prince Markus Von Dien."

I snort. "Of course, you are."

"If you're a princess, why can't I be a prince?" He wiggles his eyebrows and chuckles.

"Fine, keep your secrets. How did you find the spring?"

"A little bit of luck and common sense. There's a lot of these small springs around here. This many trees needs a large supply of water. Sometimes you can hear it if it's a large enough stream. Other times I look for animal trails or thick vegetation. And water usually collects at the lowest point, so downhill is your friend."

His voice soothes my frazzled nerves, and Markus clearly enjoys having an audience—a marked difference from our previous conversations. *Herr Bannan was nice to me too before he left me at the campsite and stole my money.* But listening to Markus is better than that deafening silence. "Why did you pick our campsite?"

He launches into an explanation of what he looks for when overnighting in the woods, pointing at parts of the ground and trees. Though I should be paying attention, I don't listen to the words, instead letting his voice wash over me and keep the silence at bay. For some reason it's not as claustrophobic in here when he's talking.

Friendly Markus is ... odd. I think I prefer the cranky, grumpy Markus. It's a lot easier to remember he's a Wolf and can't be trusted. Happy, pleasant Markus is a lot more dangerous. If I don't keep my defenses up, he'll slip right past them.

Back at the campsite, Markus dips out the stew with two bowls. He pours a packet of spices and hot water into a cup, then hands it to me. "This'll help your muscles."

A knot forms in my stomach. *Why isn't he having any? Is it poison? He knows a lot about medicines. It would be easy for him.* "None for you?" I keep my tone light.

He grins. "I usually hike a lot farther than this. Drink up, otherwise your body will be crying tomorrow."

Wary of his eyes on me, I pretend to drink, keeping my lips firmly sealed against the tin. I smack my lips. "Thanks."

I pick up my bowl of lumpy white stew and poke it with the flat spoon. It has the color and consistency of poorly cooked porridge with some odd gray morsels throughout. There's no smell to hint at what it is. I eye the concoction doubtfully. *Here goes nothing ...*

When the first mouthful hits my tongue, I swallow hard to keep from gagging. *Urgh.* The clumpy texture creates an unpleasant slime on my tongue, and the taste is a bewildering mix of bland and acidic. How something that looks so harmless can taste so terrible is beyond me. "Um, what is this?"

Markus pauses with a heaping spoonful halfway to his mouth and beams. "My own special mix of oats, nuts, jerky, and dandelion leaves. You can eat the bars straight, too. It tastes good both ways."

"Impressive." I'm not sure if I'm smiling or grimacing as I take a small bite. "Mmm."

His smile widens, his eyes crinkling in the corners. "I'm glad you like it." He turns back to his bowl with that fierce concentration men have during meals.

I force a couple more bites down, but spend most of the time pushing the congealing mush around my bowl and watching Markus out of the corner of my eye. He polishes off his portion, then goes back for seconds and thirds. When he holds the pot out to me with a questioning look, I gesture for him to take the rest.

My stomach grumbles, unhappy with the scant meal, but my tastebuds refuse to surrender. I close my eyes and remember the flatcake breakfast we had last month for Maddie's birthday: sugary berry syrup mixing with the creamy butter, finished with cups of spiced chocolate topped with dollops of cream. *The sticky buns I bought yesterday. They're buried in my pack somewhere. Thank the heavens, I won't starve. At least, not tonight.*

The hair on the back of my neck rises and my eyes fly open.

Markus stands on the other side of the fire. A dagger is in his raised right hand, the left pointing at me. His eyes shine black.

My heart leaps into my throat and I scramble back, hitting the tree, knocking over my cooled tea. *He's going to kill me. How could I be so stupid?*

His arm blurs as he throws the knife.

I can't breathe, can't move. There's a breeze as the blade flies past my cheek. A loud, wet thud. Slowly, I turn my head, coming face-to-face with an enormous brown-and-black snake, fangs dripping with venom. I shriek and fall over. The fangs fill my vision and I flail my arms, striking at anything near me. A sob chokes me before my mind finally registers Markus's knife pinning the dead snake to the tree.

Markus shakes his head sadly. "Little thing like that shouldn't be out at night. Must've been sick. Shame I had to kill it."

A shame? "It was going to kill me." My heart hammers in my chest.

"But it didn't." He pulls the knife out, then cradles the snake in his hands. "I'll give it a proper burial. It's not safe to eat it if it was sick."

He'd better be joking about eating it. "By all means, give it a burial. Say a little prayer and pass along my sympathies. You can let the next one kill me to spare it the same fate."

Markus fixes me with a stern look, his eyes narrow. "It wasn't personal. We're trespassing in its home. Mayhap you should think about other creatures before you condemn them." He stalks off into the darkness.

"Like I'm going to feel sorry for a stupid snake." A sliver of guilt creeps in, eating away at my self-righteousness. Not that I think Markus should've let the snake strike me. But I didn't have to mock him. *No.* I shake it off. I'm letting Markus get into my head. There's no reason to feel bad about the death of a horrible, dangerous snake.

I scoot next to the fire and hold my hands closer to the flames, chilled despite the warm night air. The light gives me comfort, unlike everything else in this horrible place. The minutes tick off. Imaginary creatures peer at me from behind the trees. The quiet plays tricks on my ears. Silent noises are snakes slithering closer. Every heartbeat is a boar pounding through the trees. Or wolves. Or bears. I stare wide-eyed into the darkness.

"Everything's fine." My voice is too high. "Markus said that snake was probably sick. He wouldn't leave me here if it was dangerous. We're not close to the Wolf Guard. I think." I inch closer to the fire. "It's fine. It's fine. I need to stop this. I am a princess. Princesses don't panic. Not that I was ever good at being a princess."

I take a slow, deep breath. Then another. And another. My heartrate slows, and little by little my muscles relax.

Markus silently appears on the other side of the fire, driving the last shadows of fear from my mind.

Don't be an idiot. He's one of them. But my body

doesn't listen. The bands around my chest release as he cleans out the dishes with the leftover hot water.

"What are you grinning at?" he growls.

Am I smiling? I'm smiling. Like an idiot. Stop it. "Thank you. For saving my life. The snake." *Eloquent apology, Lisette. Next time, try to actually use the word 'sorry,' fluff brains.*

While Markus processes my awkward confession, I forge ahead. "I'm sorry. For earlier. Not that you killed the snake, because I don't want to die and I—for mocking you. If you want to bury things, it's none of my business."

Markus rubs a hand across his eyes. "That's what you're sorry for?"

"Yes?"

He shakes his head, then puts another log on the fire. "Get some sleep."

What happened? "I said I was sorry."

"I heard." Markus shakes out his bedroll, then wraps himself in the blanket, his back to me.

Ugh, what now? I drum my fingers on my knee, then stalk over to where Markus is lying with his eyes closed. "What's wrong? Why are you mad?"

He doesn't open his eyes. "I'm not mad."

"You're worse than Evie. My friend pouts and pouts and pouts, and pretends everything is fine, even if she's being a brat. And I have to keep talking and asking her what's wrong, and she won't tell me until—"

"Gahhhh!" Markus scrubs his hands over his face as he sits up. "How has someone not killed you for being so annoying?"

"There's usually a guard close by." I cross my arms and stare down at him. "So?"

He glares, fire in his brown eyes. "If you get killed in the Kingdom of the Wolves, there'll be war. Thousands of lives could be lost on both sides. Does that seem like a good thing?"

That's it? "Then you better make sure I come back alive." At his snort, I cross my arms and raise my eyebrow. "Don't you think the Wolf King killing my grandmother, the Dowager Queen of Lorria, would also cause a war? Or he might be planning to start one himself? There is no winning here unless we get my grandmother safely home."

"Which I'm sure the Lorrian king and queen were working on. But you couldn't wait for someone else to come up with a plan. You wanted to play the hero." He rolls up on his knees, forcing me to take a step back. "This isn't a matter of waltzing in the front door of the palace and asking for your grandmother. I'm serious when I say we'll probably die on this trip. Are you really the best person to rescue your grandmother?"

I push away the doubts that have been plaguing me since I left home. "I'm the only one who cares enough about Oma to do whatever it takes to get her back."

"That doesn't make you right. If you die, do you think your family is going to think you did the right thing coming here? Or will their grief be that much stronger because your death was so unnecessary?"

I clench my fists. "I couldn't sit by while they did nothing. I know I'm right."

"How? How do you know?"

"Because I am!" I throw my arms out. "You're right, we're probably going to die. I've never been this terrified in my entire life and it's only been a day. I have no idea what I'm doing. I'm totally incompetent at camping, and fighting, and anything else we'll have to do out here. If you think we can't make it to the palace, then we probably won't." I puff out a small breath. "If you truly think we can't succeed, then go. I won't ask anyone else to die for Oma. But I have to try." I hide my hands behind my back so he won't see them trembling.

"I promised to get you to the palace and back. I always keep my word. Even if it's going to get me killed." He shakes his head. "If I had any sense at all, I would've left you to find your own way back to the village."

Giddiness hits me as my knees threaten to buckle from relief. "I guess it's a good thing for me you don't have any sense."

His lips twitch. "Don't break out the flattery now. If you had any other choice, you wouldn't have asked me."

"That's not true, I asked you first." *Ha, point for me.*

He pauses, his brow crinkling. "Why did you ask me?"

"Because you're a Wolf. You're my best bet for getting to Oma in one piece." Blunt and not very flattering to either of us, but it's the truth.

He nods slowly. "And I'm supposed to believe you trust a Wolf to get you to the palace and back? We're sworn enemies."

"Our kingdoms are enemies, not us." I blink as the truth of that statement hits me. In his heart, Markus will always be a Wolf. And yes, he's been rude, and harsh, and a general pain to deal with, but he's also risking his life to help me. There's not enough money in the kingdom to reward him if we actually succeed at this insane plan. "I'll learn to trust you."

His look is full of skepticism.

"Saving my life was a good first step." I give him a

small smile and lift a shoulder. "And if you're still here in the morning, you'll be leagues ahead of Herr Bannan."

That earns me a grin. "But you're forgetting the most important question. Can I trust a Lorrian? "

I tap my pursed lips, pretending to think it over. "Hmm. Hard to say. I mean, obviously you'd have no chance in a fight with me. I'd overpower you in seconds."

The corners of his eyes crinkle. "Obviously."

"And we've already agreed you have terrible lapses in judgment. Why else would you think going to the Wolf Palace this time of year is a good idea? You need me to point out when you're doing something foolish."

"Good point. I guess we better stick together then." He holds out his hand. "Truce?"

"Truce." I grasp his forearm, twitching at the tiny zap when I touch his skin. "Can you do me a favor now that we're on the same side? Could you at least try to believe we won't die some horrible death? That through some amazing stroke of luck, we'll come out victorious? Call me crazy, but it makes me a bit nervous that the person I'm depending on is convinced we're going to die any second."

"All right," Markus grumbles good-naturedly. "Now go get some sleep."

"Wait, I have a peace offering." I grab my pack and dig inside, tossing items on the ground until I find the squashed sticky buns. I grab one and shove it into his hands. "Here, you have to eat it. It's how we agree the argument is over in my family."

"With pastry?"

"It's silly, I know. But Mother always says people can't stay mad if they're eating something sweet. Actually, she says something like 'after the bitter comes the sweet,' but

I'm paraphrasing because her sayings are always cryptic and take too long to figure out. Please?"

He holds up his sticky bun in a toasting gesture. "The bite is healed, the wolf your friend once more." He smiles. "That's how we did it in my family."

I tap my pastry to his, then sink my teeth into it. *Yummm. This is what food is supposed to be.* Between bites of cinnamon and honey goodness, I ask, "Do you miss them? Your family?"

The smile disappears. He stares down at the bun in his hands, slowly tearing off a piece. "Yah." His shoulders slump, and he stares off into the distance, a lost look on his face.

My stomach twists. *It's my fault. For reminding him of his family.* I cast around for something to cheer him up, but my mind comes up blank. "Could you, um, make me more of that tea? I accidentally spilled mine."

He mutters something, then opens one of the side pockets on his pack and pulls out a small packet. There's just enough water left for a half cup of tea. This time I don't hesitate, gulping it down after it has a few minutes to brew.

A tingling tart flavor lingers on my tongue. "Hey, that's really good."

"You sound surprised." Markus pretends to be grouchy, but I can see the smile starting.

"I haven't had good tea since I left home." I lean forward and whisper loudly, "Don't tell the innkeeper, but his tea tastes like dishwater."

His eyes light up. "Yah. I don't know how anyone can stand that stuff. Tea should make a statement." He launches into a description of his favorite tea, then moves on to complaining about the innkeeper's stew. "So bland. Where's the spice?"

I turn my snort into a cough. "Absolutely."

My eyes have barely closed when Markus shakes my shoulder. "Time to wake up, sleepy pup."

I swat at him and pull the blanket over my head. "It's still dark. Go away."

"No can do. We have to get going." He pulls the blanket off and a rush of cold air sucks the heat out of my skin.

"Arrrrghhhh!" I curl up in a ball, glaring at him through crusty eyes. "You're one of those annoying morning people, aren't you?"

"If you mean someone who seizes the day and lives each to their fullest, then yah."

"More like hates themselves and likes to punish the people who actually enjoy sleep." I sit up, rubbing my arms to warm them up. My muscles protest, but they're nowhere close to the screaming agony I anticipated after our hike yesterday. Markus's magic tea worked better than I could've hoped. *I wonder what other miracles he has in his pack.*

"Where's my tooth powder …" I paw through my bag, not actually registering anything. My eyes feel like they're covered in sand, scraping with every blink.

"Here, chew on these." He hands me a small wad of green leaves with a minty smell.

I eye them suspiciously. "Is this breakfast?"

He snorts. "It'll clean your teeth."

"I'd rather brush them." I pop the leaves into my mouth. Mint. Something green tasting. Some other odd flavors I can't identify.

"Chew, chew, chew." Markus gestures, chomping vigorously on his own leaves.

After a few minutes, we spit them out. Amazingly, my mouth feels cleaner than after brushing.

"So? What do you think?" Markus smirks and rocks back on his heels.

"Meh. I'd still rather brush." At his raised eyebrow, I laugh. "You're right. Those worked great. How did you learn all this?"

Markus turns away. "Like I said, my grandmother. She was a great healer."

"I'd love to hear about her." When he stays silent, I quickly add, "Oma wouldn't know the difference between ginger and chamomile. She's hopeless when it comes to herbs."

He rummages through his pack. "What about you? Are you interested in herbology?"

I chuckle. "I'm more interested in spices. Specifically, how to make food tastier." *Mayhap I can convince Markus to let me season those bland food bars he loves so much.*

"Good herbs can be used for both." He pulls on his pack, then holds up mine. "Your accessories, princess."

I wince as the pack settles on my bruised hips. Apparently, Markus's magic tea only works on muscles and not bones.

He grimaces in sympathy. "After a couple days you'll get used to it."

Markus lied. It takes four days before the hip pain fades to match the dull ache in the rest of my muscles. With our truce established, we fall into an easy routine and our days blend together. My unforgiving guide pesters me awake before the sun has a chance to rise with his annoyingly cheerful chatter. I forgive him after my brain has a chance to wake up and there's a meal in my tummy. Hiking broken up with brief rests. Then we make camp and repeat everything the next morning.

Each day it's harder to remember Markus is a Wolf. He's just Markus. We have lively debates about desserts (he continues to incorrectly insist savory is acceptable despite my excellent and irrefutable arguments the sweetness makes it dessert). I manage to sneak cinnamon and dried apricots into the dinner pot without Markus noticing, making dinner almost tasty. I tell him about my family and growing up in the palace. He tells me how he loves to sketch landscapes and about the hidden waterfall he found near Eelan. In the few glimpses of his life in Lorria, Markus brushes over the cruelty of the villagers, but it's enough to guess at how lonely he was there. It makes me ashamed my kingdom didn't give him a fair chance. I hope he finds a warmer welcome wherever he chooses to call home next. As we walk, Markus teaches me about the different plants and animals found in the forest. Or at least, he tries to. I get the sense there's a hidden world within the forest if only I could see it the way he does.

He points to a tree off to the right. "See that bird with the splash of red on its head? That's a black woodpecker."

I squint. "I only see leaves."

"The third tree, near the middle." He points emphatically.

I dutifully scan the spot. "Is this like that lark you swore was nesting above us?"

"Is everyone in your family this blind? When you get home, be sure to ask your parents for a pair of spectacles."

"Maddie's the one who can't see across a ballroom. I have eyes like a hawk and I'm telling you there's nothing there. You should double check the mushrooms you're eating if you continue having hallucinations. Do you have any siblings?" Too late, I remember it's a sensitive topic. He's never said why he left the Kingdom of the Wolves, and I've never asked. *Mayhap it's time to broach that particular topic ...*

He stiffens, turning back into that unhappy, tense person I first saw in town. "I don't remember."

Leave it alone, Lys ... "You must remember something. You said you learned herbs from your grandmother."

He grunts.

"You weren't that young when you left here."

"Who told you that?"

"The innkeeper. He said you came to town six or seven years ago."

"Six years." He stares straight ahead.

I forge ahead, energized now that I'm getting answers. "Where did you live before that? Was it one of the villages close to the border? Will we travel near it?"

"It doesn't matter anymore." He speeds up his pace until I'm trotting to keep up.

"Markus," I pant. "Sorry. Sometimes I don't think before I talk. You might have noticed."

He doesn't look at me, but there's an infinitesimal decrease in his speed.

"I don't mean to pry. It's just, you let me talk about my

family and everything. And I don't know anything about you. It feels unfair. And if we're going to be traveling together, I'd like to get to know you better. I already know you know everything about the woods and have a leaf for every situation."

He slows down a bit more and I suck in air, trying to catch my breath. My face is burning from the muggy heat and exercise.

Markus scratches his beard, his lips tight. "It's not something I like to dwell on. I'd rather leave the past in the past."

Disappointment trickles into my chest, but I nod. "All right. I know you didn't want to come back here, so I'm really grateful you agreed to it."

He smirks. "Are you sure you wouldn't rather have Herr Bannan as your guide?"

I smack his arm. "You're never going to let me live that down, are you?"

"Never. I'll remind you about it every time you complain or second guess me."

"Then I get to complain about how you turned me down the first time when I asked so nicely."

He lifts an eyebrow. "Truce?"

"Truce." I wrestle with the words, trying to shove them back down, but they burst out. "I'll probably ask about your family again. Can I apologize in advance? My sister and I have an obsession with getting into each other's personal business and I can't help it. I'm nosey. And I want to help people with their problems. Not that you have problems. Or that they're any of my concern. I mean, I'm concerned as your friend, but that doesn't give me the right to force you to talk to me. Not that I could force you. But I don't have to nag you either. And I'll try—really, I'll try. But I'm not good at thinking before I speak." The last air whooshes out of my lungs. I want to snatch the words back, or hide in the forest, or do anything to erase my nonsensical speech.

"We're friends?"

I didn't think it was possible for my face to get any hotter. "No! I mean, yes. I think we are. Or starting to be."

Markus says, "Advance apology accepted."

His face is inscrutable. It takes everything I have not to interrogate him about what he's thinking. If he wanted to punish me, he couldn't devise a better torture.

The silence crackles. It's hard to keep my mind from analyzing every twitch and nuance of Markus's expression. *Are we friends? I think we're friends. Being friends doesn't mean anything. How does he feel about being friends?* The man should be a master negotiator, his face betraying nothing of his thoughts.

"Lisette?"

"Hmm?" I drag myself out of my head and focus on my guide.

Markus looks to the side, his brows furrowed, eyes narrowed.

"Stay close."

"Why?"

"Just … stay close."

Wolf Guard. I hurry my steps until I'm tripping on Markus's heels. "What should I do if the wolves show up?" I clutch the pack's straps to keep my hands from shaking.

"Don't move."

"But should I—"

Markus's arm snaps out, freezing me in place. "Don't. Move."

A pack of giant silver wolves surrounds us.

7

My imagination didn't do the Wolf Guard justice. The creatures are menacing enough to take on Markus, even when he's armed. They're each bigger than the largest dogs I've ever seen, closer to pony size. Their heads are almost equal height with mine. They pace back and forth between the tree trunks, disappearing and reappearing, flickering like shadows. Silent snarls are fixed on their faces. Growls fill the air.

The pack leader pads forward, its paws the size of dinner plates. The silver fur glows in the dim light. The shoulders hunch as it stalks forward, the enormous head swinging back and forth between me and Markus, its amber eyes fathomless. The bared teeth show off every canine. Its long ears are flat against its head, hackles raised down its back. A low growl, more felt than heard, comes from its chest. Wicked black claws peek between the silver fur.

The creature stops a few paces away, muscles quivering. Its nose twitches as it turns to Markus. The wolf studies him for a heartbeat, then relaxes a fraction and dips its head.

Then it turns to me.

Don'tmovedon'tmovedon'tmove. I gulp, heart racing in my chest. My muscles lock, knees shaking. Black spots float in front of my eyes. I sway closer to Markus, my feet stuck to the ground. *Don'tmovedon'tmovedon'tmove*

The wolf's eyes bore into mine. Its nostrils flare. Flare again. Its back legs tense as the growls grow louder. The other wolves slow their steps, fangs bared.

I squeak out, "Markus?"

He slowly reaches under his tunic and pulls out a thin silver whistle. Markus blows three quick breaths into the instrument, but there's no sound.

Is it broken? I shoot him a frantic look, muscles tensed to bolt despite no chance of escape.

He repeats the silent blasts.

The change in the wolf is immediate. The ears come up and the hackles go down. The deathly growl morphs to a warning rumble. It keeps its canines out as it slowly stalks up to me. The wolf stares at my face, rancid breath blasting me. Fangs linger inches from my throat. My knees tremble and sweat breaks out over my skin. I keep my eyes trained on the wolf in front of me despite the growing conviction the other creatures are sneaking up behind me, ready to pounce.

Markus says, "Hold out your hand."

I hiss, "Are you crazy?"

"She needs to sniff your scent." He keeps his tone light and friendly. "Trust me."

He's really pushing our truce to the limits. Fighting my instincts to run, I slowly hold out my hand to the beast. The wolf's amber eyes meet mine as it pushes its cold, wet nose into my palm. Hot air scorches my skin as the enormous creature snuffles my hand, its muzzle moving around and around. I close my eyes, wincing, waiting for the pain.

A warm, squishy wet thing tingles against my skin. I swallow my shriek, my eyes flying open. The silver wolf gives my palm another lick with her giant pink tongue, then sits back on its haunches, panting a smile at me. All traces of the menacing monster have disappeared. In its place sits a friendly puppy. She thumps her tail against the ground, kicking up a small cloud of dust, then scratches her ear with a back leg. The wolves around us drop their guard, sitting or flopping on the ground.

Markus's shoulders relax. "All the Wolf Guards will know to let you pass now. They'll even come to your aid if you call, or if they sense you're in danger." He grins. "You can pet her if you want."

My stomach rolls and twists. "Really? That's it?" I give him a questioning look, then glance back at the wolf. "She won't mind?" *She looks safe now, but ...*

"Go ahead. They love scratches under the chin."

I inch my hand toward the wolf, ready to snatch it back at the first sign of danger. My arm shakes. She yawns, sharp teeth in full display. I pull back, then clench my teeth and force my hand forward, refusing to play the coward in front of Markus.

The wolf's fur is coarser and greasier than expected. I tentatively pat her head, keeping well clear of the fangs. The wolf butts her head against my palm, pressing against me. As I run my hand across her head and down her back, the amber eyes half-close and she tilts her head so I can reach better. Encouraged, I increase the pressure, daring to scratch a little with my nails. The wolf leans into my touch with a happy groan, and I redouble my efforts, scratching harder as she makes little yips of happiness.

I lurch forward as another wolf rubs against my legs from behind me, knocking me off balance. With a laugh, I pet it with my other hand. More wolves crowd around us, licking everything within reach and begging for a scratch with liquid, soulful eyes. For the first time since setting foot in the forest, I'm completely relaxed and happy. There's nothing like being buried in a pile of cheerful, wriggling wolves to let you forget your cares for a moment.

Too soon, Markus touches my shoulder. "We should keep moving."

I give the wolves one final scratch, then reluctantly pull away. "Goodbye, sweethearts. I hope I see you again."

The pack leader stands on her hind legs and puts her paws on my shoulder, nearly knocking me over. She gives my face a long, sloppy lick. Before I can blink, the pack is bounding off and disappearing into the forest.

"Well," I splutter. "Well."

"Guess she liked you." Markus chuckles as I wipe my face on my sleeve.

I grin up at him. "I didn't think they'd be so sweet." I look longingly to where the silver wolves disappeared, wishing they could come with us. "I've never had a pet."

"Don't try that with the wild wolves. These are bred and raised by trainers. They're part of our family."

It's boggling to think of someone training wolves to be so menacing to strangers and yet charming to the natives. "Does everyone carry one of those whistles? How does it work? Why couldn't I hear anything? They wolves are so cute. Do you keep the ones who fail training as pets? Can people keep the ones who are too old to patrol? How do they know it's you instead of someone trying to sneak in? Why would the other wolves know my scent now? How many packs are roaming at a time?"

"Enough to keep the borders closed from anyone trying to sneak in. The wolves will recognize you, but nobody else. Anyone with you will be killed." Markus starts walking, his eyes straight ahead. "We have a long way to go before we make camp tonight."

That's it? I could've guessed the wolves wouldn't let anybody else through, but that's all he has to say about it? I frown as the truth hits me. *Unbelievable. He doesn't trust me.* I open my mouth to argue—then close it. *Markus just wants to protect his kingdom's secrets. After all, I'm the Lorrian princess. If he tells me how to let others past the Wolf Guard, he's essentially opened his border for an invading force.*

I should be angry he doesn't trust me by now, but mostly I'm tired. I rub my chest, trying to soothe away the ache. At the end of the day, our kingdoms are still enemies. I may learn things that would allow Lorria to destroy the Kingdom of the Wolves. Even the idea makes me feel slimy. *No, I won't let that happen. I may not like the Wolves, but I won't hurt them either. Not after all that Markus is doing to help me. I owe him that.*

"Markus." I pull him to a stop. "No matter what happens on this journey, I'll keep your secrets. I just—I just wanted you to know that." Heat creeps into my cheeks. I twist my fingers together as butterflies invade my stomach.

He looks away. "This may not be my home anymore, but I don't want anyone to get hurt because of me."

"I understand, I really do. All I want is to get Oma home safe. You're helping me do that. I would never betray you. I trust you and I want you to know you can trust me."

He shifts his weight, looking away before meeting my

eyes again. "You're paying me to help you."

I bite my lip to keep from smiling. "I think we both know you're underpaid. Oma and I thank you. No matter what happens."

He sets a hand on my shoulder, giving it a light squeeze. "We'll get her home."

I wrap my arms around my middle and swallow hard. "Am I crazy? Going after my grandmother all alone?"

"You're not alone. We—"

Markus stiffens. His eyes roll up in his head and he drops to the ground with a loud thump. Behind him is a skinny man holding a thick club.

He leers, revealing a mouthful of yellow teeth. "Hello, little girl."

8

The man grabs my arm. I scream and kick his legs, writhing, but his grip is iron. His fist cracks across my cheek. Stars burst in front of my eyes. I shake my head, my vision slowly swimming into focus, my cheek on fire.

Eight men surround us. They're a scraggly crew with stained tunics and crude weapons. The hard looks in their eyes make me shiver. While the others rifle through our packs, two of them quickly disarm Markus and bind his hands behind him. The ropes cut into his wrist. When they finish, the fatter man gives him a vicious kick to the ribs. Markus moans.

"Don't hurt him," I shout, jerking forward.

The man yanks me back and shakes me until my teeth rattle. "Hold still or I'll do the same to you." He holds up the club to reinforce his meaning.

The fat man laughs and kicks Markus again. Tears prick at my eyes, a lump in my throat cutting off my breath.

Markus groans when they roll him over. He blinks, then spots the man holding my arm. He growls as they haul him to his feet. "Let her go."

The bandit laughs. "Such chivalry. Where did a grunt like you find a pretty little thing like her?"

"She's my sister."

He grins, taking in the differences between us. "Not much of a family resemblance. You wouldn't lie to old Uwe, would you?"

Markus glares at him, his muscles bulging as he strains against the ropes.

"Nay, too much anger for a sister. But no mehein, so not your wife. A sweetheart then." Uwe shakes his head sadly. "You've hurt my feelings, lad. Hurt them real bad. Here sweetie, give me kiss to make me feel better."

The other men whoop and holler as Uwe leans down and slobbers on my injured cheek. I wince away.

Markus lunges at him, but the bandits are ready. Two yank his bound hands, wrenching his arms so high I fear they've dislocated them. Two more swing staffs at his legs, knocking his feet out from under him. Markus crashes to the ground with a bellow.

The bandits cheer and kick him. I swallow my fury, not wanting to provoke them into hurting Markus more.

The leader holds a knife to my throat. "Now, let's try this again."

I should be terrified, but all I feel is rage. *The scum is enjoying this.* My jaw aches and blood pounds in my ears. "You have our packs. Take them and leave us be."

"Is that a Lorrian accent I hear?" Uwe chuckles. "Today is turning out better than I hoped."

I clench my teeth. "I don't have an accent."

Markus struggles back to his knees, his usual grace lost to his bound hands and injuries. "We're from Lutach."

Uwe presses the blade to my throat. "There you go, lying again."

I grit my teeth as the steel bites into my skin. "He's not lying. I can't be Lorrian."

"And why is that?" Uwe seems to enjoy my defiance.

"I'm here, aren't I? The Wolf Guard would stop any Lorrians trying to come across the border." *The Wolf Guard. Markus said they'd help us if we're in trouble. Can they sense it?*

That stumps him momentarily, then he waves away my argument. "You could sneak by them. Enough of that." He points to the fat man. "We don't want to leave anything behind. Kill the boy and then search him."

I scream, flying at Uwe. My nails leave bloody tracks down his face.

Uwe roars, flinging me away. "Fanging wildcat." He dabs his face as one of the other men forces me to my knees. "Kill them both."

The bandits protest loudly, arguing with Uwe they should sell us both. Markus stares at me and I know—*I know*—he's going to attack them. He has no chance against the eight of them with his hands tied, but he might be able to distract them long enough that I can run away in the confusion.

He's going to sacrifice himself. He can't do that. I won't let him. I harden myself against the fear, my mind racing. There must be a way to save both of us. *We need the Wolf Guard.*

I wail as loudly as I can, startling my captor into releasing my shoulder. I fling myself at Markus, clutching his shirt. My hand inches up to his collar. "Oh, my love. My darling." I cry loud, fake sobs, burying my head against his chest. I grope for the leather cord holding the wolf whistle. I find it—then another one. Not stopping to think, I yank both out and fumble for the whistle. *Please be close enough to hear.* There's just enough time to give it a long blast before I'm jerked away, my arms gripped behind me.

The head man laughs. "All that for a broken toy?" Uwe shakes his head, then does a double take when he sees the pendant dangling on the other cord. "What have we here?" He snaps the pendant off Markus's neck and holds it up to the light. His eyes widen and he swears softly. He grabs Markus's tunic in his fist and pulls him part way up. "Where did you get this? Did you steal it?"

Markus presses his lips together.

I scan through the trees, desperately looking for a hint of silver, heart thundering. *Where are you? Are you coming?*

The men call out, "What is it? What do you have?"

Uwe's hand closes around the pendant. "The seal of the Wolf King."

The fat man laughs. "That'll be worth a pouch of gold."

"Mayhap more than that." Uwe studies Markus. "Too young to be Garit. You're Fredrik Von Dien."

My attention snaps to Markus as my stomach clenches. *Von Dien? He introduced himself as Markus Von Dien. Prince Markus Von Dien.*

Murmurs break out among the men.

No. He was teasing me.

Markus scowls at Uwe. "I'm not Fredrik."

He has the seal of the Wolf King.

Uwe gives a loud belly laugh and thunks Markus on the back. "I knew it. You're worth your weight in gold, boy."

It's a coincidence. It has to be. A pendant doesn't mean anything …

The rumors fly thick and fast between the bandits.

"I thought he died in the fire."

Another one pipes up, "Nah, that was the brother."

"There weren't no brother."

"I heard the King killed him."

"The Black Wolf killed him, not the King."

Impossible. Don't let your mind run away with itself, Lisette. Be sensible, for once. There's an explanation for all of this.

Uwe grins. "I wonder what the Wolf King will pay to get his son back?"

Markus looks at me, guilt shadowing his eyes.

All I can do is stare at him. It hits me like a punch to the gut. *He's the Wolf King's son.* Dizziness assaults me. A roaring fills my ears. I can't breathe.

I crumple to my knees as my captor drops his grip. The men look around, their eyes going wide. They back toward each other, coming together in a tight huddle. Mouths move, but the sounds are gibberish. I stare dumbly at them, my mind refusing to decipher what's happening. Markus is yelling something.

He's the Wolf King's son.

Silver wolves stalk forward. One brushes my side. The touch snaps me out of my daze. A blast of noise hits me as the men scream. Beasts and men tangle in a bloody mess as the wolf pack attacks the bandits.

He's the Wolf King's son.

I tear my eyes away from Markus and race away into the falling darkness.

9

Branches scratch my face and roots trip me, but I can't stop. I crash through the forest with no thought or regard for how much noise I'm making, or that I'm leaving a trail a blind man could follow. All that matters is I get away from them, from him, from my thoughts.

But my mind insists on grappling with the shocking news, trying to make sense of it. My heartbeat thunders in my ears, beating out Markus's secret.

He's the Wolf King's son. A hot flash sizzles through my body, scorching my skin. *He's the Wolf King's son. He's the Wolf King's son.* No matter how many times I say it, my mind can't grasp it, refuses to believe it. But the guilt was in his eyes, undeniable. *He's the Wolf King's son.*

My legs give out and I crash to the forest floor. Scraped palms and bruised knees are distant aches compared to the pain stabbing through my chest. I stagger up, immediately leaning over and retching. Bile burns my throat. I wipe my mouth against my sleeve, blinking when a raindrop hits my nose. Then another. The drops are coming down faster, thicker, making their way through the overhead canopy.

The small part of my brain still working nudges me. *Get under cover.*

I squint into the dying twilight. Open forest with low plants—no, wait. A larger grouping of rocks off to the right. I trudge over on shaky legs to find one good thing to save this burning day. A cave. *Anything is better than getting soaked.* I stumble inside and grope through the darkness until I'm out of the wind, then sink to the floor. My muscles are lead. The tightness in my chest won't go away, no matter how much I knead it. My head pounds.

I pull my legs up and wrap my arms around them. "It's not worth crying over. I knew this would happen. He's a Wolf. I just didn't know he's also a Wolf Prince. Not that I could've known, but it doesn't matter. I was a fool to let my guard down and trust him. Never again." I angrily brush the traitorous tears away. "It's fine. I can do this on my own. I don't need Mar—him. He's probably going to run straight to his father and tell him my plan to rescue Oma. Use me as leverage to get back in his father's good graces. They'll be waiting for me. So I'll have to be smarter and faster. That's easy enough. He may be good at navigating the woods, but I'm crafty. Wily. He doesn't stand a chance."

The rain pounds outside the cave, matching my heartbeat. I scrub at my dress, shaking out the dust and dirt clinging to my skirt. *As soon as the storm's over, I'll try to find a road. Speed is more important than trying to avoid notice now. Speed—and not getting lost. My pack is back with the bandits, so I'll have to figure out supplies as I go. It's fine. Everything is fine. Better than fine. It's good I found out about him now, instead of when we were closer to the palace. He's a big liar. To think I was starting to believe we were friends. Idiot. He'd better not cross my path again.*

"Lisette?" Markus's worried voice comes through the pouring rain. "Lisette, where are you?"

I shoot to my feet, back pressed against the wall. *How did he find me so fast?* I creep to the front of the cave and peer out. The trees block any moonlight. It's impossible to tell where he is in the darkness outside, but he must be close. Quickly, I scuff my footprints in the dust, hiding my tracks as I back deeper into the cave. With any luck, Markus will miss the cave entrance.

I crouch in the blackness, heart pounding, my fists clenched. *The gall to come after me. The audacity. If he thinks I'm coming with him quietly, I'll show him how wrong he is.*

A shadow appears at the entrance. "Lisette? "

I hold my breath, willing him away with every fiber of my being.

Concern fills his voice. "Are you hurt?"

Such a skilled actor. If I didn't know better, I'd believe he's actually worried.

"It's not safe in here, these mines are unstable. You need to get out before the whole thing comes down."

He's the idiot here. Well, no—I'm the idiot, but he's just as big an idiot for coming after me. Or desperate. I shift my weight, my stomach twisting. *He wouldn't hurt me.* My hand gropes for a rock. *But I also didn't think he was the Wolf King's son. Fierce face. Fierce face. I'm not afraid to fight dirty.*

A flame appears, flooding the space with light. Markus holds the improvised torch over his head, squinting my direction. Bruises cover his jaw. He's carrying both packs on his shoulders, but he's curled in on his right side, his movements jerkier than before. The pain from his injuries evident in the strain on his face.

I push aside the flash of concern for him. *Stubborn barbarian. We could've gone our own ways and never seen each other again, but he had to find me. I don't care what he says, I'm not going to follow him to the palace like a fool to be served up on a platter to the Wolf King.*

"I didn't think you would trust me if you knew who I really was."

I snort.

Markus's glance jumps to where I'm crouched.

Burn it. "Go away, Wolf. You're not welcome here."

He flinches, then his lips settle in a firm line. "I promised to take you to the palace, and that's what I'm going to do. Nothing's changed from our deal."

Is he serious? "You're fired."

Markus walks toward me, forcing me to retreat farther from the entrance. "We have a contract. Where's my payment?"

"I'm not paying you a single coin. You lied to me."

He stops in front of me and rocks back on his heels. "I didn't lie. I told you I was Prince Markus Von Dien when we met, but you didn't believe me."

Anger pounds in my head. "Don't pretend that excuses anything. You did everything you could to make sure I didn't believe you. You should've told me the Wolf King is your father."

"That has nothing to do with our arrangement."

"Are you kidding? Your father kidnaps my grandmother and you think it's not relevant?" My voice echoes off the walls. I narrow my eyes. "I knew I shouldn't have trusted you. You're just like them."

Crack!

Markus shouts and launches at me. Rocks fall from the roof of the cave. There's a painful jerk at my waist. The view changes from dirt floor to ceiling as I fly backwards. My shoulder slams into the ground, my bones ringing from the impact. Dust fills my lungs. Coughing, I put a hand to my head. *What happened?* "Markus?"

The torch flickers on the ground. Boulders are piled up, stretching for the ceiling and blocking the entrance.

Markus is nowhere to be seen.

10

"Markus!" I scramble up, slipping on the dust and dirt. My heart drums in my ears. "Markus!"

Clumps of dirt and stones drop from the ceiling. Dust fills the air in a choking haze. Rocks are stacked precariously, teetering and tilting against each other. The room is a maze of huge boulders taller than I am, with smaller rocks scattered and smashed around them. I can't spot the cave entrance under the layers covering it.

The torch splutters. I grab it before it can go out and hold it overhead, squinting into the darkness. A shadow twitches behind one of the piles. Swallowing around the lump in my throat, I scrabble over the rocks, feet sliding as I grip the stones for balance. Ignoring my scrapes and bruises, I make my way across the room to where Markus lays on his side, his leg twisted under him.

I fall to my knees next to him and shake him. "Markus. Please be all right. Markus." A sob rises through my chest.

Markus blinks slowly, his eyes dazed. "Careful. Rockslide."

I give a strangled chuckle. "Thanks for the warning."

He winces as my fingers brush over the nasty lump forming on the back of his head. I help him struggle to a sitting position.

"Fangs, that hurts." He closes his eyes, then snaps them open. "Don't let me fall asleep."

"Why not?"

"Just don't."

I glare. "Don't start this again."

He groans. "Aren't you supposed to be nice to me when I'm injured?"

"No."

"Even if I'm dying?"

The air rushes out of my lungs. "Are you?"

His grimace flashes into a smile for a split second. "Probably not."

The pressure releases me and I resist the urge to punch him. "Good. Because no matter what, I'm going to yell at you for being a burning idiot, but I might feel a tiny bit guilty about it if you died. This way I can tell you what a colossal rat you've been and not worry about it." I glare, clenching my fists. "How could you, Markus? You lied to me. About everything."

"I—"

"The Wolf King is your father. Your father! You should've told me that. You knew it was important, that I should know it, but you kept silent. I trusted you. I was the idiot who thought you didn't want to talk about your family because they'd hurt you, and I let it go. Me! I never let things go. But I did. Just like I got past that you're a Wolf and my enemy because I love Oma and need to save her. I didn't realize I was making a deal with the kidnapper's son."

Markus stares at his knees. "You wouldn't have trusted me."

It's odd to see such a large man looking so small. But I refuse to let his remorse sway me. If he betrays me, not only is my life in danger, but Oma's. I can't trust someone who's proven deceitful already. "You're right. I wouldn't have, but I might've still asked for your help." I turn away, my body shaking. "Let's just get out of here and go our separate ways."

His voice is rough. "If anyone figures out you're Lorrian, they won't hesitate to kill you, or turn you over to people who will. You need my help."

I can't talk about this anymore. "Where's my pack?" I kick rocks and shove them aside, searching among the rubble. *Food. My cloak. Whatever I need to get away from him.*

When Markus stands, I stare him down until he holds up his hands and sinks back to the ground. I spot fabric wedged under a rock. After some fierce tugs and a lot of swearing, the bag comes free. It's a tattered mess. Acidic fumes burn my nose.

I toss it at his feet. "Yours." *He can keep his stupid plants and dumb remedies.*

Markus takes the pack and starts pulling out the items. He winces and yanks out his hand. Blood drips from his fingers. "Broken bottle."

"Gimme that." I jerk it away from him and start picking through the mess. The clothes and tent inside are stained, and the majority of our camping supplies are dented, but salvageable. The medical supplies are more mixed. There're a few packets intact, and even a jar or two, but a lot of it is smashed beyond recognition. As I pull each item out, I carefully pick out the glass shards before putting it to the side.

I should just leave. But I need the stuff in my pack. Not that there's much. And it's probably pulverized. If I can even find my pack. I should go. Leave. I don't owe him anything. Except ... he saved my life with those bandits. I saved his too, but still ... We'll get out of this death trap and then go our separate ways. It's fine. I'll get him the money after I'm home. He's earned it. I owe him that much for getting me across the border, and I won't have anyone saying I don't pay my debts.

Markus's eyes watch me, but I ignore him. *It's not that I hate him, but I can't stand to be around him anymore. He lied. I can't forget that. And he's the Wolf King's son, so I'll never be able to trust him again. He can go back to Lorria, or the Wolf Palace, or wherever he wants, and I'll get Oma, and we'll never see each other again.* My stomach twists. *Don't think about it now. Get the packs. Get out.*

When Markus closes his eyes, I poke his leg with my foot. "Stay awake. Where else are you hurt?"

He waves off my concern. "I'm fine."

"Of course you are." I shove the rescued supplies at him. "Here, make yourself useful. What's useable?"

We work in silence. After the main part of the pack is cleared out, I leave Markus to finish checking the side pockets while I poke around the rocks for my pack.

I clear my throat and nod my head toward the makeshift torch. "How long until that goes out?"

He shrugs. "Fifteen minutes? Mayhap less. We can use the tent canvas to extend it."

The thought of being trapped here in the dark isn't very appealing. "Then we should get out of here sooner rather than later."

"That might take some doing." He winces, using both hands to adjust his outstretched leg.

I take a step toward him, then jerk back. "Is your leg hurt?"

"It's just a little stiff." Markus wiggles it. "See? Fine."

"You were saying about getting out of here? Can't we walk to the other entrance?"

Markus shifts his weight and massages his knee. "There probably isn't one."

"I wish you hadn't told me that." My stomach fills with rocks as heavy as the ones trapping us here.

"I'm hoping we'll find an air shaft."

"And if we don't?" I shake my head. "Forget it, I don't want to know."

We're both tired and clumsy, but manage to repack the bag with everything deemed salvageable in a few minutes. I carry the torch and Markus shoulders the pack as we head deeper into the mine.

I squint into the darkness overhead. "What should I look for?"

He holds a hand to his ribs. "Anything that looks like an opening. It should be obvious, but if the rocks shifted this far …" His voice trails off, his brow furrowed. "Say if you notice any breezes."

"Got it."

We walk deeper into the mine, the blackness circling us. Torchlight flickers against the walls. An occasional rock clatters, making me flinch. The weight in my stomach grows heavier with every step. After five minutes, we have to stop to cut another canvas strip for the torch. We keep walking, no break in the walls or ceiling.

Unable to bear the silence anymore, I ask, "Are the wolves all right?"

Markus scans overhead. "The wolves?"

"The ones that attacked the bandits. Did any of them get hurt?"

He chuckles. "I wouldn't even call it a fight. It was over in a few minutes and all the wolves were fine. Those bandits were no match for them."

One of the knots in my stomach loosens. "Good."

"That was brilliant, by the way. Signaling them."

"Thanks." My hand clenches on the torch. *Why is he making this so hard?*

"I should've thought of it. How did you—"

"Don't." My voice cracks. "I can't forgive you. I won't."

Markus hesitates a step, then regains his stride. "You don't have to forgive me. But you need me if you want to rescue your grandmother."

"I'll figure it out." I squint into the darkness, desperately seeking an opening. It's too easy to fall back into the relaxed companionship from our days camping and hiking. Too easy to forget his betrayal.

"You won't be able to cross the mountains alone. Or get into the palace. You need me."

Burn it. I'd forgotten about the mountains. "Nothing you say will change my mind."

"The Wolf Guards would've killed you if you'd tried to sneak across the border without me. You'll run into more problems. You said you needed my help."

My resolve wavers, but I pull back my shoulders. *No. I'm better off on my own.* A black patch in the rock overhead. "There."

Markus heaves a sigh of relief. "Thank the goddess. I'll

climb up and—"

"No, you won't." I square off with him, barely remembering not to poke his chest. "You can't climb with your injuries. I'm going."

"I can make it."

I cross my arms. "Lift your arms over your head."

Markus glares.

I lift my eyebrow, refusing to budge.

"Let's keep looking for another entrance. There's probably one ahead."

"You said that was unlikely."

Markus over my head. "I've changed my mind."

"So have I. This is our best option, and I'm going. Now help me up."

Markus hesitates until I give an exasperated sigh and march to the wall.

He follows me, grumbling, then sets down the pack. "Wait, wait. I can't—we'll need a rope."

He pulls out the canvas and cuts half of it into long strips. We silently work to braid the strips together, then Markus curls the rope into long loops and drapes it over my shoulder.

His hand rests on my shoulder. "I'm sorry."

I look down, my chest tight. "I know."

He waits a moment, then his hand slips away. He bends down to give me a leg up the wall. I don't miss the wince and suppressed grunt as he lifts me higher.

"Don't." I give him a fierce look. "Don't hurt yourself."

He wipes the sweat from his forehead. "We need to get out of here."

"I'll get us out." I look at the opening above me and start my climb.

My fingers are slick as I grip the rock, pressing upward.
Either the mine was roughly made, or the rock falls did
damage here, because there are plenty of cracks and crevices
to use. "Just like climbing the trees at home," I mutter to
myself. "Nice and slow." The rope throws off my balance,
knocking against my chest and knee, but I press on, knowing
this is our only chance.

When I reach the air shaft, I'm pleasantly surprised to
find it angled. I thought they would cut it straight up, but the
incline is enough to give me a little assistance as I inch my
way through.

"One hand, then the other. One foot, then the other." The
torchlight below fades. Inky blackness envelops me as I
grope forward, my muscles shaking, my fingers slipping.
"It's fine. One hand, then the—AHHHHHHHHHHHHHHHH!"

The rock crumbles under my fingers as my foot slides,
sending me plunging. My stomach drops. My screams echo
against the walls. My hands scrape as I try to grab anything
to stop my fall. I crash into Markus at the bottom, sending us

both tumbling to the ground.

"Ow." I push myself into a sitting position.

Markus is laying on his back next to me, his face creased in pain. "Are you hurt?"

"I'm fine." I scramble to my knees, my hand reaching out, but not touching him. My pulse speeds up. "I'm so, so sorry, Markus. Did I hurt you? I'm sorry. What can I do?"

He carefully sits up, holding a hand to his side. "Not your fault. Just knocked the breath out of me for a moment. Nothing broken."

My stomach twists. I swallow hard, my throat dry. "I'm sorry."

"Like I said, it's not your fault." He gives me a tight smile. "My turn."

"What?" I scramble to my feet. "No, I'm doing this."

"You tried. There's no shame in failing." Markus looks at the opening and holds out his hand. "I'll send the rope down after I do a check to make sure it's safe."

I take a deep breath, controlling my quick flash of temper. "Do your ribs hurt?"

His lips press together. "Yah."

Wow, he actually admitted it. "Then give me another chance. I still have the best shot at getting us out of here."

He gives me a long look, then nods. Markus grudgingly helps me up onto the wall again. I grit my teeth, feeling my muscles shaking as I reach for the first crack.

When the darkness slips over me again, I pause, pressing my forehead to the cool rock. *Keep going. The top is up there somewhere.* One hand, then the next. One foot, then the next. I test each spot before putting my weight on it. Sweat breaks out across my forehead despite the cool air. I grit my teeth, memories of my fall flashing through my mind. My fingertips go numb. I pull myself up, using the angle of the tunnel to take some of the pressure off my hands for a moment. My fingers flex, then I keep moving.

My legs fight for every inch, my arms shaking. When I reach the top, I flop on the ground, staring up at the trees overhead. Dampness soaks into the back of my dress, but I can't care. The air has never been fresher, the night full of a crisp, clean scent after the rainfall. I force myself up and stagger to a thick tree, wrapping the rope twice around the trunk before tying it off in a tight knot.

I stumble to the edge of the airshaft. As I stare down into the blackness, my hand clenches on the coiled rope. *If I really don't trust him, I could walk away. Nobody would ever know.*

Markus is waiting in the mine. Probably listening for me, braced to catch me in case I fall again despite knowing how badly it could hurt him. Not once did I think Markus wanted to climb up because he would leave me behind. He wanted to be the one to go because it was dangerous and he didn't want me to get hurt. Because it was hard and he would do it for me if he could.

You're fooling yourself. The rebuke is half-hearted, weak. As infuriated as I am with Markus for lying, I can't help but believe I still know him.

This is your last chance. Be smart, Lys. Oma's life depends on it.

My fingers open, dropping the rope down the shaft. I sigh. *I guess I trust him after all.*

Markus climbs up slower than expected, his face covered in sweat by the time he reaches the top. He doesn't look at me as he pulls up the pack. "I wasn't sure you were going to drop the rope."

I look away, rubbing a hand along my arm. "Neither was I."

"I should've told you about my father."

I stiffen, my pulse speeding up. I take a long, deep breath and make sure my voice is even before responding. "This isn't the time to talk about it."

"Why not?"

"I don't want to fight." I untie the rope from the tree, keeping my eyes down as I work on the knots.

"Since when? You never pass up a chance to argue with me."

"Since you're pathetic right now. It'll be harder to gloat when I win."

He raises his eyebrows. "So what you're really saying is you don't want to be humiliated when I'm the victor, injuries and all."

My lips press together to keep from smiling. "That'll never happen."

His voice turns serious. "I was worried you wouldn't understand about my father."

My fingers pause on the knot. "I wouldn't have. I don't."

He blows out a rough breath. "It's … complicated. He may be my father, but I'm not his son. At least, not anymore. Both he and my brother think I'm dead."

I spin around to face him. "That doesn't make sense. Why don't you go to the palace and show them you're not?"

He looks away, his body rigid. "They want me to be dead. I'm a threat to them."

Guilt flutters in my stomach, as though I'm somehow responsible for his pain. I can't come up with anything better to respond with than, "That's horrible." My sister and parents make me crazy, but I know they love me, just like I love them. They would never hurt me. "But why would you be a threat? Kings always need an heir. Wouldn't your brother … Fenwick? Wouldn't he be the bigger threat?"

"Fredrik. He's the heir, I'm the spare, as they say." He passes a hand over his face. "It doesn't matter. Needless to say, I don't want them to know I'm alive."

My heart aches at his anguish. I snap my mouth shut before I can barrage him with questions. It's obviously excruciating for him to talk about. And—as much as it pains me—he's right. It doesn't matter. If he needs to stay dead to his father, then he won't betray me.

But Oma's life is at stake, too. I have to be sure. "How do I know what you're saying is true?"

Markus gives me a half-hearted shrug, his face blank. His voice is hollow. "They think I tried to kill them."

12

Markus's words hang in the air between us.

He looks off into the forest. "I didn't, in case there was any doubt."

I blurt out, "I never thought you did." Mayhap I should have, but my first instinct is to believe him. That confession is practically begging me to distrust him, but it's having the opposite effect. There's a thousand other lies Markus could have told me that would have been less incriminating. His pain is so real, I could reach out and touch it. *He lied before.* Even the pointed reminder can't shake my certainty he's telling the truth now.

He rubs his shoulder, his eyes distant. "Suspicion followed me everywhere. I couldn't stay. When a fire broke out at the palace, I seized on the opportunity to make my escape. If they find out I'm alive, they'll never stop looking for me. I can't go back."

Markus is still holding back, but it's enough to convince me. The guilt inside me triples for forcing him to say it out loud. *I needed to know. For Oma.* But my conscience isn't soothed. *I needed to know.* A lump forms in my throat. *He must feel totally alone in the world. He is totally alone.*

He tries to force a smile. "Some family, huh?" Markus's eyes glisten.

Tears flood my eyes and I fling myself at him, wrapping him in a hug. "Oh, Markus. I'm so, so, sorry. That's—that's terrible." I don't know that I could've survived on my own, totally cut off from everything and everyone I knew, my closest family members preferring to believe I'm dead.

His arms come around me gently. Too late, I remember his injuries.

"Your ribs, I'm sorry, I—"

I loosen my grip, but he pulls me in tighter. Markus buries his head against my shoulder, his body shaking. My heart melts. I press my head against his, my arms stretched around him.

Markus jerks away, clearing his throat as he rubs the back of his neck. "My apologies. I didn't mean to make you uncomfortable."

"Uncomfortable? I'm not—"

He turns away. "We should make camp and get some rest. It's been a long day."

"Markus." I grab his arm, turning him back to face me. "I know words are useless, but I really am sorry. When we get back to Lorria, I'll help you, in any way I can."

He squeezes my hand and gives me a small smile before walking away. I follow behind, struggling to find the words. But there's nothing I can say that'll ease his pain. My steps are heavy with fatigue and sorrow. Knowing a small piece of Markus's story helps me understand him better, but it carries a cost. I've never had to deal with anything like what Markus is going through. How can he bear that weight every day? It would crush me.

Markus doesn't go far before finding a small stream. We wash up silently, then make camp with the supplies we have left. My pack had most of the food and I'm not sure whether to be happy those horrible trail bars are lost. We make do with a handful of edible greens from Markus's pack and a large pot of weak tea. He stares off into the woods, drinking mechanically, a lost expression on his face.

"Markus …" I don't know what to say, but I can't stand the silence. "You're still fired."

"What?" He whips around to stare at me, color returning to his face.

Huh, I guess that worked. "Go back to Eelan. I'll send word to you when Oma and I are back in Lorria."

"No."

I cross my arms. "You can't stop me from firing you."

"We've been over this. We have a contract."

"And I'll still pay you. But you need to leave the Kingdom of the Wolves." *And get as far away from your family as you can.*

A grin slowly spreads over his face. "I'm not leaving."

I definitely don't trust that smile. "You're fired. You have to leave."

"Either I'm still your guide, and I'm contractually bound to take you to the Wolf Palace. Or you fired me, in which case I can go wherever I want, including following you there."

The man is infuriating. "You can't go to the palace."

"Neither can you. But if you're going, I'm going." He settles back, smugness coming off him in waves.

I ignore the little flash of happiness in my chest and blow out my breath loudly. "You are so annoying."

"I'm your guide and the reason your rescue plan has any chance of success. You should be showering me with praise."

I arch my eyebrow. "Why start now?"

He chuckles, then puts a hand to his side. "Ouch. Let's get these injuries taken care of. We need an early start tomorrow." Markus selects a packet from his pack and mixes it with water. "This paste will keep the swelling down so you can still see out of your eye."

My hand flies to my cheek. With everything else going on, I'd forgotten the bandit hit me. Every part of me hurts in one way or another, but my face must look ghastly.

He scoops out some green gunk and smears it across my cheek. "Don't touch that."

I make a face as the clammy slime trickles down my skin. "It feels like cold porridge."

His dark eyes stay on my cheek. "It'll help."

"Don't you need to get gooped too?"

"After you. You'll need something for those cuts." He picks up a handful of green plants I recognize from our first meeting.

I wrinkle my nose. "Are you really going to chew those?"

He pops them into his mouth with a wink.

Blech. I smear a handful of the green goop across his face, snickering as Markus splutters.

I widen my eyes innocently. "Just trying to help. You said you were next, right?"

He narrows his eyes and chews furiously. When he gestures, I hold my hands out with a groan, dreading what's coming next. The smushed plants take the sting out of my cuts, but that doesn't make it any less disgusting. He dabs the goo on the scratches on my neck and arms.

I curl my lip as I stare at the nasty green dollops dotting my skin. "Your turn."

He slathers the paste on a few cuts on his arms and hands, then a nasty gash on his leg he assures me doesn't need stitches. When he makes a motion to wipe off his hands, I stop him.

"Aren't you forgetting something?" I tug at the hem of his shirt. "And don't pretend you don't need anything. Your chest must be a mess"

Markus hesitates, then pulls his shirt up on his right side. Among the mass of forming bruises is a long cut crusted with drying blood. At my shocked look, he lifts a shoulder. "It looks worse than it is. Fell on a rock."

"Hmm. Awfully straight for a rock." I grit my teeth, regretting I didn't kick more of the bandits when I had the chance. I take the paste from him and dab it along the cut. There's a shiny patch of red skin peeking out from under the upper edge of his shirt. I bite my lip and keep silent, not wanting to add to his pain by asking about old injuries. "We're going to need a lot more of that other stuff for all these bruises. And something clean to cover your cut." I hold up the filthy hem of my dress. "You're welcome to it, but I don't think it'll help with infection."

Markus cuts more strips off the canvas while I finish spreading the paste on his injury. He leans forward, awkwardly trying to wrap the bandage without putting pressure on his bruised ribs.

"Here, let me." I take the strips from him and reach around him. Even with my arms fully extended, I have to press my body against his to reach around his chest. A blush spreads to my cheeks and I keep my eyes averted. His heat soaks through my thin dress and my pulse speeds up. His muscles twitch with my movements.

I tie off the bandage and scoot safely out of range as Markus tugs down his shirt.

"Um." My cheeks get hotter as I nudge the packet. "Your bruises …"

Markus winces. I busy myself poking the fire as he turns slightly away from me. He quickly pulls his shirt up again and smears the green paste across his chest. He yanks his tunic down, his breathing heavy. I shake my head, trying to clear the odd tension.

After a few minutes of awkward silence, Markus says, "I think someone was following us."

My pulse speeds up as I look around. "Who? Where"

"I'm not sure. I don't think we need to worry about them now. They won't be able to track us after that storm."

I wrap my arms around my middle, watching the forest for movements. "Then why are you telling me?"

"I thought we were going to be honest with each other from now on."

"Are we?" I arch my eyebrow. "I don't remember promising anything."

"It was implied. Perhaps an explicit declaration would be better. To avoid confusion." Markus pushes to his feet and holds out his hand.

I look at him skeptically, then let him haul me to my feet.

He keeps hold of my hand, placing his other over his heart. "I solemnly swear to be honest."

I grin mischievously. "Does that mean you're going to tell me all your secrets?"

"No. But I'll tell you when I'm not going to tell you

something."

Do I dare? "Like the full story about why you left this kingdom and never went home?"

Pain flickers in his eyes. "Like that."

Disappointment laced with guilt slides through me. *Leave it alone, Lisette.* I broaden my grin. "I don't know. What happens if you forget your promise? Barbarians like you aren't known for having good memories."

He tugs my hand, pulling me closer, leaning down so we're eye-to-eye. "I'm sure you'll remind me." His breath brushes across my lips.

I glance away, the heat returning to my cheeks. "Of course. As a princess, I have a lot of practice ordering people around." I try to slip my hand away, but he holds firm.

"Aren't you forgetting something?"

"What? Oh!" I put my free hand over my heart, mimicking his pose. "I solemnly swear to be honest with you. Especially when you're wrong."

He squeezes my hand. "So sworn. You have dirt on your nose." He winks and releases his grip.

"I'm pretty sure I'm head-to-toe dirt. You look like one giant bruise."

"That's unfortunate. Purple isn't really my color."

I nod seriously. "It clashes with your clothing. You should really rethink your outfit if you're going to keep getting beaten up all the time."

"It seems to be a recent development. Started about the time you crashed into my life."

"Funny, the worst I ever get is some scrapes." I lower my eyes, fiddling with my sleeve. "Thank you. For saving me from the rockslide."

"What? Did you say something? I couldn't hear you."

Markus's lips twitch. "Could you repeat that?"

I bite my lip to stop my smile. "No."

"We saved each other. I meant it, calling the wolves was brilliant. I can't believe I didn't think of it."

Warmth spreads through my chest. "You're the one who told me they would protect us if they were nearby. I figured you were good for taking out two or three of the bandits, but not all of them."

"Only three?"

I fight a smile. "Maybe four."

"Clearly you don't know the extent of my capabilities if you think four of those ruffians could take me." He wiggles his eyebrows.

"Barbarian you may be, but even you have your limits." I turn away, picking up my empty cup and reach for the tea pot.

He scoffs. "If you hadn't distracted me, I could've protected you."

I look over my shoulder and flutter my eyelashes. "I didn't know you found me so distracting."

To my amusement, his ears turn red. *What are you doing?* I snap my gaze back to the pot and busy myself scooping up a cup of tea. A breeze rustles the branches overhead, making me shiver. I peer into the darkness. Shadows thrown from the fire flicker between the trees. "Are you sure we lost whoever was following us?"

"For now. They'll have to search to pick up our trail again."

"Is it the man from the village? The one in the green shirt. Or one of the bandits?"

He frowns. "I'm not sure. I haven't caught a glimpse of him, but I suspect it's the man from Eelan. It's not impossible to sneak by the Wolf Guards, especially if you're patient."

"Why do you think someone would follow us?"

Markus hesitates, then says, "He knows who one of us is, and he's going to try and capture us."

"He must be after me then. If everyone thinks you're dead, there's no reason to look for you."

"You're probably right." It pains him to admit it.

A giggle bubbles up. "Finding this honesty thing harder than you thought?"

He groans. "Extremely."

"It's to be expected. I imagine you've been lying to everyone most of your life out of necessity." Survival is a good reason to become a practiced liar. A much better reason than the councilors and toadies at court have.

"Yah, but I've never enjoyed it. Not that people in Eelan sought me out for conversation. I'm a bit out of practice." He shrugs good-naturedly.

Sparks of anger flicker in my chest. "They had no right to treat you like that. I hope you'll spend more time in Lorria before you leave so we can make it up to you. Not everyone is that cruel."

Markus raises an eyebrow. "I thought we were being honest with each other."

"We are. I think you should come to the palace. Take some time to decide where you want to go."

He shakes his head. "I'm not welcome anywhere in Lorria. The moment they find out I'm a Wolf, they'll turn on me."

"No!" I bite my lip. *Honesty. Even when I don't like it.* It hurts to admit the shameful faults of my kingdom, but I can't deny them. Not to Markus. "Perhaps. But once they get to know you, they'll love you."

"First they'll try to run me out of the kingdom. No, it's better I disappear. I've put it off too long already." He stares into the fire, his eyes dark. "It's time."

"But first I'm sure my parents will still insist on a feast and a ball and a hundred other celebrations to thank you for helping to rescue Oma. And saving me, too. Father will want to give a speech at all of them and Mother will use them as an excuse to force me into a new wardrobe. Then there's all the small talk, and pretending to care about the court gossip. Jaw aching from smiling for hours upon hours. Hmm, perhaps I should go with you." I nudge him, earning a small smile.

"I think you'd miss your family too much to leave."

"I miss them now, but not as much as I thought." It's something I hadn't realized before. "I've been so focused on rescuing Oma, and having one adventure after another, I haven't had time to miss them."

"Adventure is an odd word to describe our travels so far."

I chuckle. "Some were more adventurous than others. We might be a little banged up and bruised, but we're not broken. And since it was my pack that was destroyed, I don't have to carry anything until we buy supplies. It could be worse. Although my dress would probably disagree." I wrinkle my nose at the dirty and ripped fabric.

"That reminds me." He digs around in his pack, then holds out the stained clothes I saw earlier. "I was putting this off, but I think it's time." He shakes them out, revealing a small pair of trousers and a shirt, both a rusty red that matches his clothing.

A sinking feeling hits my stomach as I realize there's no

way the tiny leathers will fit Markus. "What are those for?"

"You'll be more comfortable in these. And we'll make better time." He eyes me critically. "They might be a little large, but they'll still be better than that dress."

Of all the supplies to survive a rockslide, why did it have to be those? I bury my hands in my skirt, clutching the filthy fabric. "I'm fine. I won't slow you down."

The patient tone is back. "Lisette, the terrain is going to get rougher. Trust me, you'll want pants for this."

I scoot back, shaking my head. "My mother would skin me alive if she found out I was traipsing around in trousers."

"You're invading another kingdom and you're worried about what your mother will think?"

"You don't know her. Believe me, the trousers are the worse offense." I put my hands behind my back. "No. Just no."

13

"I can't believe you talked me into this." I yank on the trousers, trying to get them into a more comfortable position. "These things are ridiculous. How do you walk around in them all day?"

"Men like pain." Markus holds out a sheathed dagger hilt-first to me. "Now that you've decided not to stab me in my sleep, I thought you might want this."

"Aren't you the trusting one. I might change my mind about stabbing you if you spring anymore surprises on me." I reach for the knife.

He slides it out of reach, then grins and hands it over. "Just remember, only I know the way out of the forest."

"I guess you're safe for now." The dagger is lighter than expected. I'm not much of a weapons expert, but the hilt is a lovely pattern of overlapping leaves between engravings of the moon's phases. There's a large ruby set where the full moon would appear. On the blade are some inscriptions, but I don't recognize the language. "It's so pretty. What does it say?"

"Something cryptic that takes too long to figure out." At my snicker, he says, "It's a blessing to protect whoever carries it."

"I love it." I try to figure out how to attach the sheath to my trousers, fumbling with the leather cords.

After I drop it a second time, Markus steps closer. "Here, let me help."

As he takes the knife, his fingers skim my hand. My heart stutters. This close, I'm overwhelmed by his scent of leather and musk, a hint of mint on his breath. His hands brush my waist, my stomach, until I gasp at the intimacy of it. My knees go weak and I have to fight the urge to press against him. *What is wrong with me? Did I get hit on the head without noticing?*

"Did you see how I tied it?" Markus's dark eyes capture mine, pulling me into their depths.

"Yes." Self-conscious of how shaky my voice sounds, I step back and clear my throat. "Thanks. I can manage it next time."

"If you have any trouble, let me know. Sometimes it takes a few times to get the hang of it." Markus turns to finish burying the smoking remains of our fire, taking his warmth with him.

We set out, my mind whirling. I must be weak from hunger. Dehydrated. Something caused an allergic reaction that muddled my brain. Markus isn't the type of man I normally fancy. While there aren't many who've caught my interest, the ones who have were scholarly types. The ones who read in the library instead of going on a hunt. Not a man who'd rather sleep in the forest and could kill a striking snake from thirty paces. No, something must be wrong with me.

Heat floods my cheeks. It's clear the delusion is one-sided. Markus didn't have any reaction to touching me, another reason I'm surely mistaken. It's impossible he could ignore that much desire when it nearly knocked me off my feet. I have to get control of myself. The last thing I need is to embarrass myself by attacking him in some misguided lustful haze.

It's because I'm not used to being friends with a man, that's all. Sure, I've been friendly with them. But traveling day after day together, getting attacked by bandits and trapped in the mine, it's no wonder my feelings are getting a little mixed up. Yes, that must be it.

Feeling better now that I have everything figured out, I hum as we stride through the forest. It's nice having Markus as a friend. I'll be sad to see him leave Lorria. *Now I just need to remember not to mix up friendship with ... whatever that was.*

After several hours of walking, a patch of sunlight makes my eyes water. I hold up my hand, squinting at the dark green leaves clustered around the base of one tree, bright red berries poking through the foliage.

I grab Markus's sleeve. "Look, look. Sunshine. Actual space between the trees. And bushes. Does that mean we're through the forest?"

"The Black Forest covers the entire kingdom; that's why it's so hard to conquer." At my crestfallen expression, he chuckles. "There are parts where it thins. We'll see more of them the farther we go."

The scenery continues to change. More sunlight breaks through as the trees spread out. Blooming bushes pop up regularly, and bluebirds and shimmering spiderwebs make an appearance. The changes soon turn from a celebration to a punishment as the brush thickens, creating impenetrable walls of branches and scratchy thorns. I almost start missing the endless twilight of trees where the only obstacles were roots to trip over.

I shove through the growth, grudgingly admitting the leather shirt and trousers are easier to move in through the new obstacles than my dress would be. Not that I'll ever tell Markus. He's already enough of a know-it-all for all things forest, his ego doesn't need any help.

Then a miracle happens. We find a road.

It stretches off into the distance, curving out of sight. I stretch my arms out and spin around, relishing the freedom of movement and sign of civilization. I trip on a rock, staggering to the side. I catch my balance before I tip over, my clumsy movements and Markus's guffaws doing nothing to dim my happiness.

"Where does it go? Will it take us to the palace?" *Please, please, please say it'll take us to the palace.*

He shakes his head. "It goes to Lutach, then east, away from our destination."

My spirits sink. "But we can still follow it for a bit, right?"

"Not if we want to avoid people." He gestures to the other side of the road. "If we keep to the forest and stay off the roads, nobody will spot us."

My dreams of waltzing down the open road are slipping away. "Surely there's going to be more people in the forest now that we're closer to a town. More bandits. Hunters and people gathering berries and—and doing other forest-y things."

His brow wrinkles. "What do you think—never mind. Even if there's a few people, we can easily evade them in the forest. We'd run into people on the road. There's no way to avoid it."

"Won't that be suspicious? Two people traveling through the forest instead of on the roads."

"Not if they don't see us." He waves again.

I look at the thick brush he gestured to, then the welcoming, wide road, and back to the brush. "We'll make better time if we stick to the road. And we need supplies."

He looks at the sky and groans. "Fangs and fur, how did I end up with the most foolish princess this side of the forest?" He motions to the road. "Go ahead, take it. Save me the trouble of trying to get you to the palace. The first person that lays eyes on you will spot you for the foreigner you are."

I put my hands on my hips and stare him down. "Oh, yes. I'm sure their first thought at seeing me will be 'this must be that Lorrian princess. I've seen her picture *everywhere*.' These people don't even know I exist, much less what I look like. I'm not walking around waving the Lorrian crest, or carrying a sign declaring 'I'm from Lorria.' As long as you can keep from calling me princess again, we'll be perfectly safe. You're more likely to be recognized than I am."

"Fine. But if we get caught, I'm going to tell you 'I told you so' twice a day until we're executed."

"As long as you don't give us away. Besides, we won't get executed. I'll tell them I'm the princess and they can send a ridiculous ransom demand to my parents. You'll claim you kidnapped me and they'll declare you a hero. Problem solved."

Markus grabs his hair with both hands and glares as I smirk. He stomps down the road, cursing and muttering as I saunter behind, humming a cheerful tune.

After a few minutes, Markus slows his pace so we're walking side by side. "If we stay on the road, eventually we're going to run into people. Agreed?"

Not trusting his cheery tone, I hesitantly nod.

"And it's better if they don't find out you're from Lorria, right?"

This reminds me of too many conversations with my mother where I came out wishing I'd kept my mouth shut. There's a trap here, but I don't know what it is. "Yes."

"Then you're going to have to change some things to fit in here. Starting with that accent."

Of all the ridiculous— "I don't have an accent."

"Yah, you do. And you keep saying 'yes' instead of 'yah.' You might as well wear a tiara."

"That's just proper grammar."

He gives me a critical look. "We'll also have to work on your look. It's so … girly."

I smack his arm. "I'm wearing trousers."

"And another thing. You're too clean." He waves his hand up and down at me. "It's unnatural." His lips twitch.

I squish the laugh threatening to break out. "Hmm." I tap a finger to my lips. "That is a dead giveaway. Should I roll around in the dirt? Put twigs in my hair?"

"Twigs will look like you're trying too hard. But a good dirt bath is just the thing. Here, let me help you."

He reaches for me and I dart away with a laugh. "Don't you dare!"

"Come on, one good roll across the road and you'll fit right in."

I draw my new dagger and wave it at him. "Now that I've found the road, your value as a guide is in question. I'm definitely rethinking whether I can stab you.”

He throws his hands up in surrender with a chuckle. We settle into a pleasant walk, Markus naturally slowing his stride to match my shorter one.

He says, “In all seriousness, you need to be careful if we see people.”

“I will.” It’s obvious Markus is debating something with himself. I roll my eyes. “Like what?”

“You’re too quick to meet people’s eyes. Most people try to avoid eye contact except with close family and friends.”

“Huh.” *This might be tougher than I thought.* “What else?”

“In the market, don’t ask the price of anything. Wait for them to offer it. Always handle money with your left hand. The seller will criticize their merchandise, but you praise it. Some hand gestures are inappropriate. Try not to talk with your hands.” He gives me a quick look. “It’s probably better if we skip meal etiquette completely, since that can get complicated.”

My head swims from the instructions. So many things feel backwards. “How long did it take you to figure all this stuff out?”

“I didn’t have to figure it out. It’s the way I was raised. It’s all the Lorrian things that confused me. I’m still not sure I have most of it worked out.”

“You seem perfectly normal to me.” When he gives me a warm smile, I elbow him lightly in the ribs. “You know, except for being a giant. I hope not everyone in this kingdom is as big as you or I’m in danger of getting stepped on.”

“Just stay by my side, little lady. I’ll protect you from the big, scary wolf men.”

"I bet they're all bears like you." I wait until his chest puffs out, then add, "Big ole squishy pet bears."

He pretends to be hurt. "You forget I'm a scary guy."

"Big, yes. Scary?" I shake my head. "I'm more afraid of getting a rash from one of these bushes than you. You're a softie, through and through."

He scratches the back of his neck. "Nobody's called me soft before."

"That's because you growl at everyone."

"You screamed when you met me."

"I did not." *Perhaps a little.* "It was a yelp. Because you surprised me. And you were waving that giant axe around."

"It was strapped to my back."

"You tell it your way, I'll tell it mine. In either version, I wasn't scared."

Markus walks quietly for a bit. "Will you tell me about your grandmother?"

That's definitely not what I was expecting. "Why do you want to know? "

"She's important to you. I'd like to know who's so special you'd risk your life for theirs."

I smile to myself. "Oma would say that anybody is worth risking your life for, even if they're a stranger."

At his encouraging look, I tell him. How Oma's laugh can fill a room. Her way of talking you into doing anything she wants. All the community projects and charity work. The way she used to tell me stories until I fell asleep. How she tells me I'm her soul's twin. That she's the only one who really understands me. The words pour out of me like the rain after a drought, and Markus listens. Not out of polite interest, but because he seems to care. I hope he can see Oma the way I can with every story, every description.

"She sounds amazing."

I wipe the tears off my cheek with my sleeve. "She is. That's why we have to rescue her."

He stops and puts his hands on my shoulders, bending down to meet my eyes. "We will. I promise."

I grip his arm and squeeze, silently thanking him. We turn and continue down the road, each lost in our own thoughts. I kick the small rocks, watching them skip through in the dirt. It should embarrass me, being so emotional in front of someone, but Markus is so easy to talk to. There's no judgment, no belittling. We tease, but there's no edge to it. It feels like we've been friends for years, not days.

Markus casually says, "When we're in Lutach, I thought we could get rooms at the inn for the night. Get a hot meal and a proper wash."

The mention of a bath makes my skin ten times itchier. "But the people …"

"As someone loudly reminded me, it's unlikely anybody will know who we are or pay us any attention. And there're a lot of things we need to buy at the market, so we might be in town for most of the afternoon, anyway. A new pack and bedroll for you. Food. Minthrush for toothpowder, sindsine for mountain sickness. Mayhap elderflowers and willow bark."

His mind is always on plants. "How do you keep them all straight? The plants, I mean."

"Practice and study. You have to be careful because the wrong ones can kill you."

Markus's eyes light up as he describes the differences between belladonna and blueberries, and how to identify poisonous mushrooms from edible ones. The amount of information and detail is amazing. I'd bet he knows more than the palace doctors or town midwives. *Mayhap I can convince him to train the doctors at the palace before he moves on. His knowledge could save lives.*

Markus says, "Aurelia was telling me—"

"Who's Aurelia? Your grandmother?"

He snorts, then coughs quickly. "No, ah. I spoke with her back in Eelan. You saw her, it was at the inn."

I frown, thinking back to that night. He talked to the older woman and that stunningly beautiful girl. "The woman with the white hair?" I ask hopefully.

My heart twists when he shakes his head. "No, the one close to my age with the blue eyes."

"Oh." *No wonder he was oblivious to my reaction earlier. He already fancies someone else.*

"She has an interest in healing and wanted to learn about the plants native to our kingdoms. Nicolas, her fiancé, spent some time in Germania, but they're both from Floren."

"Ah." My step lightens, the bands around my chest loosening. *Enough about her—er, them.* "You said we can get all our supplies in Lutach. Is the village that big? I thought everyone in the Wolf Kingdom lived in family homesteads far away from other people."

Markus breaks into a loud laugh. "Where did you hear that? Fangs and fur, next thing you'll tell me, you think we're all illiterate."

My cheeks heat. *Yes.* "Of course not."

He shakes his head good-naturedly. "Come on, what else have you heard? Might as well get all the rumors out of the way now before you accidentally ask someone if they've given birth to wolf pups or howl at the moon."

"Howling is only for special occasions, right?" I giggle. "What's life really like in the Kingdom of the Wolves?"

"Basically, the same as Lorria. Lutach is bigger than Eelan, but probably smaller than the town near your home. We have different customs and beliefs, but there are farmers, craftsmen, shops, weavers, and healers. People are people, no matter where you go."

"It sounds so ... boring." I wrinkle my nose. "Don't you have anything special? Magic healing waters, or demons that haunt the fields, or selkies that offer you a favor if you give them a fish? "

He chuckles. "Sorry to disappoint you."

I search my memory for all the Wolf lore I've heard over the years. "What about witches that tell your fortune?"

He shifts his pack and runs a hand across his beard. "Not exactly. When we're born, a soothsayer reads the signs around us. It's not witchcraft."

Ooh, a real fortune teller. They're obviously charlatans, but it would be fun to experience it. "Do you think I could meet one? I'd love to know my fate. What did they say about you?"

He frowns fiercely. "It's not a game." Markus stomps ahead.

Geesh, I didn't realize he'd be so sensitive about it. I hurry to catch up. "Markus, I'm sorry. I didn't mean any offense."

He slows his pace, then pats my shoulder. "Some things are not to be trifled with." Markus checks the sun, then looks to the thinning forest on either side of the road. "We're getting close to the village. I have some money, but it won't be enough to cover everything, and we can't use Lorrian currency this close to the border or people will be suspicious. We can pound out the stamps on the Lorrian coins and trade on the metal's value. If you don't mind working on the coins, I'll refill our waterskins."

"Done and done." I drain the last warm drops from mine, then happily hand it over.

Markus disappears into the trees as I settle in the shade to work. Brute strength isn't something I'd normally list under my skills, but the metals are soft. It only takes a few blows with a flat rock to remove the Lorrian crest. In short order, the coins are shapeless lumps. As I wait, my guilt pokes at me, nagging me. It takes a few minutes to remember the coins I held back from Markus, now sewn into the waistband of my dress. Those fears feel three lifetimes ago and are silly now that I know him. Using my new dagger, I free the coins and add them to the pile before turning my thoughts to Lutach.

It's been so long since I've been around other people. At least, people who aren't criminals and trying to kill us. I wiggle with excitement, letting daydreams of the village dance through my mind, wondering what marvels I might spy at a marketplace in the Kingdom of the Wolves. *Surely Markus was downplaying the differences between our homelands. Any kingdom with fortune tellers must be full of mysteries waiting to be discovered. I'm going to find every one of them.*

There's a rustle across the way as Markus works his way through the bushes. He steps onto the road and I blink.

Markus shaved his beard off.

Nothing else has changed about him, but it suddenly hits me he really is my age. Clean-shaven, he looks a little boyish, something I'd never have thought before. His dark eyes gleam, drawing all the attention to them. A girl could drown in those eyes. The edge of shyness to his smile is in full view, making my heart skip a beat.

"New look?" I ask breathlessly.

He rubs a hand across his chin. "I always shave before going into the village. Only married men have beards. If I suddenly show up with a beard now, it might call too much attention to us if someone recognizes me."

My stomach twists. "Right."

"Does it look funny?" He rubs his hand across his jaw again.

"No, no. It looks fine. I'm just used to the beard. It'll take a minute to adjust. I might not recognize you if we get separated."

"Then you better stay close." He winks.

"Uh-huh." Not one teasing comment or witty comeback. It's not often I'm speechless, but my mind is blank.

He darts a look at me, then scoops up the pile of metal on the ground.

My cheeks burn. "I had a few extra coins."

His eyebrows raise slightly, but he doesn't otherwise react to my confession. "We should get moving. Your bath and bed await you. And they usually have dancing and singing at the inn in the evenings."

Dancing? He wants to go dancing? Is that why he shaved? Now the girls in town will know he's unmarried. They can flirt with him and dance all the local dances I don't know. Is that why he wants to go to Lutach?

Feeling completely unlike myself, I stumble along in a daze as he sets a jaunty pace down the road. Going into the village suddenly seems like a terrible idea.

I can't be jealous. It's ridiculous. We're friends. I'm hungry and that's making me cranky. Yes, that must be it. Silly of me to think it could be jealousy when nothing could be further from the truth. Whew, I'm glad I figured that out before I made a fool of myself.

I search desperately for something to bring back a sense of normalcy. "Do you visit Lutach often?" When he hesitates, I tease him, "This is where I remind you about our oath."

"I knew I'd regret that." He grins. "Yah, I come to this village or another one close to the border every few months. I like to catch up on the news and eat familiar foods. Every time, I swear it's the last time, that it's too dangerous to return. But something keeps pulling me back."

"Home has a way of doing that."

"This isn't home anymore, but it's nice not to feel like an outsider for a few days. And the festivals! We throw the best parties in the world. You haven't lived until you've attended a Silvester here. And there's Karnival, Maifest— oh, and Carnavalle is happening soon. There are bonfires and dances and food. Everyone sings and toasts and has fun until dawn."

And he tries to claim this isn't still his home. "That sounds fun. We never have anything like that at the palace. It's all boring balls and musicals and readings. I think Mother would faint if we tried to light a bonfire in the gardens. I'll have to try it when I get back." *If he misses his home so badly, why leave at all?* I twist the tunic into my fist as I debate whether to ask, finally giving into my curiosity. "Why did you come to Lorria? Why not stay hidden in one of your remote villages?"

He lifts his shoulder in a half-shrug. "At first, all I

thought of was getting away from the palace and my family. I didn't plan to stop in Lorria, but then the fever took me. By the time I recovered, Eelan seemed safe enough."

And he can't abandon the hope he'll get to go home one day. My heart squeezes. I wish I knew why Markus is convinced he can't tell his family he's alive. The more I think about it, the more I'm sure he hasn't told me the entire story. I still believe Markus didn't try to kill his family, which makes me wonder why they'd assume he did. I'm dying to hear the full story, but I won't push him. As annoying as it is, and as painful as it can be, I trust him to tell me when he's ready.

Ugh, I hope he's ready soon.

The village is tucked at the bottom of a small hill covered with tall brown grass. Homes and shops cluster tightly together, the thatched roofs mingling at the eaves like they can't bear to be apart. It's hard to believe it's big enough to support a market and shops, but Markus swears it's the central trading spot for several smaller towns and homes scattered in the area.

Unlike Eelan, Lutach is a riot of colors. People are dressed in bright shirts and dresses in every shade of the rainbow. Every structure features long window boxes with cascades of ivy and flowers, the fronts painted bright pastels.

I'm suddenly very aware of my stained tunic and trousers. I whisper to Markus, "Mayhap I should change into my dress."

He waves me off. "It's common for women to wear trousers when traveling."

I purse my lips. "If you say so."

Though I'm covered from neck to toe, I feel naked as we walk into town. People give us curious looks. I'm thankful

Markus's instructions give me permission not to meet anyone's eyes, no matter how unnatural it feels. My skin crawls and I shrink closer to Markus. *Stop it. They don't know who you are. Strangers are always a curiosity. I'm probably imagining their stares.*

Markus walks confidently down the street, taking seemingly random turns, which leads to the small marketplace. Stalls with striped awnings are built onto the backsides of the buildings bordering the space. The market is crowded for so late in the day. Seeing the familiar press of shoppers and stalls restores my poise. This, at last, is something familiar.

I push a strand of hair out of my eyes. "What should I buy? Elderflowers and willow bark?" My stomach grumbles. *Good reminder. The heavens know what we'll be eating if I leave him in charge of our food. Mayhap I can actually get something edible.* "Actually, I'll buy food. You're the plant expert, after all. It makes sense you get those."

He hesitates, rubbing the back of his neck. "It would be better if I do the bartering. It's a different style than you're used to."

"Nonsense, negotiating is negotiating. I can be complimentary to the person while still getting a good price. If we want to have enough money left for our rooms and my bath, you'll need my help."

"But we should stay together. You might not recognize me again if you wander off on your own."

"Nice try, but I've had enough time to get used to your baby face. It's not like we speak different languages in our kingdoms. I'll be fine." I hold out my hand and wiggle my fingers.

"Fine. Use the money I have from this kingdom. It'll call

less attention to you."

He reluctantly drops a few coins into my palm, explaining the values versus Lorrian currency. He offers again to do the shopping, but I wave him off, eager to test my skills in a foreign market. I walk away, choosing my first target with care.

The man is old enough that he knows the value of his wares, but young enough to still be influenced by a pretty face and some light flirting. Plus, he's handsome, so bartering with him won't be a chore for me. I slowly make my way through the market to him, inspecting stalls and taking a circuitous route so he won't suspect he's my intended destination.

There's an excellent selection of herbs and spices arranged on the side of his stall, with fruits and vegetables on the longest table and trinkets on the far side. I let my eyes roam over the dolls, pots, fancy lace pieces, and wooden nesting bowls. My eyebrows rise as I note some of the work looks as good or better than what I'd find at the marketplace by the palace. A rack of bracelets shows off the exceptional craftsmanship of the kingdom. The silver strands used to create the braided design are as fine as spider's silk, so delicate they look like they might shatter at the lightest touch. Each one has a tiny colored stone between two clear beads. There's a bracelet with a red stone that exactly matches the ruby in the dagger Markus gave me.

Enough distractions. I survey the fruits and vegetables out of the corner of my eye, mentally compiling a list of things to purchase. *Keep my hands still. Handle the money with my left hand. Don't ask about prices. Praise the merchandise.*

All the advice flies out of my head when I spot a set of

charcoal pencils and a sketchbook perched on the end of the table. *Markus would love those.* After he told me about his sketches, I've noticed him tracing in the dirt when he thinks I'm asleep.

I'm looking too long. He knows I'm too interested to get a good bargain. Move on. But I can't leave without getting the art supplies for Markus. *Don't ask for prices. Give them compliments.* I give the stall owner my brightest smile. "Good day. Your selection is exceptional."

He shrugs. "They're flawed, but one must make do with what's on hand."

Markus wasn't joking. They really are weird here. I gesture to the bracelets as a diversion to my real intent. "I've never seen finer workmanship. Whoever crafted them is truly gifted."

The stall owner makes a slashing motion. "Barely apprentice work. A true master would hide them until he could toss them out on the waste pile."

I will never understand the Wolves. "It'd be an honor to wear something so beautiful. At the palace—"

"You're from the palace?" He looks at me closely.

"No, no." *Burn it. Trying to play these silly games has me all jumbled up.* "I was trying to say I'm sure there's nothing finer in all the land, even at the palace." Before he can puzzle through my explanation, I hurry on. "Do the different colored stones mean anything?"

His eyebrows slam together. "They're Carnavalle Mehein."

The words are obviously supposed to mean something to me, but I'm at a loss. "Ah. I don't think we have those in my village."

"Where's that?" His eyes narrow.

I make a vague gesture west, my stomach twisting. Inching away from the bracelets, I ask, "How much for a sack of oranges?"

His eyes darken. "There's nothing here for a Lorrian."

My laugh is too high-pitched. "Lorrian? Why would you say that?"

A large woman with ruddy cheeks at the next stall looks over her shoulder at us. "Lorrian? Did you say Lorrian?"

The man points to me as the blood drains from my face. The woman shudders. She hurries over to another shopper and starts whispering furiously in her ear, darting glances at me.

He pulls a large blanket from underneath the table and tosses it over the table. "You need to leave."

"Wait a minute. I just—"

"Leave. Now." The man stands at the back of his stall, arms crossed, refusing to look my direction.

I spin around, determined to find Markus and get out of this horrible place. Villagers stare at me, talking in tight clusters. Frightened faces slip into anger. A warning bell bangs in my head as my muscles tense. I glance frantically around, trying to remember which direction we came from. Colors blur together. The market shrinks as people move closer in fits and starts. I swallow hard as my mouth goes dry. A shiver runs over my skin as the crowd grows, the rumblings pulling more people in.

Markus elbows his way through the people gathered around me. He puts a hand on my shoulder, coldly surveying the people surrounding us. "Everything all right, Lisette? "

Even standing still, the threat coming off him is impossible to miss. The murmurs quiet. The people closest to us shuffle back a few steps.

I bite the inside of my cheek to keep the tears from spilling. "Yes, fine." My voice is a whisper.

"Are you done shopping?"

"Yes."

Markus keeps his hand on my shoulder as we walk out of the market. The people blocking us fade away. Mutters chase our steps. I'm desperate to leave the stares behind, but I keep my steps even, refusing to give them the satisfaction of making me run. It's impossible to hear anything over my thundering heartbeat.

When we reach the last building, I don't pause, hurrying across the road and pushing into the brush, Markus following. Branches and thorns scratch at my skin, my face, my clothes, snagging my hair. I can't stop. Deeper and deeper into the forest I go. When I finally stagger against a tree, panting, the bushes have disappeared, and the forest is back to its eternal twilight. I slide down the trunk to the ground and bury my face in my hands. Markus sits next to me, his warmth reviving my chilled skin. Instinctively, I press against his side, seeking shelter from the emotional storm. He stiffens.

I jerk back, my head shooting up. "I forgot, I'm—"

"No, I'm sorry." He wraps his arm around my shoulders. "Are you hurt?"

"I'm fine." A shudder runs through me, remembering the cold eyes of the villagers. "I should've listened to you. The man figured out I'm Lorrian, but I don't know how. He said something about corny veils I didn't understand and I think that tipped him off."

"Carnavalle?"

"That's it."

I allow myself one deep breath of his leathery scent

before I ease away from him. His arm tightens for a moment, then drops to his side.

"It's a big festival to celebrate the end of the harvest." He rubs his arm, then scratches his chin.

I give him a small smile. "Don't worry, it'll grow back."

"Huh?"

"The beard. I can tell you miss it."

"It's actually a lot cooler without it. I might keep shaving for a bit."

"That's too bad. I kinda liked it." I hurriedly add, "I mean, you look nice without a beard, too. With a beard, without a beard. Both are good." *Ugh, what are you doing?* "I can wait here if you want to go back to town and finish buying supplies."

He shakes his head. "I'm never going back there again."

I wrap my arms around my legs, resting my chin on my knees. "I don't understand why they reacted like that. Even if I'm Lorrian—and I didn't tell them that—why would that make them so angry?"

"I told you, it's the accent." His elbow nudges my ribs.

I roll my eyes and bump him with my shoulder. "I don't have an accent." His chuckle eases the tension from my body. "Really, why?"

"They're afraid of Lorria and being this close to the border puts them on edge. It makes them paranoid. They think the Lorrians steal their livestock and spoil their harvest."

My jaw drops. "But nobody from Lorria would dare come here. Everyone's terrified of the Kingdom of the Wolves." I bristle, remembering the stories I heard in the inn. "If anybody should be scared, it should be us. They're the ones coming into our kingdom to burn fields and—and kill the livestock, and cause other mischief."

He snorts. "You've been listening to Herr Dunst's stories. Wolves aren't crossing into Lorria, and Lorrians aren't coming here. Each side blames the other for their misfortunes."

"But—but they were so sure." Even as I say it, doubt creeps in. Markus would know if people were coming into Lorria that often. And while Markus has proven it's not impossible to travel between the kingdoms, it doesn't seem worth the danger just to cause some trouble. Still, I can't underestimate people's pettiness and foolishness. Only suspecting I was from Lorria was enough to turn the villagers into a mob. That level of hatred is enough to drive people to do irrational things.

"We should keep moving." I stand up and offer him my hand.

He looks at me with amusement, then takes it. There's a little zing as our skin touches, but I pretend not to notice. I lean backward, straining, while he sits unmoving on the ground.

"Burn it, you're heavy. Get up, you big oaf."

He yawns. "Keep going. You almost have it."

Markus lets me grunt for a few more seconds, then clambers to his feet with a groan, throwing me off balance.

"Whoa." He grabs both my arms, steadying me. "Careful, princess."

I ignore the way my heart flutters. "It's your fault, barbarian."

He snickers. "Truce?"

"Truce."

He takes a second smaller pack off his back I hadn't noticed until now. "I bought a few things before we left."

I slip the pack on and settle the weight on my hips. It's
lighter than it should be. I bite my lip and look down. "I'm
sorry."

"Don't be. Really, it's my fault. I should've realized how
suspicious they would be of any visitors. We'll be fine with
what we have." Markus squeezes my shoulder. "Let's leave
this place behind us."

Walking gives me too much time to dwell on what
happened in the village. So much anger. My hands shake,
remembering how helpless I felt. I cling to the backpack's
straps, trying to hide my fear from Markus. I alternate
between berating myself for running away like a coward,
and quaking at what could've happened if I'd stayed a
moment longer. Fear piles on top of fear until my lungs
struggle for air. Their faces flash through my mind, blinding
me. Accusing eyes. Hands on knives. Muttered threats.
Moving in closer and closer and cl—

Markus's deep voice shatters the hurricane of emotions
trapping me. "I wouldn't have let them hurt you."

"I know." And I do. "I'm just glad they proved
themselves to be cowards. I wouldn't want to put you in any
danger."

"No, let's save that for invading the Wolf Palace."
Markus chuckles.

I stumble. *I can't ask him to go to the palace, not after
everything I've learned about his family. I didn't realize
what I was asking. But there's no way I can make it without
him, as our recent visit to the village has so aptly proven ...*

*As long as he gets me close enough, we can part ways
before we get to the palace. Oma and I can find our way
back to Lorria. We'll take the roads, since speed will matter
more than hiding.* My shoulders relax and the knot in my

chest loosens, knowing Markus won't be put in danger. I spend the rest of our hike debating whether I should ask Markus to leave before we go through the mountains, and calculating how fast Oma and I can travel.

My aching legs are ready to give out when Markus finds a campsite for the night. We silently split up the tasks, with Markus hunting out a water source while I gather firewood. The comforting routine keeps my fears shoved to the back of mind, temporarily restrained, but not banished.

As we walk back from washing up at the spring, I nudge him. "Not exactly the bath you promised me."

"It would be if you'd dunk your head underwater." A mischievous grin breaks out on his face, making my insides warm. "I'll help you next time."

"There'll be no dunking unless you want to get stabbed in your sleep." I pat the dagger on my belt.

"In that case, maybe I can make it up to you." He hurries over to his pack and pulls out a bundle of bright red fabric.

I raise an eyebrow. "That doesn't look like a bathtub."

"No, but it's a present." He unfolds it, revealing a long cloak lined with thick gray fur. "I had to guess your size."

My eyes widen, taking I the beautiful garment. "For me? Really?"

"You don't think I'm going to wear this tiny thing, do you?" He holds it out.

I slip it over my shoulders, marveling at the soft fur and beautiful stitch work. It's been so long since I've worn something colorful, I forgot how it can instantly lift my mood.

I clutch it closed, a lump forming in my throat. "Thank you. Really, thank you. This means—thanks."

He rubs the back of his neck. "No need to thank me.

You'll need something warm when we go to the mountains."
Markus meets my eyes, then quickly looks away.

I smother my grin, not wanting to embarrass him further.
"Red's becoming my signature color. First the leathers, then
the dagger, and now the cloak. You really know how to
coordinate an outfit."

"It suits you. Here." Markus takes the whistle from
around his neck and drops it into my hand. "You're a Wolf
at heart and that's all that matters. I'm, uh, going to get more
firewood." He hurries away.

I look at the large pile of branches next to the fire and
shake my head. *Boys*.

14

"Lisette." Markus shakes my shoulder. "Lisette, wake up."

I bat his arm away. "What is it? It can't be morning already." I slowly sit up, staring groggily at the embers of our dying campfire. It's hard to tell time under the canopy, but even I know it isn't dawn yet.

"We have to go. Someone's coming."

I grip my blanket, knuckles white, heart jumping to a gallop. "Is it the villagers? Did they follow us?" A cold sweat breaks out over my skin as the blur of angry faces flashes through my memory.

"I didn't get close enough to recognize them and I'm not planning to." Markus yanks me out of my bedroll. "Hurry. We only have a few minutes."

Jolted out of my shock, I roll up my bedding and cram it through the backpack straps, not wanting to waste the time to tie it in place. Markus shovels dirt over the embers until the last trace of heat and light disappears. He grabs my hand and leads me into the night.

It's a waking nightmare. I can't tell if the thundering in

my ears is my heartbeat or feet pounding after us. Imaginary shadows reach for me. Fear and darkness make me clumsy, and I trip every few steps. My eyes adjust to the scant moonlight filtering through the leaves overhead and my feet become surer. Markus increases our pace, zigzagging through the trees.

After an hour, Markus's shoulders relax and he slows to walk. The icy coldness around my heart drips away and my muscles loosen. *We lost them.*

He stops near a large boulder. "That should be far enough."

I grip his hand. "I can keep going. We don't have to stop."

"No need. The ground is too hard to leave tracks. We can leave before dawn to make sure they won't find us again." Markus releases my hand and puts his pack on the ground. "There's not enough time for a fire, but you should get a few more hours of sleep. I'll scout back, see if I can find out who they—"

"No. We stay together." When he hesitates, I grab his arm. "If we lost them, it doesn't matter who it was. And you could end up leading them back to us if you're snooping around and they spot you. Let's keep our advantage and leave them behind."

He nods reluctantly.

I poke his chest. "And don't think about sneaking away when I'm asleep. Honesty, remember?"

"Fine," he grumbles. "Get some sleep. I'll keep watch."

"I'm too nervous to sleep." I fidget with the leather cords on my trousers. "Markus …" *He's not going to like it. Is it weird? It's not weird, but it's still weird. It's weird for me. I shouldn't ask. But I have to. Is it too much to ask? How can it be too much—he's taking me to the burning Wolf Palace for burning sake. Just ask. Ask. Ask now.*

Markus raises an eyebrow. "Is there something you wanted to ask me?"

Do it. Say it, you coward. "I want you to teach me how to defend myself. I don't know how to do anything, and I hate feeling helpless, and I want to be able to fight off an attacker if I have to."

"I'll do it."

"And I know you'll be there to help me when I need it, but it would make me feel better to know how to do some fighting things, and then you won't have to worry about me if we get into trouble, and if I get good enough, I could even help you a little if there's a fight, or we need to run away, or if we get separated and I need to find you, and it's just a good idea, like a life skill, that everyone should know, especially me, because everyone assumes I'm small so I can't fight, and they're right, and I hate that—"

He holds up his hands against my verbal assault. "I said I'd teach you."

"And—oh. Um, thank you." A little ball of warmth glows in my chest. I bounce on my toes, my muscles full of energy. "Right. Right. What do we do first?"

"First, you take off your pack."

"Right." I drop it on the ground. "What's next?"

He studies me for a moment. "You're better suited for a hit and run technique. Don't get caught if you can avoid it. You're fast. Hard to catch. If you have the chance, run away."

"Not very heroic, but something I can definitely do."

"Heroics get people killed. The important thing is to do whatever you can to survive." He folds his arms and looks me up and down. "I seem to recall you like kicking people in the shin. Kick whatever you can reach. And bite. And scream."

My enthusiasm dims. "I'm pretty sure I could've figured this out on my own."

"Then here's something new. As a last resort, play dead. It's an old battlefield trick to pretend to be dead, and then sneak off when they're not looking, or attack when the enemy turns their back." He leans down and stares me directly in the eye. "But you won't fall for that. You will always check that your opponent is actually dead."

I nod solemnly.

"Say it."

Geesh. "I will always, always, always check that my opponent is dead after I stab him with my dagger. Or my sword. Do I get a sword?"

He chuckles. "It'll have to be a short sword. A regular one would drag in the dirt."

I swipe at his arm. "I'm not that short."

"Yah, you are. That's enough for tonight. Tomorrow, I'll show you how to hit someone without breaking your fingers."

I dance from foot to foot. "Next time someone tries to grab me, they won't know what hit them. Bandits, beware." I throw punches at the shadows.

"We'll turn you into a weapons master in no time. Or at least, make it so you won't stab yourself."

I ignore his teasing, dreaming of glorious swordfights. "Mother and Father will have to let me go on trips with Oma if I can prove I can protect us both. I can't wait to show them when I get home."

"They'll be very impressed." Markus's smile doesn't

quite meet his eyes. He turns away, scanning the trees. "I'm going to take a quick look around."

I try to shake off the odd mood hanging over us. "But not too far?"

"Right." He disappears into the trees, leaving me gazing bewilderedly after him.

15

I tie back my hair, marveling that my legs aren't as tired tonight. I haven't needed Markus's special tea for almost a week—which is good, because I suspect his supply is running low. Are there other medicinal properties, or did Markus bring it on the trip especially for me, because he knew I wouldn't be used to the long days of hiking? Even better, Markus caught a rabbit, meaning we'll have fresh meat for the first time in ages.

Staying away from the villages has made traveling harder than it should be, but I can't shake my fears. Every time I think about going to a village, my hands shake, and Markus refuses to leave me long enough to go by himself. When we come across the occasional farmstead, I stay hidden in the trees while Markus barters for oatmeal, dried fruit, and whatever foodstuffs travel well. I long to have a proper bath, but we make do with scrubs in the springs and streams.

Setting up camp is a well-practiced routine. At my insistence, I've done every chore except finding water, a skill which still eludes me. Knowing I have to convince Markus to leave before we get to the palace has added urgency to mastering the tasks. I need to be able to do everything if Oma and I are going to make it home by ourselves.

Markus grins. "I have a surprise for you."

I stretch my back with a grunt. "Is it a horse? Because I would love it if we could ride the rest of the way."

"Better."

"We'll see." His excitement is contagious. A smile spreads across my face as I look around our campsite. Nothing looks new or out of place. "Where is it?"

He points to the stewpot. "I found coriander."

As far as surprises go, it's not life changing. But knowing supper will have fresh meat and a new spice makes my mouth water. "You're a magician." I take an appreciative sniff. "I've never had coriander before. What does it taste like?"

"It's … Hmm … It's, ah …" Markus shrugs, holding his hands up. "It's coriander. There isn't really anything like it."

I eagerly wait for the stew to finish simmering over the fire. He's surprisingly cautious about making sure the rabbit is cooked thoroughly, lifting a shoulder and mumbling something about fevers when I insist it's done. After torturing me with the delicious smells for what feels like hours, Markus finally declares the meal ready.

The steam from the bowl bathes my face in a delicious aroma, wonderful scents tickling my nose. Only knowing Markus will tease me endlessly keeps me from shoving my face into the bowl. As I take the first bite, I close my eyes, savoring the taste. A groan escapes my lips. *I forgot how good fresh meat is.* It transforms the wilted greens into a gourmet meal fit for the palace. There's a strong, tangy citrus flavor mingling with the others that must be coriander. It leaves my mouth tingling. It's not unpleasant, but I can't decide if I like it or not. Too soon, my bowl is empty and I eagerly hold it out for a refill.

Markus snickers. "Did you even taste it?"

"I did. Delicious. More, please."

"Only if you promise to slow down and actually enjoy it."

I snort. "That was me, enjoying it. I didn't know you were so sensitive about your cooking."

"It's about the experience, the tastes. It's nourishment for the soul, as well as the body." Markus dips out another bowlful, then teasingly holds it out of reach. "Better than a horse?"

"No, but I couldn't eat a horse. This is wonderful."

"I knew you'd like coriander."

Rather than spoil his mood, I settle for, "It's unique." I scratch my neck. "I can't help but feel like we should make more progress. We're not even at the mountains."

"Avoiding the villages and towns slows us down some. There's more the closer we get to the pass. We can use some roads near here to make better time. It'll mean going through a few villages, but the traveling will be faster and easier."

I clutch my red cloak tighter around my shoulders and grip the bowl. "No. No villages. You remember what happened last time." The tea does nothing to ease the growing lump in my throat. *I never want to feel that helpless again.*

"We won't stop. We can—"

"No." I shudder, feeling those villagers' hatred-filled eyes on me again. "The closer we get to the palace, the more likely the Wolf King will hear rumors about us. We both need to be careful." I take another bite of stew, appetite gone.

Markus sets his bowl aside. "You're not thinking clearly. Lutach is weeks behind us. If you want to get to your grandmother, this is the best way." His voice softens. "I'll keep you safe."

My insides twist. "I know you will. But you need to be safe, too. If the King ever finds out you helped me, it would put you in danger. More danger, I mean." I rub my chest. *It hurts to admit it, but ...* "I'm scared. I don't like to think about what those villagers could have done to me."

"They never would have laid a hand on you. I swear it. At the next village, I won't leave your side. We'll go straight through. You'll be safe." His eyes, so intent, make my stomach jump.

Can I face them again? Picturing Markus by my side makes the mob less threatening, but no less frightening. *I can do this. For Oma. For Markus.* I point my spoon at him. "You better not step more than one foot away from me. I mean it. I'm counting on you."

His face breaks into a beautiful smile. "It's settled, then."

While I have every confidence in Markus, the thought of going back to the village sends prickles over my skin. "The worst part was knowing there was nothing I could do if they attacked me. Before that moment, I thought I was brave. I think I'll have nightmares about it for the rest of my life."

His hand twitches, then stills. "But now you know what to do. You're getting good at fighting with your dagger. And soon you'll be home, and surrounded by guards, and you'll never have to think of them again." He turns his back on me, refilling his tea.

A wave of nausea and dizziness assaults me. "Markus?" It's hard to form the words. My voice sounds fuzzy. "I don't feel good." My pulse races. Sweat breaks out all over my body.

"What's wrong?" His eyes narrow. He drops his cup and dives across the small space between us. "Are you sick? What do you feel?" He holds a hand up to my damp forehead.

I nod, the movement nearly making me pass out. "Dizzy. Sick." My breath wheezes in and out, rasping through my chest.

Markus curses, then flies to his bag, coming back with a thin clear vial. He pours it into my mouth, then forces my jaw closed and plugs my nose. I squirm against the assault, but he holds firm, frantic apologies pouring out of his mouth. The liquid burns as it trickles down my throat. When he releases me, I sputter, trying to suck in air.

He scoops me up in his arms. We're racing blindly through the darkness.

"Keep breathing. You'll be all right. Keep breathing." Markus keeps repeating the mantra.

I cling to his chest, the edges of the world going soft. "Markus? I'm sorry." The words are slurred.

His arms tighten. "For what?" When I don't answer, he gives me a little shake. "Stay with me. What are you sorry for, Lisette? "

An invisible hand squeezes my insides, and it feels like they're going to burst. I curl up tight with a groan.

"We're close. You'll be all right. Keep breathing."

As the darkness creeps over my vision, his words fade into a high buzzing. "I'm sorry …"

The world slips away.

16

Voices murmur around me as I swim up through the darkness. *I'm so tired.* There's a weight pressing down on me, pushing me back. Memories of Markus carrying me through the woods flood in. *I can't breathe!* I jolt up, gasping, my hand pressed to my chest.

"Easy, easy." A woman in a yellow skirt and blue top hurries over, pressing me back down on the bed. "You're all right. Take a deep breath. Keep breathing." Her blond hair is twisted into a knot at the base of her neck, and there are deep lines around her mouth.

Her words are eerily familiar to what Markus kept repeating. "Where am I? Where's Markus?" I clutch the blanket to me, shrinking back against the pillow.

"Nevenberg. Your friend brought you to the healing house." She moves to the side, revealing Markus slumped over in a chair a few feet away. At my alarmed squeak, she shakes her head. "He's fine, just exhausted. He carried you here and then watched over you while you slept. He finally fell asleep not too long ago."

Knowing Markus is here helps me push back on the panic threatening to overtake me. I relax my grip on the blanket, breathing easier. "What happened?"

"We think it was a food allergy. You're lucky you were so close to the village, otherwise it could've been deadly. Even so, I'm amazed he got you here in time."

I try to recall what happened. "We weren't close. Markus had me drink something as soon as I had trouble breathing. I think that helped."

"Oh no, dear. You're mistaken. I'm sure his homemade remedies are good enough for cuts and coughs, but this required proper medicine. He was smart to bring you here. He saved your life."

I press my lips together. "His grandmother was a really knowledgeable healer. He learned everything from her." *I'd bet he knows more than you.*

"Isn't that sweet. I'm sure he did." Her patronizing tone sets my teeth grinding. "It's almost time for tea. Try to eat something, but go slowly in case you have another reaction."

Rude. I stick out my tongue at the woman's retreating back.

Markus snores softly, his head slumped forward, chin resting on his chest. He has dark circles under his eyes, his skin ashy underneath his tan. Even his beard looks tired. My heart twists, wondering how far he had to carry me. I wrap my arms around my waist, remembering how hard it was to breathe, how everything hurt.

It's tempting to call out and wake him. To let him know I'm fine and thank him for saving me. See those dark eyes and know he's all right too. But the air of pure exhaustion around him keeps my lips sealed. His ordeal was probably harder than mine. I just had to pass out and not die. *He saved me again*. My debt to Markus keeps piling up higher and higher. I'll have to find another way to thank him besides his payment.

The healing house is a large, open space with beds every few feet around the perimeter. Most of the beds are empty; the few other occupants are on the far side of the room. Men and women are carrying trays, rolling bandages, and performing other tasks. Yellow and blue seems to be some kind of identifying uniform, as they're all dressed in similar colors to the woman who spoke with me.

I curl up in the bed, content to watch Markus sleep. Not for the first time, I'm thankful Herr Bannan left me in the forest. Markus is the best guide I could ever hope for. Despite our differences, we're friends. If only our friendship wasn't so one-sided. Markus does everything for me, but there's so little I can do for him. Even being a princess, I'm not used to being so dependent on someone else. He's the expert in camping, navigating the kingdom, medicine, everything. He can do anything. Compared to him, I'm a silly little girl who can't even set foot in a marketplace without starting a riot.

A hand brushes a strand of my hair behind my ears. My eyes fly open to find Markus watching me.

He gives me a tired smile. "They said you woke up."

Heat floods my cheek as my pulse speeds up. "I must've fallen asleep again." I sit up, feeling suddenly nervous. *Don't be silly, you sleep a few feet away from him every night. You're friends. It's fine.* "You're awake too." *What is wrong with me? Nobody else can make me trip over my words so badly.* "You saved me. Again."

A dark cloud covers his face. "You wouldn't have needed saving if I hadn't poisoned you. I nearly killed you."

"What? No! If I didn't know I was allergic to coriander, how were you supposed to? It was an accident. The important thing is you helped me and I'm fine."

The tightness around his eyes doesn't ease. "How do you feel?"

"Fine. A little tired. And thirsty. That woman promised me tea, but I think she lied." I smile, trying to reassure him.

He jumps out of the chair. "I'll check on it."

My heart sinks as he disappears out the door. It never even occurred to me to blame Markus for what happened, or that he would blame himself. I don't want to cause him pain. Yes, it could've turned out badly, but it didn't because he knew what to do. If the situation were reversed, things would have been much worse.

I fidget in the bed, waiting for Markus to reappear with the overdue tea. Minutes tick off. The room has emptied of the staff, leaving only the sleeping patients across the way. I drum my fingers on the bedsheet, leaning forward to better see through the doorway.

"I have to do everything myself," I mutter, throwing back the blanket. I stand—and my knees buckle, plopping me back onto the bed.

A different woman appears in the doorway and *tsks* as she walks over to me with a tray of food. "Careful there, dear. Last night took a lot out of you. Rest now. You should be back to normal by tonight."

I grumble as I crawl back between the blankets, and she settles the tray across my legs. "Where's Markus?"

"Is that your friend?" When I nod, she tilts her head to the side. "He asked me to bring tea now that you're awake, then left." She hurriedly adds, "But I'm sure he'll be back later."

My stomach twists, and for a moment I'm afraid I'm having another attack. But no, I haven't eaten anything. I absentmindedly thank the woman who promises to return soon.

I manage a few sips of tea to ease my parched throat, but push the food around on the plate. Every time I think about taking a bite, my throat closes and my chest tightens. I reduce the small bun to crumbles as I stare unseeing at the tray.

Where did he go? He wouldn't abandon me now, would he? No. Not Markus. But he also promised not to leave me alone in the village. What's so important that he would leave? And why didn't he say anything to me about it?

The woman comes back and clucks over my lack of appetite before taking the tray away. I try to rest, but every voice has me leaping up in bed, every creak makes me cringe against the headboard. I pull my red cloak off the side table and wrap it around my shoulders, running my hands across the soft fur. A man in one of the other beds watches me, making my skin crawl. *Do they know I'm Lorrian?* Markus wouldn't have told them. But I might have let something slip again. *I shouldn't have talked. Was I making eye contact? Burn it, I was. What else am I messing up?* My heart thunders in my ears. *I can't stay here.*

I slide over to the edge of the bed and find my shoes on the floor. I stand up carefully, clinging to the headboard in case another dizzy spell hits me. Once I'm steady on my feet, I check for any of my other possessions that might be lying around. Nothing. If they have any of my belongings somewhere else, Markus will have to retrieve them. If he comes back.

I lift my chin and walk calmly across the floor, through

another room, and out the door. I don't look back. People are bustling down the streets, the crowd thick. Tall buildings stretch on either side of the road, with more roofs peeking behind them. It reminds me of the town around the palace with its bright colors and storefronts.

There's no sign of the forest. The buildings block the view. Too many curious stares crawl over my skin. I pull up my hood, setting out at random. I keep my eyes down and try to blend in, following the flow of the crowd. *The town must end somewhere. I need to find the forest, where it's safe.*

The stream of people spills out into a large marketplace. Striped awnings and bright shades fill the square. Vendors call out to potential customers. Faces flash past as people bump into me from all directions. Ice runs down my spine and I put a hand to my chest, reminding myself to breathe. My elbow knocks against someone's basket, a shove from behind sends me stumbling. I press my lips together and wrap my arms around my middle, watching for signs the crowd is about to turn into a mob as I back away. I break out in a sweat. *I have to get out of here.*

"Your first time here, dearie?" The woman at my side looks at me with sympathetic eyes. Her brown braids are streaked with gray and she has laugh lines around her mouth and eyes.

"Um, yes. Excuse me, I have to be going." I inch backward.

"Nonsense. Everyone should experience the Nevenberg market, and there's no better time than at Carnavalle. That's why you came, right?" She doesn't wait for my response. "It's a bit more crowded today, but everyone will have their best wares out. And, if you're lucky, your sweetheart will gift you a mehein tonight."

I keep my lips pressed together, too scared to say anything more. *Where is Markus?*

"Don't be intimidated, I'll help you with your shopping. I know everyone here." With a light laugh, she loops her arm through mine, carrying me deeper into the marketplace. "You remind me of my daughter, Petra. My favorite—don't tell her sister or brother—but she sometimes has to be nudged into things the first time, too."

The woman seems to expect a response. I squeak out, "I usually don't think things through." *Like now. I should've stayed in the healing house.*

She pats my hand. "That's the best way to have adventures. I'm Ingrid."

"Lisette."

"Where are you from, dear?"

I blurt out the first town I can remember. "Lutach."

"Ah, that explains the accent. Wonderful. Now, let's go by Monika's stall first, because she makes the best custard wheels in the kingdom, and it'll break my heart if I don't get one before they sell out."

Ingrid keeps up a steady patter, leading me around the market from stall to stall. At first, I worry I'll slip and she'll figure out I'm Lorrian, but gradually my fear fades. She's not the least bit suspicious and doesn't press me for details, seemingly simply enjoying having company on her shopping trip. Her willingness to befriend a complete stranger and easy manner reminds me of Oma. My grandmother makes friends everywhere she goes, giving a comforting arm and sympathetic ear to anyone in need.

Being with Ingrid also makes me look less conspicuous than if I was on my own. People aren't looking at me closely anymore. The ebb and flow of the people, the smells, even the bickering shoppers remind me of the market at home. The press of the crowd is uncomfortable, but no longer frightening.

Ingrid buys me a flavored ice after I offer to carry her shopping basket. I worry about another allergic attack, but she reassures me it's simply ice and blueberries crushed into a sugar syrup. After a small taste doesn't elicit a reaction, I quickly gobble down the rest of it, marveling at how it soothes my throat and cools me in the hot market. I make a note to suggest it for the next summer gala at the palace.

The mix of familiar and new fascinates me. There are fancy bowls and plates like I'd see at home, but the patterns are floral instead of geometric. Instead of sugared apples, the vendors fry the apple peels with honey. Ingrid smiles and points out the specialty items brought out for Carnavalle, including a display of bracelets, each one with a tiny colored stone between two clear beads, like the ones I saw at Lutach. I push the dark memory away and focus on the decorations. Markus mentioned something about Carnavalle being a festival, but I didn't realize what a huge event it is for the Kingdom of the Wolves. I'm dying to ask Ingrid more about it, but keep my lips closed, stockpiling the questions for Markus.

Time passes quickly. Before I know it, the merchants are bringing out torches as the sun sets.

Markus must be back by now. He won't think to look for me in the marketplace. "Ingrid, I'm sorry, but I really do need to go now. Can I help you to your home?"

"Oh dear, I've kept you all day. Let me make it up to you. Why don't you join my family for the bonfire? Petra always brings too much food."

"That's very kind, but I need to find my friend."

"A friend, ay?" She gives me a knowing smile. "I bet he's handsome."

My cheeks heat. "I—I suppose some would think so."

"Very handsome, by the look of it." She sighs longingly. "I remember blushing like that over a boy. Youth has some advantages." She takes my arm again. "I'll help you find him."

"No, please. It's fine. I don't want to trouble you."

"I won't be able to enjoy the festival if I'm worrying about whether you found your friend. And in this crowd, two sets of eyes are better than one. Now, what does he look like?"

"Um, well, uh … Markus looks like a bear, but in a good way. Dark hair, almost black. And dark brown eyes. He's tall. Gigantic even." I hold my hand over my head for emphasis. "A nice smile."

"And handsome?" Her eyes twinkle.

The blush reaches the tips of my ears. "And handsome."

"He sounds easy enough to spot."

Ingrid suggests different places to look as we leave the market and walk through town. My companion keeps up a steady chatter about festival events she's looking forward to. The healing house is the first stop. I duck my head in just long enough to confirm Markus isn't inside, then hurry along, afraid the healers might try to drag me back into bed.

It's not until we loop to the end of town and come near the healing house again that I finally spot a clean-shaven Markus looking frantically around. He sees me a moment later, relief quickly replaced by annoyance. Guilt creeps over me realizing how late it is and how much he must've worried when he discovered I wasn't at the clinic. But I push it away, my annoyance building. *He left without telling me. Serves him right if he got a little scare out of it.*

Markus storms over to where I'm standing with Ingrid. She watches his approach with bright eyes, curiosity growing every second.

He gives Ingrid a perfunctory nod, then turns on me. "Where have you been? Fangs and fur, do you realize what could've happened? Why didn't you wait for me?"

I cross my arms and narrow my eyes. "Me? You were supposed to be getting us tea. The next thing I know, you've disappeared without a word. What was I supposed to think?"

"That I wouldn't have left you if you weren't safe, and that I needed to get our supplies from the campsite."

I throw out my arms. "Why didn't you tell me that? Going back for our gear isn't a secret mission. I only knew you left because that woman in the clinic told me."

"So you knew I was going back to the campsite and thought it was a good idea to go traipsing around town alone?" He looks at the sky. "Why are you always do the most foolish thing you can think of?"

"I didn't know where you had gone, or when you were coming back. And did it even occur to you I would've felt better waiting somewhere else? Somewhere I could have some privacy instead of people staring at me?"

He runs a hand across this chin. "You needed to be around people who could help you if something else happened."

I poke his chest. "I'm fine. They said so. There was no reason to leave me there. I could've waited in the woods, or an inn, or somewhere that wasn't full of creepy people. And if you were in such a hurry, why did you stop to shave? Where are our things?"

He grumbles, "The innkeeper's holding them for us."

"Our packs can go to the inn for safekeeping, but I can't. Perfect."

Markus and I lock eyes, glaring at each other.

Ingrid says, "It's a pleasure to meet you, Markus, dear. Lisette was telling me such lovely things about you."

I mutter, "I don't remember saying anything nice."

He breaks off our staring contest and greets Ingrid with a smile and an elegant bow. "My apologies. I'm afraid I allowed my concern for my friend to overwhelm my manners. May I have your name, if it pleases you?"

Ingrid offers him her hand. "Ingrid. I do hope you and Lisette will join us for the festivities. Nevenberg is famous for the Carnavalle celebrations."

"It's been many years, but one of my fondest childhood memories is coming here and watching the performances. It was a marvel that's never been matched."

"I think this year's show might just do that. Oh, you must come."

Markus's face lights up. He looks at me, then shakes his head. "We're honored by the invitation, but I'm afraid we have urgent business in Badenberg."

Ingrid's smile dims. "I understand. If you both are passing through here again, please come visit. I have the little farm on the west side. You can't miss the apple trees."

"We look forward to it." Markus bows over her hand, then steps away, giving me privacy to say goodbye to Ingrid.

She takes my hands. "Such a handsome and considerate young man. I can see why you're so taken with each other."

I barely stop the snort. "No, um. We're friends. Just friends. We can't spend five minutes together without arguing."

Ingrid gazes into the distance, a fond smile on her face. "My friend and I used to bicker like that. I finally married him. It made it more fun to make up. I really loved him." She shakes her head, her eyes full of memories, then squeezes my hand. "My mistake. Enjoy yourself, dear."

I glance over at Markus. He's gazing around with a hungry expression, his eyes bright. How long has it been since he's attended a celebration like this? It's a small gift I can give him to start repaying everything he's done for me. And I want to leave him knowing I brought him a little happiness. *The day is already lost. A few more hours won't hurt anything.*

As she turns away, I put my hand on Ingrid's arm. "Wait, please. We'd love to join you for the festival, if it won't be an inconvenience."

Her face breaks out into a broad smile, the wrinkles at the corners of her eyes deepening. "No inconvenience at all. But are you sure, dear? I get the impression the urgent business is yours, not his."

"It's too late to travel, and I could use a little more time to rest." It's not entirely untrue. Walking around town tired me out more than expected. I'd hate to think I lost my newfound endurance so quickly. *We'll make better time tomorrow if I can rest tonight.* "I want to meet the family you've told me so many stories about."

After a questioning look at me, Markus quickly agrees to the change in plans. He and Ingrid chatter about the differences between the Carnavalles in different towns, and their favorite parts. Listening to them brings back memories of Oma's stories. Bonfires with singing and stories, everyone sharing food and toasting each other. A weight settles in my stomach, knowing Oma is still at the Wolf Palace with no idea I'm coming. I almost regret telling Ingrid we'd stay, but the reasons are still valid. I send a silent message to Oma that we're doing everything we can, then decide to enjoy the evening. It's a chance to learn more about the Kingdom of the Wolves and I've always loved a party.

Torches sit outside most shops, and a number of people are carrying them, making the way easy to navigate. I keep close to Markus and Ingrid, nervous about losing them in the crowd. Our route takes us to an enormous field. People have spread out blankets around a large pile of logs and branches at the other end of the space. Ingrid weaves through the families, waving hello to her friends in the crowd, and leads us to her family.

She quickly makes introductions to Petra and her husband, Otto, and their little three-year-old Christina. Anja and Kurt join us, bringing large baskets of food to add to the growing pile and extra blankets for everyone. Petra looks exactly like her mother, down to the brown braids. Anja and Kurt must take after their father with their golden hair and noses that turn up at the tip. Everyone has warm, open expressions and greets us enthusiastically. There's no surprise that Ingrid invited strangers to join them. Markus makes quick friends with them, sharing stories of the villages he's visited and a bit of wood lore. He's so at ease around them, like he is in the forest. Conversation flows between the family members, and they pepper us with questions about where we're from and our destination, offering advice and sights to see along the way.

They're the expected questions, but my sense of wariness creeps in. I inch closer to Markus and let him answer, keeping my comments short and vague to avoid drawing any attention to myself. They're friendly enough, but that could change in an instant if they discover I'm Lorrian.

At some unseen signal, the torches are extinguished and darkness falls across the field. The only light left is a line of lamps around the large woodpile. A woman dressed in black and white, bells chiming on her sleeves, bounds in front of the crowd.

"Welcome to Carnavalle!"

The crowd roars back at her, clapping and whistling.

The master of ceremony raises her arms for silence. "Tonight, we celebrate. We celebrate family and friends. We take time to appreciate what we have and remember those we've lost."

Petra puts her hand on her mother's shoulder. Ingrid's eyes shine with tears as she covers her daughter's hand with her own.

"Family comes in all shapes and sizes. It's children and grandparents. Siblings and cousins. Friends and neighbors. The people who love and support you. It makes us strong and helps us thrive. Even if a disagreement about the prettiest mule comes to blows" —she pauses while the crowd laughs at some shared joke— "they're family. You have to put up with them, because nobody else will."

The crowd applauds and cheers.

"Family makes us strong. Which is why it's fortunate this year's celebration is to commemorate the thirtieth anniversary of our Wolf King's victory over Lorria." The speaker pauses until the cheers die down. "King Wilhelm and the Black Wolf fought the Lorrian invaders, pushing them out of the Black Forest, proving once again we remain strong, while always being the leader of peace. We will not let Lorria and their bloodthirsty ways corrupt us."

What invasion? That never happened. We haven't had a battle with the Kingdom of the Wolves since my great-grandfather's time. We've never even had a skirmish with King Wilhelm and his brother, the infamous Black Wolf. Besides, we would never attack someone unprovoked. I hide my clenched fists under my cloak. *How dare they spread these lies about my kingdom.*

Little Christina whimpers, burying her head in Otto's shirt. At my concerned look, Otto shakes his head. "She doesn't like that name." He mouths 'Lorria.' He lifts her into his lap and rubs her back as she peeks to the side, then hides her face again. "She'll be all right when the singing starts."

I give him a tight smile, my eyes straying back to his daughter. *She's terrified of us.* Lorria is the monster in the dark for the poor child.

I want to stand up and shout that their king is a coward. That he kidnapped Oma as a show of power. That all we want is peace, but their kingdom won't leave us alone. I'm ready to explode at the next accusation—and then I see Ingrid. She's slicing up pears and cheese, nodding and shaking her head along with the crowd. Ingrid, who's been so kind and welcoming, believes everything they're saying about Lorria.

If we were in Lorria, my people would have the same accusations about the Kingdom of the Wolves.

It hits me like a blow to the chest. I suck in my breath. When Markus gives me a concerned look, I shake my head and try to smile. It's something I knew, but never realized. Our kingdoms blame each other for everything, regardless of whether it's likely to be true. Everyone is wrong ... *But the king kidnapped Oma ... Why? Is he really planning an invasion? Or is he afraid we're going to invade and wanted to protect his kingdom?*

Ingrid pauses to smile and pat my knee before returning to her task.

"Lorria wants to destroy us." The master of ceremonies lets the boos grow before pressing on. "They burn our fields. Destroy our crops. They think to weaken us. We won't let that happen. Our king and the Black Wolf guard our borders so we can live in peace. Tonight, we remind Lorria they will never defeat us!"

The crowd explodes in cheers and the bonfire is lit with a *whoosh*, flames shooting high into the night sky.

Everyone stomps their feet and cheers. A nervous knot forms in the pit of my stomach. I move closer to Markus. All my fears from the marketplace come flooding back, turning the friendly crowd into a mob. Cheers turn into taunts. My teeth chatter.

Markus slips an arm around my shoulders, pulling me closer to him, his heat seeping through my clothing. Clutching my arms, I fight the urge to press against him. His support gives me enough control to wrestle the fear down. I let out a shaky breath. *They don't know me. They don't know my kingdom. This isn't about me.*

A hidden band plays, music filling the night air. The crowd claps along, breaking out into a song. I've never heard it before, but the beat stirs my blood, begging my feet to tap along to the rhythm.

People stream down to the area in front of the bonfire, waving ribbons and throwing confetti. They sing and dance, raising their arms and spinning to the music. Everyone is happy and at ease.

Anja and Kurt stand up. "Come on," they cheer, laughing as they run down to join the dancers.

I don't want to think anymore, be afraid anymore. If I sit here, I'll drown in fear. I want to move and empty my mind and rid myself of this terror. "Let's go." I jump up and tug on Markus's hand, trying to pull him up.

He tilts his head to the side, a quizzical look on his face. "We don't have to dance."

"I want to." A thought hits me. "Do you like to dance?" He said something about enjoying it before.

"Yah, but are you sure?" His eyes are full of concern.

I give him my best sassy smile and ignore the knot of fear in my chest. "Definitely."

He grins and lets me pull him to his feet. I grip his hand as we move to join the dancers. When we reach the group, Markus spins me around, making the world blur. There are no choreographed movements like the dances at home. Everyone steps and twirls and moves as the music demands. I let the song carry me, emptying my mind of everything but the need to dance. Markus is always within arm's reach, his face glowing, a smile on his lips. His grace in the woods shines through as he moves easily with the crowd. We come together and part again, but are always close enough to reach out to each other. The singing and dancing go on for hours until my tired legs are ready to collapse, but I keep going, reveling in the freedom and joy.

The crowd finishes the last song with a rousing chorus. The master of ceremonies steps in front of the bonfire, ushering everyone to return to their seats. "And now, our featured performance."

I drop onto the blanket with Ingrid's family, my cheeks flushed, trying to catch my breath. A group of players take their places in the now-vacant area in front of the fire. A man in a long black cloak and mask leaps forward with a dramatic bow.

"Long ago, it so happened that a little girl was sent to carry bread and wine to her ill grandmother, who lived across the woods."

I look up at Markus excitedly. "I know this one. Oma used to tell it to me before bedtime."

"It's one of my favorites. I always wondered what kind of silly girl would go wandering into the woods on a whim." A slight smile plays over his lips.

"Obviously, a very wise and caring one," I reply with a laugh. I'm suddenly very aware of how close he is to me. My heart kicks into a gallop. Heat explodes across my skin, immediately replaced by ice as I shiver.

"Here, let me." He reaches behind him, then drapes a blanket across my lap. "The chill in the valley gets unpleasant after sundown."

His fingers brush my skin as he ties the red cloak closed at my throat. He freezes and our eyes lock, our faces inches apart. My breath catches.

Markus drops his hands. "It shouldn't get much cooler tonight." He quickly turns to Otto and strikes up a quiet conversation.

My face burns and mortification washes over me. *Why do I keep throwing myself at Markus when he's clearly not interested? All I'm accomplishing is making a fool of myself and making him uncomfortable.* I keep my eyes lowered, hoping nobody else witnessed my humiliation.

Petra passes me a wooden platter loaded with nuts, pear slices, chunks of cheese, apple slices, cheese rolls, and sticky buns. I nibble on a piece of creamy white cheese as everyone digs into their meals with gusto. The performance plays out with enthusiastic support from the crowd, ending with an enormous round of applause for the acting troop. The evening ends with a lovely song about peace falling over the land as it rests.

Ingrid catches my hands as we finish packing everything up into baskets. "You and Markus must come stay with me tonight."

I shake my head. "We've intruded on you enough."

"I insist. The inn will be booked, and there's no point in sleeping in the woods when I have unused bedrooms. Please."

A proper bed ... I sigh longingly.

"And there's enough time for a bath if you won't fall asleep in the tub."

The last of my resistance melts as the smile spreads across my face.

She knows she's won. "Wonderful. It's settled."

Markus says, "What's settled?"

"You're both coming home with me tonight. No use arguing, young man. Lisette needs a good rest, and I dare say you could use the same." She pulls me along, calling over her shoulder, "Come, come. We should hurry if you want a bath, too."

Ingrid and I chat on the way to the inn to get our packs, Markus trailing behind carrying Ingrid's market basket. Her home is only a short walk from town, a cozy two-story cottage with a thatch roof and tulips in the front yard. Ingrid ushers us inside to find a neat kitchen off to the side and a large, open living room. The banked fire fills the home with a lovely warmth and we shed our cloaks by the door.

Ingrid claps her hands. "Markus, I'll show you to your room and then get Lisette set up in a bath by the fire. You can have your turn after her."

We insist she bathe first, but she waves away our protests. Ingrid ushers Markus upstairs with ruthless efficiency, then we fill a hip bath with the water warming over the fire. She busies herself in the kitchen, frequently peeking her head up the stairs to 'make sure that boy is a gentleman.'

Her antics make me giggle. There's just enough room for me to sit in the tub, and I sink into the bath with a sigh. The warm water is heaven after all the slapdash scrubbing in icy springs. I'd love to soak for hours, but exhaustion pulls at my eyelids, and knowing Markus is waiting for his turn keeps me from lingering too long. My muscles are loose and warm when I finally climb out of the water and towel off in front of the fire before donning a borrowed nightgown. Being truly clean makes me feel content and at home for the first time since I set out to rescue Oma.

Ingrid shows me to one of the tidy bedrooms on the second floor, then sends Markus down for his bath. "And get behind those ears, young man. I don't want to see a speck of dirt on you."

Markus gives a meek "Yah, ma'am," from the hallway. Imagining him staring down at the tiny tub in dismay sets me giggling again.

Ingrid shuts my door with a grin. "The big ones need the most mothering."

"I think he secretly likes it."

"Me too."

She shoos me to the vanity tucked along the wall. When I sit down, the image in the mirror surprises me. It's still me, but with all the softness gone. My cheekbones are highlighted, my skin rosy and tanned, my eyes a smidge wider. I hadn't thought about it before this, but the muscles in my legs and arms are more defined, too. It's an odd feeling seeing the physical changes in me, like I need to get to know this new version of myself. Ingrid picks up the brush from the table and goes to work on my hair, taking care to get the tangles out.

I let my eyes drift shut and relax back in the chair. "Markus keeps trying to convince me to dunk my head in springs. He has no idea how long it takes hair to dry."

Ingrid chuckles. "Most men don't. My Jonas was helpless in the kitchen. I'd swear the man could burn water. But you never met a finer metalsmith or a kinder soul."

"He sounds wonderful."

"He was. Love of my life." Her hands pause. "When you find love, grab it. Fight for it. That's what I tell my children." She chuckles again. "Not that they listen to me."

"My mother says the same thing about me. Mayhap mothers should switch children. Advice is always easier to take when it comes from someone else."

"Wise for one of so few years." Her nimble hands quickly bind my hair up in a loose braid tied off with a red ribbon. When she sees me admiring the ribbon, she says, "To match your cloak."

"My signature color." I smile at my private joke. "Thank you for today. For helping me in the market, and then inviting us to stay with you and your family. It was wonderful."

"Nonsense. I'm always happy to have a new friend. Especially one who cares so much about others. You do a good job protecting him. Markus."

I look up at her in surprise. "He's the one that defends me. I mean, he's Markus. And I'm, well." I gesture at my slight frame. "Nobody is going to bet on me to win a fight."

She chuckles. "Yah. Anyone with eyes can see that boy is ready to scoop you up and protect you at the first hint of threat. But you, you're subtler. You're looking after his heart."

Heat floods my cheeks. "We're friends, that's all. Friends look after each other."

"And I'm happy to count you both among my friends. With an enemy on our doorstep, you can never have too many friends." She gives a small shake of her head. "Forgive me, I don't mean to cast a shadow. Lorria seems to be on my mind tonight."

"Ingrid. Do you … Have you …" *How do you ask someone to stop hating who you are?* A yawn escapes as exhaustion slams into me.

"Would you like a cup of tea, dear?"

"No, I better get some sleep. Markus will want to have an early start." I turn and squeeze her hands. "Thank you again. For everything."

"You're part of the family now. No need for thanks." She drops a kiss on my head. "Goodnight."

I stare at the closed door. I can't hate the Kingdom of the Wolves anymore, not after today. I can hate the king and his terrible decisions, and whatever he did to make Markus think he was better off dead to his family. But the people here are like the ones back home. Even the ones in Lutach. My stomach clenches remembering the mob, the looks in their eyes. *But it wasn't about me.* It was the lies they've been fed about Lorria that drove their fear and hatred. If they knew the truth, there would be nothing to fear. Perhaps the kingdoms would never like each other, but we'd never know until the truth is revealed.

There must be a way to cross the divide between our

kingdoms, but I can't see it. Even kind, sweet Ingrid might turn on me if I tell her I'm a Lorrian princess. Wouldn't I have done the same thing before I spent this time in the Kingdom of Wolves? I believed they wanted nothing more than to destroy my kingdom. That they couldn't be trusted and any acts of kindness would be lies to lull me into a false sense of security. Why would they think differently about me? And any suspicion about me would fall on Markus.

But when do the lies stop? Does it start by telling one person? Changing one mind? *If I'm wrong, Markus and I will be dragged into town in chains and then ...* I gulp. Not only will we suffer, but Oma is depending on me. *But if I don't do it now, then when? When will it finally be time for things change?*

17

Ingrid ladles a spoonful of eggs onto my plate. "You're so quiet this morning. Did you not sleep well?"

I stifle a yawn and give her a bright smile. "It was the most comfortable bed I've had in weeks." Not technically a lie. It was comfortable, but unfortunately my worries wouldn't let me enjoy it. As Markus comes through the front door, I add, "I should've warned you about Markus's snoring."

"I think you're placing the snoring blame in the wrong bed." Markus winks at me as he heads to the sink to wash up.

"I don't snore!"

"Did I say you did?"

Ingrid loads another plate with food. "Did that winch give you any trouble?"

He scrubs his hands with soap, digging at the grease under his nails. "The mechanism was rusty. It's working now."

Ingrid pulls his head down and plants a kiss on his

cheek. "You saved me from another one of Petra's lectures."

A blush runs up Markus's cheeks to the tips of his ears. "Least I could do."

He glares at me as I snicker. Ingrid puts a platter of sausages next to the plate of sliced apples. Markus slides onto the bench next to me as our hostess sits across the table.

She touches her forehead, then her lips. "May today bring health and happiness."

Markus makes the same gestures, and I quickly mimic the movements. Before I can dive into the eggs, he clears his throat, his knee bumping mine under the table. As Ingrid chatters about the festivities planned for the rest of the week, Markus catches my eye. He makes sure I'm looking before moving his fork to his left hand, holding it upside down. With exaggerated slowness, he uses the knife to push eggs onto the back of the fork.

I wrinkle my forehead, then quickly clear my expression. *He can't be serious. Meals would take forever if you have to balance a tiny bite of food on the back of the fork every time.* I copy his technique. The fork is halfway to my mouth when the eggs drop into my lap. *Ridiculous.*

Markus's lips twitch as he answers Ingrid. "We wish we could stay, but we really must move on. Lisette's family is waiting for her."

"Then you must promise to visit me the next time you're near here. I won't take no for an answer."

We promise. It saddens me I'll never see Ingrid again after today. *Markus will visit her for me ... unless he really leaves.*

I try another bite of eggs. This time the food slides off after I've barely lifted the fork. I sullenly stab a sausage as Markus methodically devours his eggs, sausages, and fruit.

There must be a trick I'm missing.

Ingrid pauses, looking at me. "Oh, how pretty. What is that?"

The whistle slipped out from under my tunic sometime while I was eating. "Oh, ah, it's a wolf whistle." I pull it off and hand it to her.

She turns it over in her hands, studying the simple metal cylinder. "It's beautiful. From a very skilled craftsman. A wolf whistle, you say? I've never seen one before. I thought only the royal guards kept these. Wherever did you get it?"

"It, um, was a gift." I shift on the bench, keeping my gaze away from Markus. *Can she connect Markus to the palace with a whistle?*

She holds it up to the light. "Really beautiful. My Jonas was the finest metalsmith in the kingdom, and this reminds me of his work." Ingrid hands it back to me with a smile. "A very special gift."

I silently hang the cord around my neck, unsure how to respond. Markus changes the topic, asking about the roads ahead, keeping up our cover story of traveling to Badenberg.

"How have the storms been this way? Should we plan for rain?"

I tune them out, determined to finish my food even with all the ridiculous etiquette rules. When I pick up a piece of cheddar, Markus nudges me with his knee. He casually picks a slice of cheese with his left hand without breaking off his conversation with Ingrid. His lips twitch.

I narrow my eyes as I switch the cheese to my other hand. *Is he messing with me, or is this really how they eat?* Ingrid spends so much time gesturing and talking, I can't tell if she's following the same rules Markus keeps hinting at.

Markus sits up. "The King, you say?"

Burn it, what did I miss?

Ingrid nods. "It's all rumors, mind you. But they say King Wilhelm has closed up the palace. Nobody is going in or out these past few weeks. Everyone's speculating whether there's illness inside, or if there have been threats against the King or his son. That's the one I'm betting on. Ever since his youngest died in that fire years back, King Wilhelm has kept Fredrik at the palace. Too afraid something will happen to his surviving son to let him have a life. It's not right."

I grip my fork, my knuckles white. "Have you heard of any visitors before they closed the doors? Or prisoners?"

Ingrid's brow furrows. "Nothing like that. There haven't been any ambassadors or visitors outside the kingdom since we shut the borders, however many generations ago. The only one is the Black Wolf, but he's their family. He practically lives there when he isn't patrolling the borders."

Markus leans forward. "But the King is safe? And Fredrik? Nothing's happened to them?"

Ingrid shrugs and takes a sip of tea. "I haven't heard anything. I hope they're all right. The King has been good to us. I'm sure Fredrik will make a fine king one day, but we haven't gotten the chance to know him. It's not like the old days when the heir would do tours of the towns so we could meet him."

My heart picks up speed. "Do you know why the Wolf King would want to start a war with Lorria?"

Ingrid's eyes widen. "Wherever did you get such an idea? He makes sure those greedy brutes don't cross our borders, but King Wilhelm wants peace. He would never start a war."

I bite my tongue. Ingrid may feel righteous in her hatred for Lorria, but I wonder how she'd feel if she knew her beloved king kidnapped my grandmother. Lorria has done nothing—*nothing*—to deserve this.

Ingrid sniffs the air, then glances over her shoulder at the tidy kitchen. "Where is my mind today? I forgot the cinnamon apple crumble. I hope it hasn't burned."

"I'll get it." I jump up from the bench, relieved to have a moment to myself. My mind whirls as I grab a towel to hold the hot cast-iron skillet. We've been carefully avoiding talking about Markus's family, dancing around the topic, but never venturing too close. But now I have to know. *He doesn't have to tell me everything, but I have to know what kind of danger we're walking into. If the—*

Flames rise in front of my eyes. Heat scorches my skin. I scream and drop the burning towel. I grab the pot of water and dump it onto the fire. The flames sizzle in protest. The fire sputters, then dies, leaving the charred towel in the puddle on the counter.

Ingrid hurries over. "Are you hurt? Let me see."

"No, no, I'm fine." I press my hand to my chest. My heart is racing and I can't seem to catch my breath, though the danger's passed. I gulp in air, my pulse slowing. "I must have held the towel too close to the stove's flame." *Idiot. That's what I get for being distracted.* There's a large scorch mark on the counter where I dropped the flaming towel. I bite my lip. "Oh, Ingrid, I'm so sorry."

She waives away my concern. "Don't give it another thought. I'm just glad you're not hurt. Here, let me see your hand." She studies the pink skin. "It doesn't look too bad. You should put some aloe on it to be safe." She hurries off up the stairs.

Markus is standing at the table, the bench knocked over behind him. He's staring past me, his eyes locked on the stovetop.

I grimace. "I can't believe I did that. I'm such a klutz. Poor Ingrid. I wish there was something I could do to make it up to her before we go."

He doesn't react.

"Markus?" I touch his arm.

He keeps staring at the stove, his face covered in sweat. "The fire. It's here." His voice is a whisper.

"Markus." I shake his arm, but he doesn't move. "Markus, what's wrong?" I grab the front of his tunic and yank his face down to mine. "Markus, look at me."

His eyes snap into focus. He grabs my shoulders. "Lisette."

Thank the heavens. "What's wrong?"

He twists his head, grimacing. "It's not safe. I have to go." Markus's hands tighten on my shoulders, then he stares at me. "I need to go."

Ice spreads through my chest. *All this talk of his family must have changed his mind about helping me.* My heart gives a hollow thump as a lump grows in my throat. *Don't cry now. Wait until you're alone.* "I understand. I can find my own way from here. Thank you for all your help. I wouldn't have made it this far without you."

He blinks. His hands drop so quickly I stumble back a step.

"What? No. I'm still your guide." He shakes his head. "We need to leave." Markus dashes past Ingrid as she comes down the stairs, leaving me wondering what happened.

By the time Ingrid smears aloe on my hand and wraps a simple bandage around it, Markus is back, our packs in his hands.

Ingrid tries to convince Markus to finish breakfast, but

he's adamant we leave immediately. I give her a tearful hug goodbye, sorry to leave, but eager to continue to the palace.

Whatever fascination Nevenberg held for him yesterday has vanished. Markus is silent as we walk, directing us down an overgrown road. I wait until the town has disappeared before breaking the quiet.

"That was an exciting morning."

Markus grunts.

"I still can't believe I set that dishrag on fire. Good thing it wasn't my sleeve." I force out a laugh.

He doesn't respond.

Isn't he supposed to be the cheery morning person? "First bandits and cave-ins, and now I almost destroyed Ingrid's kitchen. Disasters seem to follow us wherever we go. Makes me wonder what's coming next."

"The fire was an accident." His pace increases until I'm trotting to keep up.

"Obviously. It's not like I would try to burn Ingrid's house down."

He clenches his fists, the muscle in his jaw ticking. "I warned you. I told you it would be dangerous coming here."

My temper flares at his sharp tone. "I know that. It's not your fault."

"That's what you're implying."

Don't kick him, don't kick him, don't kick him. "I'm not implying anything. Why are you deliberately misunderstanding me?"

Markus takes a controlled breath. "I'm sorry. It seems I'm not fit for company today. I'll scout ahead."

He strides off as my mouth drops open. *Where did that come from?* Something is off with him, but I can't put my finger on it. It could be the reminders of his family, but it feels like something more. I shake my head. *That man is one frustrating mystery. Mayhap it is better we spend the morning apart.*

I catch glimpses of Markus as the day wears on. He checks on me frequently, but is never close enough to call out. It's odd hiking by myself. A bit lonely, but not terrible. I can't remember the last time I was by completely alone. Probably the night I left home. After that, I was traveling in public coaches and inns. Even at home, people are always just a few steps away.

A strange thing happens as I walk. The forest seems to open up to me. It's easier to spot the birds in the trees and the lizards running through the grass. I even spy a few rabbits in the brush and a deer grazing in the distance.

The time alone lets me ponder everything we've gone through on this journey. I'm not as brave as I thought, but I am stronger. I could have turned around anytime and nobody would have blamed me. But I kept going. Yes, I was scared, but I pushed on. If I can go through these things and come out better on the other side, nothing can stop me. My steps lighten, like I've set down a burden I didn't know I was carrying. I'm centered and at peace with myself in a way I've never felt before.

When twilight falls and I find Markus setting up camp, I greet him with a smile. His face is blank. Obviously, his time alone wasn't the healing experience mine was. I shrug it off. We still need to talk, but we have time. I can wait until he's ready. We silently finish setting up camp. By unspoken agreement, we skip my nightly defense training.

As Markus cleans out the bowls from supper, he clears his throat. "Sorry about today."

"Thank you, but you don't have to apologize. You

needed time for yourself. And actually, I had a good think. It worked out for the best."

He raises his eyebrows. "Come to any epiphanies?"

"As a matter of fact, yes. I got to know myself a little better." I narrow my eyes and say in a mock stern tone, "But don't think this means you can wander off by yourself every day. I don't want to get lost in this barbaric forest of yours."

He gives me a ghost of a smile. "Absolutely. I know how helpless you princesses are on your own."

Not as much as I used to believe. "Good. Now get some sleep. We have a lot of ground to make up if we want to rescue Oma this century."

I busy myself setting up my bedroll, letting him have a few moments of privacy. There's a tension in the air that's been absent since our friendship started. Markus is in such an odd mood. *Will he still be here in the morning?* I don't know what's changed with him, so I don't have an answer. I stare wide-eyed into the firelight, frozen, listening for any movement.

"No … Stay away … Get out …"

The low voice yanks me from sleep, the pain and distress sending my heart hammering. I shoot up, searching for the threat. The campfire coals give everything eerie shadows, soft orange light flickering to show and hide the details around me.

Markus thrashes. "Don't … Run …"

I crawl over to him, avoiding an arm as it flings out to the side. "Markus." I shake his shoulder. "Markus. It's a dream. Wake up."

"No!" He lunges at me, grabbing me by the shoulders, fingers digging into my skin with bruising force. His dark eyes stare at me, unseeing, trapped in some nightmare.

I shriek, "Markus!" Fear for him sends chills over my skin. He's locked in some internal battle, unable to break free. "It's all right. Come back to me."

His hands squeeze. Markus flinches, eyes focusing on me at last. "Lisette." He crushes me to his chest, arms wrapping around me tight, stealing my breath. "You're safe."

The shock of being so roughly handled disappears at the sob in his voice. "Yes, yes." It's hard to keep my voice from shaking. "I'm here."

His heart thunders, lungs bellowing. "You're safe." Markus buries his face in my hair, his body shuddering.

I rub his back the way Mother used to rub mine when she found me crying after a fight with Maddie. "You are too."

He keeps me pressed to his chest while I murmur reassuring nonsense. His pulse gradually slows, the tension draining out of him, though his hold on me doesn't loosen.

"Markus," I whisper. "What's wrong? What is it?"

"You were trapped. In the flames." His breath is hot on my neck, the words coming out in gasps. "I couldn't get to you."

His arms tighten to an uncomfortable degree, but I don't protest, knowing what it is to need physical touch for reassurance.

Markus takes a deep breath. "That's how my brother was almost killed the last time. A fire. In the palace." His voice is almost nonexistent. "It was my fault."

I swallow down the protest. He needs to get the story out. Any interruption might break the thin strand he's clinging to.

"It was King's Day. It was the biggest celebration the kingdom had ever seen. Food and wine all day for the thousand guests at the palace. There were nonstop acrobats and tumblers and dancers." He takes a deep breath. "The main attraction was the fire dancers. It enthralled my brother and I. Torches whirling through the air, spitting flames into the sky. They were exotic and dangerous and mesmerizing. The crowd went mad every time they appeared."

I tighten my arms around him, wanting to stop what's coming next, but knowing he needs me to hear it.

"Fredrik" —his voice cracks— "was my hero. I worshipped him the way only a little brother can. We snuck out of bed and stole torches to practice. Spent hours trying to spin and toss them. I was terrible." A ghost of a smile flashes across his lips before disappearing. "My brother was so good at it. Rik was good at everything. The perfect son. My father's favorite, but I never resented him because he was my favorite, too."

That's exactly how I feel about Maddie. It's impossible to hate her, because I love her so much. Being my parent's favorite hasn't done her any favors. If anything, it's made it easier on me. They were so focused on her, I had freedoms I wouldn't have had otherwise.

"Rik wanted to go to sleep, but I was determined to practice until I had it down perfectly. I could barely lift my arms by the time I finally gave up. I thought I put the torch in the fireplace with the others, but ..." He goes silent.

Nonononononono. The story doesn't have a happy ending, and there's no way to change it. The ache in my chest grows.

Markus's wound may be old, but it still causes him in agony.
I'd do anything to erase the shattered look in his eyes.

"It's all jumbled after that. Rik shaking me awake and
yelling to run. Heat. Smoke. So many flames …" His eyes
go distant, his jaw tight. "I should've waited for Rik. I
thought he was right behind me. I—I went back. To find
him." Markus's eyes are shadowed as he rubs his shoulder.
"He was unconscious, the flames burning all around him.
His tunic caught fire. I put it out, but he was hurt. I managed
to drag him out, but just barely. That's when I knew I had to
leave them. I ran. I ran away and never looked back." His
shoulders slump. "Eventually I made my way to Lorria, and
you know the rest."

*That's why he had such a powerful reaction to the fire
this morning.* "But Markus, you don't know the fire was
your fault. And even if it was, it was an accident. Your father
and brother would have understood. You didn't need to
leave."

He swallows hard. "That wasn't the first time. You
remember I said soothsayers read the signs around our
births? Most people learn they'll be artists, or great
craftsman, or lead a happy life. Mine said I was destined to
kill the king. Accidents have followed me my entire life.
Saddle straps that snapped when we were riding, poisonous
mushrooms mixed in with the edible ones, ladder rungs
breaking. Everywhere I went, something bad happened.
Someone usually got hurt."

Markus grabs my hands, eyes glistening. "People
counseled father to send me away for their safety and mine,
but he wouldn't hear of it. He and Rik loved me, and I
couldn't bear to be parted from them. Until the fire. That's
when I knew I was too much of a danger to them. If I stayed

any longer, they might not be so lucky the next time. I knew it would hurt them less if they thought I died in the fire."

When his head drops on my shoulder, I stroke his hair. "It's not your fault."

"It is. I—"

"No." I grip his head and bring his face up, my eyes boring into his. "It's. Not. Your. Fault."

Such pain, so much anger at himself. I won't convince him tonight. The wound is too deep and infected. But I can help start the healing. Reassure him and remind him. Show him I believe it until it sinks in, just a little. Once it has a hold, he won't be able to shake it loose. The road won't be easy, but Markus has walked in the shadows long enough. He's carried a burden that doesn't belong to him for far too long.

How to make him understand? "You love your father and your brother. You would never hurt them." I wait until he gives a slow nod. "I don't know how that fire started, or what caused those other mishaps. Neither do you. Accidents happen. People are quick to blame. If they didn't have you, they would pick some other mischief to lay the responsibility on. Fredrik and your father love you. They wouldn't want you to be chained by this guilt forever. They would want you home, with them." I can't believe I'm campaigning for him to return to the man I hate most in the world, but it's what Markus needs. It's what will make him happy.

"I can't go back." Markus pushes to his feet and paces. "It's best I stay dead. The soothsayer was clear. I'll kill my father. I can't be responsible for that. If I did, I couldn't live with myself."

I get in his way, forcing him to halt his steps. "Is that what's stopping you? You're going to believe some charlatan's rubbish and abandon your family forever? Do you really think you could kill your father, no matter what he does?"

"No, but—"

"Then that's that. You should to go home." He looks away, but I pull his face back around to mine. "You deserve to be happy." I press my hands to his chest. "Your family wants you to be happy. I want you to be happy."

There. A crack. The words found a way past his wall, creating a tiny opening for the future. I wrap my arms around Markus and rest my head against his chest, willing the change to take root and grow. I want Markus to be happy. He's helped me so much; I can only hope I've given him a little something back. *Something to remember me by.*

His shirt is damp. *When did I start crying?*

"I'm sorry it took this long to tell you. I know you've been curious."

Understatement of the century. "It's your story to tell. I'm grateful you trusted me."

"You showed remarkable restraint."

"Don't count on that in the future. I'm not usually patient, but for you" —I hug him tighter— "I'm willing to try new things. Like wearing trousers."

"Does that mean you're going to let me win all our arguments?"

"Don't press your luck. I like you, but not that much."

Markus laughs, just like I wanted him to. "It was too much to hope for." He yawns. "We should try to sleep. There's a few more hours before sunrise."

"How can you tell?" I say with a mock grumble. Markus seems more settled, but he's hard to read when he wants to hide his feelings.

He taps the side of his head. "I am one with the forest. I know all."

I snicker. "You're something, all right."

He looks at his bedroll, then at the forest. "We should start keeping watch. There'll be patrols near the palace."

We haven't even crossed the mountains yet ... oh. "Good idea." I drag my bedroll next to his. "We should stay close together, too. That way, if we need to wake the other, we do can it quietly."

Taking my time, I make a big show of fluffing out the pack I'm using as a pillow and shaking out the blankets before climbing into them. Markus sits stiffly on top of his bedding. Closing my eyes, I yawn and stretch, leaving my hand out on the edge of his blanket. After a few minutes, he lays down with a sigh. His hand slips over mine.

He whispers, "Goodnight." His breathing slows, deepens.

A light snore joins the night noises.

I smile and drift off to sleep.

18

Markus reappears on the path ahead of me. I huff and puff my way to him, cursing the Wolf King for building a palace on the other side of the mountain. *He could've at least made a tunnel, or built a lift. Or make the trails wide enough for horses. But no. I have to haul myself up the mountain because his royal pain-in-the-rear doesn't believe in good infrastructure.*

"There's a camping spot this way."

While my legs and lungs are ready to collapse in relief, I can't help myself. "It's too early. If we're going to get across the mountain, we need to push on."

"I don't like the look of that storm." Markus nods at the gray clouds gathering overhead. "And this might be the last water until we get until we get to the other side." He grins. "Don't worry, you'll get plenty of punishment tomorrow when the real climb begins."

I groan. "I thought we were already past the steep part."

"This? Pfft." He waves a hand dismissively. "Only a flatlander would think this was steep. It barely qualifies as a hill.”

“Only a barbarian would think that’s a hill. It’s all that mountain air, it’s addled your brains.” I pat his arm as I shake my head sadly. “Unfortunately, there’s no cure once you’ve hit the delusional stage. All we can do is wait for it to run its course and see if you come out sensible on the other side.”

“The girl who hired an insane barbarian to take her through the wolf-infested forest shouldn’t talk about being sensible.”

“Who better to lead me through a savage kingdom than a wild beast?” I sweep my arm through the air dramatically. “Lead on, ruffian.”

“My pleasure, milady.” He drops into an elaborate bow.

Markus follows some invisible trail, twisting and pushing through the thick bushes. I stick close behind him, ducking the occasional errant branch, as he shoves deeper into the thicket.

The last bush hides the opening to a tiny pocket carved into the mountainside. I take a deep breath of the humid air. A small stream of water escapes the rock and spills down to a wide, clear basin lined with gray stones, creating a soft musical backdrop. Dark green plants crawl over the walls and blanket the ground. Tiny light blue and lilac flowers with yellow centers scent the air with a light perfume.

“Wow, this is beautiful.” I wander closer to miniature waterfall. “How did you find this place? “

“Game trail.” Markus pulls out the small shovel, then touches a pocket on his pack. “If you can get the fire pit ready, I spotted berry bushes higher up the trail.”

He disappears back through the undergrowth, taking his pack with him. I quickly set up camp. He returns shortly with a triumphant smile and a huge collection of blackberries.

My mouth waters looking at the pile of berries. "We should probably save some for tomorrow."

"We could do that." Markus pops one in his mouth, then another. "But they're so fragile. It would be a shame if we waited, and they were damaged." He winks. "Better eat them all now."

I grin. "If you insist." I bite into a blackberry, savoring the explosion of sour-sweet juices.

We speed through our nightly fight training, both eager to get to supper. Markus is so distracted I even score a hit on him for the first time and celebrate with a victory lap around him as I mimic a crowd chanting my name. He declares us done for the night and wraps up the session with his usual reminder to always run away if that's an option.

We add the berries to the bread, cheese, and pears left from our last trade, creating a small feast. The cozy little space is warm even without a fire, so we only build a small one for light and tea. I lean back against my pack with a contented sigh, tossing the last blackberry into my mouth. Never in a thousand years would I have pictured myself here. My dreams of traveling with Oma involved inns and families, not the wilderness. I'm proud I've challenged myself in a way my grandmother hasn't, despite her exciting life.

Markus pats the pocket on his pack. "More tea?"

"None for me." I rub my bulging belly.

Instead of the normal graceful efficiency, Markus bumbles his way through preparing his cup, dropping the pouch of herbs twice and spilling water over the side of the pot. Once it's ready, he sets the cup aside untasted. He walks over to the water's edge and dips his hands in, then rubs the back of his neck.

I purse my lips, watching him move around the camp. *Is he hurt and hiding it?* Markus isn't one to complain except to tease me. There isn't any pain in his movements, just clumsiness. If anything, I'd say he's … nervous?

Markus twitches when he notices me watching him.

I narrow my eyes. "What's going on?"

"What do you mean?"

"Are we camping in the middle of a den of poisonous snakes?"

"No."

"Are bears going to come crashing in here and attack us while we sleep?" I stand and plant my fists on my hips.

"No, again."

"Then why are you so jumpy?"

"I'm not." When I lift an eyebrow, he shrugs. "Really. It's safe."

I eye him skeptically, then shrug. "Do you have any more of that special tea that helps my muscles? If that was the easy part, I'm going to need all the help I can get to climb over this mountain."

His brow crinkles. "That's it? No interrogation or driving me crazy until I tell you what's bothering me?"

"You're not mad at me, and those berries were amazing. I'm too happy right now to pester you into submission." I point a finger at him. "Don't think that'll work all the time, though. Usually my minimum bribe level is cake." I gasp. "Wait. I just remembered. You promised to buy me spiced chocolate. There must've been a shop in Nevenberg. Ugh, I can't believe I missed it."

He rubs the back of his neck again. "I—I forgot. We can

go back. Or at the next town. There's one on the other side of the mountain. It's small, but I'm sure someone will have it. We can ask one of the farmers. On the way back to Lorria, I'll buy you twice as much."

He's actually upset. I tug his arm down, immediately regretting my joke. "Markus, I'm teasing you. I don't care about it, I promise. Being there and seeing Carnavalle with you was better than any spiced chocolate."

He looks down at me, moonlight shining in his eyes. "Still. It was rude of me to forget." The air is suddenly warm between us.

My breath catches. *He's being polite. It's all in my imagination. Don't make him uncomfortable.* I roll my eyes and give him a little shove, trying to break the moment. "Yes, well, I'm sure I'll think of a way for you to make it up to me."

"Mayhap this will earn my forgiveness."

Markus slips an item out of a pocket on his pack as he pulls my hand close. With a featherlight touch, he fastens something around my wrist. Heat spreads across my skin. I keep my eyes on his hands, afraid of what they'll reveal if I look up. His fingers brush my palm. Markus jerks away, revealing an elegant silver bracelet resting around my wrist.

The delicate silver wires are like strands of starlight, braided together and then braided again to create an intricate pattern. A flawless, deep red stone sits between two thin metal beads engraved with dainty flowers, then a clear stone on both sides, capped off on either end with two more metal beads etched with the phases of the moon.

The tips of his ears burn red. "I was going to buy one before we left Nevenberg, but Ingrid insisted on giving this to me. Her husband made it. I should've given it to you at

Carnavalle, but—you don't have to take it. Or I could get you something else. It's silly."

He reaches for it, but I twist it out of his reach. "It's beautiful. And it's my signature color." While the marketplace bracelets looked incredible, this is a showpiece fit for a king. That it also came from Ingrid makes it even more precious. "I love it."

He hems for another minute as a smile grows on his lips. I quickly drop my eyes, running my fingers over the beads. "The ones I saw in the marketplace only had one stone and no beads, but this one looks more … complete? No, balanced. Do they mean anything?"

When the silence stretches too long, I look up to find Markus busy with his pack. *Burn it, what did I say? I need to stop tripping over my tongue.* "Markus?"

"They symbolize different phases of, um, friendship. Every bracelet is unique. They're for different events and milestones you experienced together and want to remember."

"Aww, that's so sweet." My heart flutters before I can stop it. "What do these represent?"

"Can't you guess?" His teasing tone returns. "You can't expect a big oaf like me to explain it to a sophisticated princess like yourself."

I nod wisely, fighting the smile trying to break through. "So true." I touch the stones, trying to guess their meaning. The red is a joke between us, so that one is easy. The moon stone matches the dagger's engravings. The two clear stones are a mystery. Stars? Water? The moon again? And the flower beads are pretty, but I can't attach any deeper importance to it. "Not that I'm giving up, because obviously I can figure this out on my own, but perhaps a hint would be helpful."

"Hmm, I guess I can give you a hint." His eyes crinkle with amusement as he points to the flower beads. "They're spicy, but deadly."

I gasp. "Are those coriander flowers?"

He rubs a hand across his face, hiding his lips.

"You horrible, rotten beast." The laughter grows until I'm crying. "You're terrible."

His deep laugh joins mine. "You have to admit, it was memorable."

"I spent most of it unconscious, but you have a point." I spin the bead and give him a mischievous smile. "Speaking of which, I think almost dying warrants me winning at least ten arguments."

"You must still be disoriented from the coriander. At most, you would get three."

"You're forgetting I met Ingrid and got us the invitation to Carnavalle. Surely that's worth at least seven." When he makes a face, I add, "And I'm being forced to climb a mountain tomorrow."

"Five arguments." He leans forward, eyes narrowed, and holds out his hand.

"Deal." We shake, the little zing when our skin touches making my heart sing.

His hand lingers on mine. I reluctantly slip away, determined not to misunderstand his actions again. I've embarrassed myself too many times and I don't want to ruin our friendship over a silly mix-up.

To cover my heating cheeks, I return to admiring the bracelet. "You're spoiling me. Is there an equivalent for men?"

"No." Markus doesn't move, his eyes still locked on my

face.

"That's unfair." My pulse speeds up, my body fighting to move closer to him while my mind keeps it frozen in place. "Why should I get all the pretty things? I should get you something so you can commemorate our adventure, too. The men at court are fond of overly tall hats."

Markus starts, then draws back a step, clasping his hands behind his back.

I flinch. *I always say the wrong thing to him.* "No hats. How about a whistle that actually works to replace your wolf whistle? One that can mimic bird calls."

He crouches and pokes the fire with a stick. "I don't need anything."

Rocks fill my stomach. My head spins at how easily we shift from a fun, light evening to this grim atmosphere in the blink of an eye. Something sends Markus into these dark moods, but I don't know what's triggering him. And yet, I keep stumbling into it. I thought by now Markus would be comfortable enough to tell me if I'm being a brat, but he flips to sulking while pretending he's not.

Enough. "I can't stand it anymore. What's going on? We're having a friendly moment, and then you suddenly act like I'm a stranger."

He keeps his eyes averted. "I don't know what you're talking about. Everything's fine."

Don't kick him, don't kick him, don't kick him. I set my feet and stare him down. "You know I'll harass you until you tell me what's bothering you. It's best to admit defeat early and avoid the suffering." I sigh. "Markus. I'm trying. But I don't know what I'm doing that offends you so much."

He bends his head forward. "It's not you. Not really." He snaps the twig and tosses the pieces into the fire. "You're going back to Lorria. To your family."

When he doesn't continue, I prod him. "Yes. After we rescue Oma, of course I'll go home. And you'll start a new life somewhere, or stay with your family at the Wolf Palace." My heart twists as I say the words, preferring to pretend he'll change his mind and come with me back to Lorria. Perhaps even agree to stay at the palace.

Markus is quiet, staring into the flames. I settle on the ground next to him, resisting the urge to fill the silence.

His shoulders droop. "I keep forgetting we're from different worlds."

The unhappiness in his voice melts my resolve to keep my distance. I press my shoulder against his, letting his leather and musk scent wash over me. "I know. When it's the two of us out here, it feels like … like …"

"Like this is our kingdom. Like Lorria and the Kingdom of Wolves don't exist."

"Exactly." The rocks turn to butterflies. "And we've always been here. It's terrible and unforgivable, but sometimes I forget we're here to rescue Oma. It's just you and me, traveling and exploring. Then I remember and it's a punch to the gut. When Oma's safe, everything will go back to how it was." *And I don't want it to.*

"I don't know what's waiting for me outside Lorria. Or if going back to my family is the right thing to do. Everything is muddled."

I twist to look up at him. "You don't have to decide right away. Why not make your home in Lorria for a while? I know Eelan wasn't welcoming, but you could live somewhere else and have a fresh start. We're not all bad."

He glances down at me. "It's tempting."

My pulse speeds up. I shift up to my knees so I can look

him directly in the eye. "Come to the palace. All the healing techniques you know are remarkable. You could share that knowledge, make a real difference for everyone. You'd be working with people who would respect you and be excited to learn from you." *And I'd have you a little longer.* I hold my breath, daring to hope.

He stares into my eyes … then shakes his head. "It's a pretty picture, but I'd never fit in there. They'd hate me for being a Wolf."

I open my mouth to argue, then sink back down with a sigh. "They'd learn, like I did. But I can't pretend it would be easy on you. There's been hatred between our kingdoms for too long." It's my turn to stare into the fire.

He nudges me. "You're right about one thing. Nothing needs to be answered right now. Tonight, I want to live in our kingdom and talk about what our next adventure will be. Because tomorrow …" He chuckles. "You'll see."

A groan escapes my lips. "You're trying to torture me, aren't you? You're mad that I'm right about everything and this is your way of getting revenge."

"Is it working?"

"Unfortunately." I bump my shoulder against his. "Do you want to tell me now? How about now? Is now good? What about now?"

He smirks. "Save that energy for the hike tomorrow."

"Annoyance is not my fuel of choice."

"And yet it works so well."

"At making me not sleep." I nudge him again. "If you won't tell me what punishment is waiting for me tomorrow, tell me about an adventure we'd go on in our kingdom."

Markus inclines his head toward the small trickle of water coming down the rock wall. "If you like waterfalls, there's an amazing one near the canyon …"

19

I never thought I'd long for more trees.

The dusty, open trail was fine when we started out this morning. Though I missed the shade, it was nice to see more than five feet of terrain at a time. That was before it turned into a deathtrap.

I toss back the cloak's soggy hood, so drenched at this point it doesn't matter if the rain falls directly on me. The drops pummel my head relentlessly. My leathers rub and chafe with every step. I send a silent plea to the heavens the bedroll inside my pack stays dry, otherwise it's going to be a chilly night.

Markus slips, dropping to one knee. He braces himself as his legs splay in the mud. "Slippery right here." The words are barely audible over the pounding raindrops, despite our being a few feet apart.

I hurry forward to help him. My foot shoots out, the pack's weight overbalancing me. My arms windmill as I teeter, threatening to tip over. "Aaarrrrggghhh." My other foot skates sideways and I crash face-first into the cold sludge.

Spluttering through the downpour, I push up on my arms, flipping my dripping curls out of my face. He grins, face smeared with muck. Rivulets run down his hair, creating clean trails through the filth covering him from head to toe.

He offers me a hand. "Should we swim for it? "

"Don't tempt me."

Markus hauls me up with ease, steadying me until my feet have a tenuous grip on the marshy ground. My foot comes free from the mud with a loud, sucking pop. The wind howls, sending me staggering into Markus's chest, knocking us both back down into the clammy sludge.

I sit up and sigh. "I give up. I'm crawling the rest of the way. It'll save me the trouble of falling down every other step."

He looks at the sky, then frowns as he checks behind us. "We need to keep moving."

Markus scrambles to his feet, pulling me up with him despite my grumbles. Another blast of wind sends me reeling. I brace myself, leaning forward into the squall, my boots sliding through the mud. Markus grabs my waist, preventing me from being swept off my feet as the wind continues its assault. Gusts blast from the side, then the front. Each onslaught pushes me a new direction with no opportunity to brace against it. If not for his firm hold, I'd be tossed around like a ragdoll.

I cling to his arm, tucking my head down as we forge ahead. We creep forward, losing two steps for each one gained. The wind howls its rage, throwing rocks, dirt, and sticks to stop us. Every inch is a battle. My teeth chatter from cold and terror. Everything is numb. I can't tell if I'm moving my legs anymore, or if Markus is simply dragging me along.

Lightning flashes, illuminating the sky for an instant. I jump as a deafening boom sounds.

I yell, "We have to get under cover."

He shakes his head, bellowing, "We have to move. Someone's following us."

Great. If I wasn't already terrified, this news would've done the trick. But there's no room in my fear for a vague shadow behind us when nature is doing its best to murder us right now. "They can't kill us if the storm does it first."

Markus glares. Another flash of lightning and a roar of thunder clash in the sky. He grabs my hand and drags me off the trail. "Stay low."

We struggle up the hill. Markus finds a low overhang of rocks just high enough for us to crawl under. The sudden cessation of rain pounding on my head makes me dizzy and my ears pop. I untie the pack, the knots slimy and tight. I drape my cloak over the top of the bag, the vibrant red lost under the layers of mud.

Markus pulls the canvas out of his pack. "We should be safe here. Or at least, safer than on the path."

He peels off his wet cloak and sets it aside before pulling the canvas sheet over his broad chest. I'm too numb to blush as he tucks the rough fabric around and under me, trapping our heat inside. Everything is damp leather, wet hair, and frozen skin. Lightning strikes something on the next hill. A metallic scent fills the air and the hairs on my body tingle. I gulp and huddle next to Markus.

It takes a few minutes before Markus's heat penetrates my icy skin. The first tendril of warmth sets my teeth chattering. I rub my hands up and down my arms and scrunch down, trying to preserve as much body heat as possible—if I ever start generating any.

I blow on my hands. "Who's following us? Is it the same people from before?"

Markus peers out, although it's impossible to see anything more than a few feet away. "It's just one. He's too far behind to recognize any features."

"I can't believe he would travel into this storm just to chase us."

"I want to know how he found us again."

"If it's the man from Eelan, he probably knows we're traveling to the palace. I left a note for my parents explaining where I was going. If my father sent him, he knows our general direction and could track us that way." I silently curse my earlier self for being so foolish.

"That's only if he's after you. If he's trying to find me, he wouldn't know where we're going."

"He can't be after you. You're dead, remember?"

"Mayhap." Markus looks unconvinced. "In any case, we'll have to stay alert. The storm should slow him down, but there are a lot of opportunities for him to catch us on the way to the Wolf Palace, or on the way back."

After I rescue Oma, it won't matter if he catches us, as long as Markus isn't with us. "Hmm." I lapse into silence, debating whether it would be better to contact my father's man before I rescue Oma, or right after. I could use his help getting Oma, but not until Markus leaves me. My father's man will view anyone from the Kingdom of the Wolves as an enemy, no matter what I say. I can guarantee my and Oma's safety, but not Markus's.

It's imperative Markus leaves me once we're close to the palace. If he isn't going to return to his family, they can't find out he's still alive. Selfishly, I want to keep him close as long as I can. My muddled feelings aside, he's my friend—the closest friend I've ever had, if I'm being honest with myself. The thought of never seeing Markus again makes me feel hollow. But I won't let him put himself in unnecessary danger. *Markus will be safer on his own.*

The storm rages around us. My shivers slowly disappear, leaving me clammy in my damp clothing. It even resists Markus's tremendous body heat, refusing to dry. He doesn't seem to be faring much better with his soggy leathers. We huddle together, watching the power of the squall. Lightning crackles and thunder shakes the air. Rocks tumble down the hill and slide onto the path. Branches tangle as they're thrown through the air. I should be petrified, but it's impossible with Markus's solid presence next to me, reassuring me.

He pulls the canvas tighter around us. "We're safe here. You don't have to worry about the storm."

A warmth blossoms in my chest, chasing away the lingering chill. "I'm not. One of the advantages of my being small is you're big enough to block anything the storm blows this way. And you're definitely going to get struck with lightning first. If anything, you should be worried."

"Good point. Although if we get buried in a mudslide, I'll be able to climb out easier."

"Then I guess I better hang on to you. In case there's a mudslide."

"Don't expect me to pull you out."

"You will." I close my eyes and listen to the rain pounding on the rock over my head. "You promised to take me to the palace and you never break a promise."

"Yah. Lucky for you. You're not worth all this trouble."

"Yes, I am." I nudge him with my elbow without opening my eyes. "You also swore to be honest with me."

"Fine," he pretends to grumble. "You're worth it."

I smile. "I'm glad we're in agreement."

Markus pulls the canvas off us. "The storm's let up enough
that we can keep traveling."

I groan. "Do we have to? Things are finally getting
better. I'm only half frozen now."

"We'll get sick if we stay out here all night. We need to
find a place where we can build a fire."

The promise of being dry and warm again is enough to
move my stiff muscles. I take a last look around our
overhang, then sigh and duck out into the pouring rain.

The chill hits as the torrent pounds on us, determined to
make us miserable. It's hard to say if the tumbles into the
mud and the accompanying bruises are worse than the slips
and strained muscles. Markus keeps looking off the path—or
what's left of the path. Almost an hour later, he gives a
shout, pointing to a dark shape tucked into the hillside.

It's a snug hut with a wooden roof. Markus shoulders the
door open against the howling wind. I stagger inside,
promptly bouncing off something as he wrestles the door
closed, leaving us in darkness. The howling drops to a dull

throb. There's thunking and clunking as Markus moves around. He bumps into me twice, muttering some creative oaths I make a note to remember for future use, then a lamp is lit. Instead of an abandoned shack, it's a well-appointed one-room cabin, complete with a bed, two chairs, a table, and a tall stack of chopped wood next to a fireplace.

I pause in the middle of removing my sodden cloak. "What is this place? We're not in someone's home, are we?"

Markus hangs the lamp on an overhead hook. "There are a few cabins like this along the mountain trail. They're used for winter hunting, and people foolish enough to cross in summer that get caught in the storms."

"Clever. And nice." There are a few routes in Lorria that would benefit from something like this. I'll have to suggest it to Mother and Father after they're speaking to me again.

I arrange the wood in the small stone fireplace while he works on getting supper ready. Filling the pots is as easy as holding them outside the door. I sit as close as I can to the fire, my teeth chattering even with the heat pouring into the room.

Markus warms his hands at the fire. "No practice tonight. We need food and rest."

Thank the heavens. "If you're not feeling up to it, I guess I can let you skip it. It's too bad, I'm feeling lucky. I was definitely going to win tonight." My muscles protest as I stretch the aches out.

He opens a small chest tucked under the bed I hadn't noticed and pulls out a stack of fabrics. "The goddess is looking out for us tonight." He shakes out several blankets and two oversized nightshifts that lace up the front.

I launch myself at him and rip a blanket out of his hands, burying my face in dry fabric. "I love this cabin. I love the

Wolves. I love everything about this kingdom and all its weird customs."

He chuckles. "I can only imagine your gratitude after you get a hot meal."

"I may never move out of here." I dance in place, desperate to get out of my filthy, soaking leathers and into something clean and dry and not smelling of several weeks of travel.

As he retreats to the other side of the cabin, Markus points a warning finger at me. "Don't look."

"I didn't know you were so modest, Markus," I tease him with a laugh. I check he's facing away, then grab the other robe and turn my back to him.

"We should keep watch on the fire tonight. One good downdraft and the cabin could catch fire."

Even the disappointment of not getting a full night's rest can't dim my excitement. The leathers peel off with a wet *squelch*, loathe to release my skin. I dive into the blanket for cover, using the corner to quickly dry off. A quick glance over my shoulder without actually looking, then I slip the huge nightshift over my head, instantly feeling warmer. It's the most luxurious feeling in the world, the thick fabric enveloping me, the hem pooling on the ground and the sleeves falling well past my hands.

I tug the fabric, futilely trying to keep the neckline from slipping down my shoulder, then shrug. It's still more demure than the current fashion at court. I stretch with a giant yawn, sleepiness creeping in. "You can turn around now. Can I take the second watch? I'm ready to fall asleep on my feet."

He points to me, a horrified look on his face. "What happened?"

"What? Where?" I whip my head down, pulse racing. Peeking out from the fabric is my shoulder, now a dark purple color. "Huh." I push up my sleeve, examining the purple and green bruise extending from my shoulder to my elbow. "Where did that come from?"

He growls as he digs through the pack, glancing at pouches before throwing them to the side. "Why didn't you tell me you're hurt?"

I frown, confused at his reaction. "I didn't notice it."

He shakes the small yellow bottle in his hand as he turns his glare on me. "You deliberately hid it from me."

Anger shoots through me. "You're being ridiculous. I've had worse bruises from falling off my horse. I'm fine."

"You are not fine."

He reaches for my arm and I jerk away.

"Don't tell me what to do."

"I will if you won't take care of yourself."

I poke him in the chest, fury filling every fiber of my being. "I don't need some overprotective oaf to tell me what I need."

We glare at each other, eyes locked. Tension simmers between us, a powder keg threatening to explode. Hidden behind the rage, rising and mixing with the emotion, something else swirls. Something dangerous. The air crackles with energy. I desperately cling to the anger, but it slips away, a storm of need and hunger erupting.

Markus looks gorgeously disheveled. His hair is a mess of damp curls, his eyes dark pools. His gaze flits to my lips. The heat in his eyes blazes and his breath quickens. I've never understood the power of desire until this moment. An urgency I've never felt before fills me, fueled by a strange current of desperation.

I love him.

The knowledge steals the breath from my lungs as I stare into his beautiful eyes.

Affection and respect have grown into something deeper, something wonderful, and terrifying, and incredible. It's thrilling and just a bit scary, realizing I handed him my heart without noticing. A nervous knot forms in the pit of my stomach. I've always been petrified of letting someone have power over me. Loving someone gives them the ultimate control. It's something I've instinctively avoided, shying away from any flirtation that might lead to something deeper. But with Markus, I was helpless to avoid the plunge. It was impossible not to fall in love with him. He's exactly what I need, what I crave.

He brushes a strand of hair back, his hands lingering on my skin. "Lisette …" His voice is a low rumble I feel deep in my belly.

I can't speak, can barely breathe. My heart slams against my ribs.

All uncertainly melts away as he pulls me closer, his heat seeping through my clothing. Loving Markus is the opposite of terrifying. It's easy and comfortable, and feels exactly right. It's harmony, setting something to rights I didn't know was wrong. A tingle spreads across my skin. I press my hand to his cheek, trying to seal my touch into his soul.

Markus cradles my face in his hands, his lips a breath from mine. His eyes search mine until I might die from anticipation. Finding the answer he needs, Markus smiles before he kisses me.

The world explodes in a haze of desire and passion.

This was the kiss I'd longed for my entire life. I'm

probably doing everything wrong, but the thought is lost in a sea of lips and hands and heat. My arms circle around his neck, pulling him closer, everything in me craving more of this, more of him. His growl shoots straight through me. He buries his fingers into my hair and I go boneless, his body warm and solid against mine.

After an eternity, and much too soon, Markus breaks away with a regretful sigh. He buries his face in my neck, murmuring my name. I close my eyes against the dizziness and gasp as his breath brushes against my skin.

I run my fingers through his thick, dark hair, my cheek pressed against his. "Wow."

His chuckle vibrates against my throat, tickling my skin. Markus pulls back, his eyes dancing with humor and heat. "Yah."

"That was" —I capture his lips again— "really" —and again— "really nice."

His lips tease against mine as he says, "Nice is not the word I'm thinking of."

"Pleasant? Enjoyable?" I smile and lean back, my arms still looped around his neck. "Agreeable?"

"More like … wow."

"And all this time I thought you didn't fancy me."

"Didn't fancy—" he groans. "Do you have any idea how hard it was? Feeling this way and not daring to—" He shakes his head.

It's my turn to groan. "Why didn't you say anything? You must've known I how I felt."

He turns the bracelet on my wrist, the stones flashing in the firelight. "I knew we didn't have a future. You're a Lorrian princess and I'm—well, you know what I am. I didn't want either of us to get our hearts broken when we were doomed before we started."

My heart leaps even as my stomach twists. *He knows it too, how big this is*. It would never be a simple dalliance. Not with him. "What changed your mind?"

"You did." His eyes crinkle at the corners. "You're brave enough to take on the Kingdom of the Wolves and compassionate enough to see the truth about my people. About me. If you can do all that, then we can figure this out. Together."

That word echoes harshly through my head. "Markus." I bite my lip. *There are so many things keeping us apart. Our families will never understand.* As he said, we should figure this out. But not now. Now, I want to enjoy the moment. I run my hand down his cheek as his eyes slide closed. I whisper, "Make sure you don't forget … I was the first one to say I liked you."

"Never." He nips my neck, making me yelp and sending desire shooting through me. "I better clean our clothing before that mud sets."

I slide away from him with a grumble, knowing we need space to clear our heads. He scrapes the leathers clean while I get the tea ready and explore the rest of the cabin. There's an abandoned mouse nest in the bed's stuffing, and a tiny cupboard next to the door with jars of dried leaves and other concoctions.

Markus pronounces the jars unneeded since he has the same or better in his pack, and leaves them for the next visitors who might need them. "I could teach you about healing plants, if you'd like."

"You could try, but I'm afraid it would be an exercise in frustration. I've never been able to tell one plant from another to my mother's eternal shame. I destroyed half the plants in the hothouse before she gave up.”

“And how many of those were on purpose?”

I grin. *He knows me so well.* “Most of them.”

“The offer stands if you’re interested.” He lays my shirt in front of the fire with the rest of the clothes.

It feels strange to eat at the table after all our campfire meals. Almost formal. But Markus digs into the stew with his normal gusto and everything in me unwinds. We pass the evening talking and laughing, mutually agreeing without words to let the future wait. It’s hard to keep my mind on the conversation. Knowing what it feels like to kiss him, to be in his arms, it nearly drives me mad to keep my distance. Every moment is delicious torture. Every few minutes Markus sends me heated glances, then shakes himself.

After we clean up the dishes, he wraps a blanket around my shoulders, tugging me closer while pretending to smooth out a wrinkle. “I’ll take the first fire watch. Sweet dreams.”

I tilt my face up and scrunch my nose. “Don’t I get a kiss goodnight?”

He wraps his arms around me and lifts me off the ground. I grip his shoulders and giggle as he swings me around. He leans closer, closer, closer … and kisses my forehead.

“Spoilsport,” I pout.

He slides me down until I’m standing on the floor. “I’m trying to remember I’m a gentleman.”

“I stand by my comment.”

He taps my nose. “Go to bed.”

I tug his shirt until he leans down, then brush my lips against his. “Goodnight.”

“Dream something beautiful.”

I curl up on the bed, watching Markus tend the fire and

check our drying clothes. My eyes grow heavy in my warm drowse, but I can't fall asleep. Ideas and worries about the future keep slithering into my mind. We can't stay in the Kingdom of the Wolves. It would be hard for Markus to be in Lorria, but not impossible. But it wouldn't be fair to him, especially if he has a chance to reunite with his family. Should we both leave Lorria and start a new life somewhere else?

Where do we belong?

The morning starts off with a rosy glow. There was a small worry in the back of my mind that the magic of the prior evening would disappear, that I might feel differently about Markus in the daylight. But if anything, I'm even happier and more confident. When Markus slips his hand into mine, it's only surprising how natural it feels. The lone thing casting a shadow across us is the future. Since I can't do anything about it now, I'm going to enjoy the moment and let tomorrow take care of itself.

Markus never woke me for my turn to watch the fire. I briefly consider chastising him, but the full night's sleep in a real bed felt too good to even tease him about it. We steal glances at each other as we pack up, eating a quick breakfast of tea and dried fruit as we prepare to depart. I pat the hut's wall as we leave, missing it already.

Evidence of the storm is everywhere. It's like a giant swept his hand across the land, carelessly flinging the forest around. Boulders and mud from the hillside hide the trail. Fallen branches and downed trees cover the ground. We pick our way through the pass, Markus insisting on staying close by my side and helping me over the fallen trees.

I laugh when he lifts me over a small puddle. "I think I could've made it around that one by myself."

"Better to be careful. Lots of loose rocks and mud around."

His serious tone catches me off guard. "I remember. Yesterday we spent half the day swimming in that muck. I've heard people like taking mud baths, but I don't see the appeal."

Markus's chuckle is forced. "People like strange things."

What's going on with him? Did I accidentally insult his culture again? "Are mud baths popular in the Wolf Kingdom?"

"Not that I know of." He rubs a hand across his chin.

Hmm. "Well, there's one thing for sure. I'll never complain about having a lukewarm bath again. Anything is better than snow melt." As I slow my steps again to allow Markus to catch up, I realize he's walking at half our normal speed. *Is he injured?* He didn't mention anything, but it would be just like him to pretend he's fine.

I tug on his hand. "Why are you walking so slow?"

"I thought we should keep an easier pace today. There's a good place to stop for a break about a mile ahead."

I tilt my head. "It's too early to take a break."

"We need to conserve our strength if we want to be rested when we get to the palace. It won't do any good to show up exhausted."

"We'll rest when we're close. Right now, we need to get out of the mountains."

"If that's what you want." Markus's bland tone sets my teeth on edge. "Here, drink some water." He tries to hand me his waterskin.

I push it away. "I'm not thirsty."

He rubs his chin again. "Is your pack too heavy? I can carry it." Markus grabs the top of the bag, knocking me off balance. He puts a steadying hand on my shoulder. "Sorry, sorry."

I pull away from him. "What is wrong with you?"

"What? Nothing."

I study him with narrowed eyes. "You're acting strange. What is it? "

"Nothing is going on." His eyes briefly meet mine before jumping away to the trail as he rubs the back of his neck.

My stomach twists. *Is it me? Is he trying to work up the courage to tell me he doesn't like me after all?* "Do you regret kissing me?"

He flinches. "What? No! No, nothing like that."

"Then what is it?"

"Nothing." When I keep staring at him, he adds, "I'm trying to be nice."

I cross my arms. "By knocking me over and ordering me around?"

He throws his hands up in the air. "Can't I do something for you without you making a big deal out of it?"

"Not if you're going to act like a different person. What are you doing? It's like you think I'm incapable of walking without falling over."

He snaps, "You're important to me. I want to take care of you."

"But I want you to be you. This isn't you."

"I help you all the time."

I press my lips together. "Not like this. Stop acting so

strange."

He rocks back on his heels. "Do you regret kissing me? Is that what this is about? Are you trying to push me away?"

"Of course not!"

"How can you be sure?"

I snarl, "Because I think I love you, you big barbarian."

He growls, "And I might love you, you spoiled princess."

"All right then."

"Good."

Markus loves me. I grin stupidly, happiness filling my chest, lifting me so high I'm surprised I'm not floating. His expression is equally dopey, his eyes soft and his smile loopy.

I press my hand to his chest. "See? I didn't break. We're the same people we were yesterday, except now I can kiss you whenever I want to."

To prove my point, I pull his head down to mine. My lips brush against his, featherlight, loving the way his eyes drift closed. Heat curls inside my chest. He pulls me to him, his warmth soaking through me. Every kiss is a thrill, new and exciting and perfect. I hope this feeling never goes away. It's so tempting to get lost in us, but guilt tugs me away regretfully.

"We need to keep moving." I steal one more kiss and sigh. "We've already lost too much time."

He presses a swift kiss to my lips. "We're getting close. The worst is behind us."

I arch an eyebrow. "Promise?"

He opens his mouth—then shakes his head. "I'd better not. I'd hate to lie to you, even accidentally. The way this trip is going, I'm afraid to guess what'll happen next."

"At least tell me it's downhill."

"Mostly." His lips twitch.

"Ugh. That means we're going to climb three mountains before noon."

"Only a flatlander would call them mountains. But if we're being honest, then I have to confess something to you." He looks at me seriously. "You snore."

I gasp. "I do not."

He grins. "It's a very polite snore. Ladylike."

I put my hands on my hips. "There is no way you can hear me snore—which I do not—over yours. You're so loud, the trees shake."

Markus slaps his chest. "It's the sign of a healthy body."

"More like clogged airways. You should see if you have an allergy remedy in your pack."

"I'll see if I can find some … for you." He nimbly avoids my swipe at his arm. "Come along, princess. We have a lot of hiking to do."

I chuckle as I follow him up the trail.

22

I plop on a rock, wiping my forehead on my sleeve. "Markus, wait. There's a stone in my shoe."

"We're due for a break anyway." He settles next to me. "We have a long climb, and then we'll reach the bridge. If we make good time, we should make it down the other side by nightfall."

"How much farther to the palace?" The boot's laces are thick with burrs, stinging my fingers as I pluck them out. The landscape has morphed into some alien world. Dusty orange rocks and skeletal spiny plants cover the ground in every direction.

"About three days, if we don't run into any more storms."

Three days to Oma. I suck on my throbbing finger as I shake the pebble out of my shoe. The clear blue sky makes it hard to remember the danger from a few days ago. "Can we go any faster? Take a shortcut?"

"This is the shortcut. The main bridge would add another three days."

"Then why doesn't everyone come this way?"

"It's a rope bridge. No way to get a horse or cart across. It's not for the faint of heart." He grins. "How are you with heights?"

Terrible. "The higher, the better." I take a long draw on my waterskin, then dig out some jerky, handing him half. The dried meat tastes like the dust coating my tongue.

Markus's gift for understatement is apparent as we hike up the hill. Most of the landscape is too vertical for a direct climb, so we switchback along the face, barely making any noticeable progress despite hours of walking. Every step kicks up clouds of orange dust. I let Markus get ahead of me, tired of the constant coughing and dryness in my throat. *When I set out to rescue Oma, I didn't think it would involve this much walking. I'm not built for hills.*

The ground finally levels out just as I'm about to collapse. I brave a look back over the edge. The hill is even more intimidating from the top. On the return trip, I'm going to have to slide down on my backside if I don't want to tumble head over heels to the bottom. It's hard to imagine Oma camping out in the woods and hiking across the kingdom in secret. My grandmother gets attention wherever she goes. People are drawn to her, like moths to a flame. I'll have to convince her to be careful.

Markus looks over his shoulder. "Not too far now."

"To what?"

"You'll see."

It's nice to have Markus back to normal, but the glee in his voice has me worried. I push it aside. *He wouldn't be this excited if it were actually dangerous.*

And a little teasing goes both ways ... "Ouch." I sit in the dirt, hands gripping my head. "Aaargh."

Hurried footsteps come closer. "Lisette, are you hurt? What happened?" He crouches next to me, hands on my shoulders. "What is it?"

I grab his shirt and pull him down, my lips molding onto his. There's a surprised "Mmph," then he's melting into me. He wraps his arms around my waist. The awkward position and extra weight from the pack throws him off balance and we crash onto the ground.

He rolls to the side, panic in his voice. "Did I hurt you?"

"Yes, you hurt me. You stopped kissing me." I tug his shirt again, my eyes narrowing on his mouth tempting me back.

"We have to keep going," he murmurs, his eyes darkening.

"Right … Right … Just—" I kiss him, letting the moment linger. Then I push to my feet. "Ready."

He stares up at me. "Right." He blows out a big breath. "Right. Let's go."

I take his hand and walk beside him. This could be a normal day where we're out exploring the wilderness, discovering what's around the next corner while enjoying the day together. *If life were that simple ...* I shake my head. It's so easy to get lost in the daydream until I start thinking about Oma, what we might find—no, what I might find. Because I'll be alone. Markus can't risk going to the palace. I've been ignoring the future as hard as I can, but the nearness of the palace brings Oma, and Markus's needed departure, to mind too often.

Markus squeezes my hand. "Are there more of those distractions in my future?"

"If you're lucky. Now, what's this high thing you're threatening me with?"

"A little walk on air." Markus pulls our linked hands up and kisses the back of mine. "Don't worry, I'll catch you if you fall."

"I think I'll be the one doing the catching. I've seen how clumsy you are."

"Oh, really?" He picks me up and swings me around, making me laugh. "Who's clumsy now?"

I plant a kiss on his nose. "I'm corrected."

It's only a few short minutes before we round a corner and the roar of water fills the air. I run ahead, thick mist rolling around the rocks. The cool breeze feels amazing. Twenty feet away, the ground disappears. A huge canyon stretches a hundred feet across, dividing the land as far as I can see in either direction. Across from us, a rushing river turns into a pounding waterfall, cascading a thousand feet to the ground below. It's incredible, unlike anything I've ever seen. I always thought the city and palace were beautiful, but the wild nature in the Black Forest mesmerizes me. There's a peace to it, even as it stirs the blood and sends a thrill through my soul. No wonder Oma loves traveling so much. How many more places like this are waiting for me to find them?

Markus puts his arm around my shoulders. "Like it?"

"I love it. It's almost worth the hike up here."

"You're one of the few people who have seen it."

I raise my eyebrows. "But it's along the trail."

"Like I said, not many people use this crossing because you can't use horses. That's good for us. Less chance of being spotted."

"Is that something we need to worry about? That man tracking us is long gone, and nobody else will recognize us. There are a thousand blond-haired and brown-eyed girls in both our kingdoms, and we're not close enough to the palace for anyone to identify you as their long-dead prince."

"I—" Markus frowns, then looks over the side. He walks along the edge, glancing at the canyon, then to the right, then back to the canyon. "This can't be right. There should be a rope bridge." He stops and points to the ground. "You can see where the poles were. Where is it?"

We spot the rope dangling down the canyon wall on the opposite side at the same time. My heart plummets to the canyon floor below. Markus swears quietly under his breath and I nod in agreement. The palace is somewhere on the other side. We're so close to Oma, and then this.

"The storm must have knocked it down." Markus curses again. "We need to turn around."

My pulse speeds up thinking of all time we'll lose. "What—no. We have to get across. Can we climb down? "

He shakes his head. "It's too dangerous."

"We're breaking into the palace to rescue my grandmother. I don't think anything is too dangerous at this point."

"This is. We're not climbing down."

I put my hands on my hips. "Because you can't, or because you don't want to?"

"Both." He runs a hand over his face, fatigue deepening the lines around his mouth. "I've done a little climbing, but something like this takes skill. We might get down, but we wouldn't be able to climb up the other side. Not without a lot of equipment I don't have."

Burn it. "Is there another way across?"

"The main bridge. It's about two days." He gestures to the right.

"There's nothing else closer? No other rope bridges, or

tightropes, or, or a catapult?"

That gets a quick smile. "Not that I'm aware of. It would probably be faster to get to the main bridge than build a catapult."

"Not as exciting, though."

"I'll suggest that as a replacement." Markus turns to me, rubbing the back of his neck. "You should hike back to our last campsite. There was plenty of water, and nobody will be in the area. I can get your grandmother and meet you there."

My stomach clenches. *He's trying to get rid of me.* Bitter betrayal floods my mouth and I swallow hard. "No."

"It'll be easier if I go alone. I can move faster by myself."

Because I'm slowing him down. "Oma won't trust you. You need me to convince her to come with us."

"She will when I tell her you're waiting for us. Besides, she'll be so happy to be rescued, it won't take much convincing."

I cross my arms, ignoring the cold crawling through my chest. "You don't know Oma."

"You're putting her and yourself in more danger by coming with me. If you really want to rescue your grandmother, you'll stay here."

He's right. My lungs freeze. I spin around so he can't see the pain on my face as tears flood my eyes. *What made me think I could rescue Oma? I'm only good at is disappointing my parents and getting my sister into mischief. Really, it's Markus who's rescuing Oma. All I'm doing is making things harder and slowing him down.*

I straighten. *No. I might not be the best person to rescue Oma, but I'm still going to try. I won't let anything stop me. But that doesn't mean Markus should risk everything to go with me.*

Markus puts his hands on my shoulders. "I'm sorry. I shouldn't have said that." His voice thickens. "There are so many things that can go wrong. If you were hurt or captured …"

"No, you're right. I am slowing you down. But I'm still going to rescue Oma." *I can't put this off any longer.* I swipe at the annoying tears as I face him. "But you're the one who should leave. Markus, think about it. Someone will recognize you if you go anywhere near the palace. The worst that'll happen to me is the King will have another hostage until my parents arrange for my release. If your family knows you're alive, they won't stop trying to find you. You'll spend the rest of your life on the run."

He tilts my chin up to meet his gaze. "That's no danger to me and you know it."

"But it is." I struggle for the words. "You left your family because you were terrified about what would happen to them if you stayed. I don't agree with you, but it's your choice. Now I'm taking that choice away from you. I won't do it."

He takes my hand, running his thumb over the bracelet. "This is my promise I'll help you when you need it. I won't let you walk alone into danger when there are other options."

"Do you think I can ever be happy if I know you're trapped where you don't want to be? If you're terrified every day you'll hurt your family? I can't, Markus. If something happened to you …" I shake my head. "No."

Markus sighs. "How do you do that?" He wipes away a tear on my cheek.

"What?"

"Tell me I'm wrong without telling me I'm wrong." He

wraps his arms around me, pulling me close. "Do you think you mean any less to me? I was being selfish. I'll never stand in the way of something you need to do, no matter how much it frightens me. I won't try to stop you now. But fangs and fur, I won't stay behind when I can help. You need me at the palace, whether you want to admit it or not."

I thunk my head against his chest. "I hate it when you're logical and thoughtful and sweet. It makes it hard to stay mad at you."

"Being right helps too."

"It really doesn't." I swallow around the lump in my throat. "Why did you come here? You should've stayed away."

"And miss all the fun?" The smile slips from his lips. "We're stronger when we're together. Don't forget that."

Markus isn't going to leave willingly, and—no matter how much I'd like to deny it—I need him if I'm going to have any hope of getting Oma home. Still, I'd try, if I could convince him to go. What does it say that I'd put myself and Oma in danger to keep him protected? I brush the guilt aside. Oma wouldn't want to put innocent lives at risk. If I can't keep him away, then I'll keep him close.

He's never going to let me live this down. I frown at him. "I hate you."

He kisses my forehead. "I know. Now let's go invade the Wolf Palace."

The trees trap the heat under their branches, blocking any whisper of a breeze, making the air sizzle. The rushing river in the canyon next to us taunts us, making my mouth ten times more parched.

Markus swears he's told me everything about the palace that might be even remotely relevant. The layout is useful, but it's frustratingly light on the other details. Not that I'd be able to describe my home any better. A palace is a small city, a thousand different tasks being carried out simultaneously all over the grounds. Who pays attention to guard patrols and when the staff arrives? We have a slapdash plan that has no hope of working, but it's comforting to have something, anything.

He nods at the horizon. "The secret entrance to the palace is over that last hill." Markus takes a long drink from his waterskin, then swipes the back of his arm across his forehead, leaving a dusty smear. "If we're lucky, it won't be guarded. And it'll still be intact. And they haven't thought to block the other end. Then we just have to free your grandmother, sneak back out before anybody notices, and race back to Lorria before they can catch us. So, perfect plan. No chance of failure."

"It'll work. And if there's a problem, we'll come up with a new plan. We're good at that." I take a small sip, swishing the water around my mouth. *Only a few hours to Oma.* While getting her out of the palace is intimidating, the journey after is what's making me lose sleep. She's always been a good traveler, but a tour around the countryside doesn't equate to being on the run with deadly enemies nipping at our heels.

"At least we won't have to worry about the Wolf Guards around the palace. The border wolves will have passed your scent on to them by now. They shouldn't bother us."

"I hope they come by. I'd love to be smothered in an enormous pile of puppies again." *Mayhap I can convince one of them to follow me home.*

Markus shakes his head. "Unlikely, since they already know us. They aren't as aggressive as the border wolves. These mostly support the palace guards. After all, it wouldn't be good to have wolves attacking every person who wants to visit the palace."

"Do you need the whistle back?" I tug on the cord around my neck. "I don't know any of the signals."

"I'd feel better if you keep it. If we need help, give it a big blast." Markus looks at me, the crinkles in his forehead smooth and his eyes warm for a moment. He shakes his head, the serious expression returning. "It'll be better if we travel light for the next part. Steep descent. Loose rocks. We can hide our packs here and pick them up on the way back."

I pat the dagger on my hip. "I'm ready."

He chuckles. "We're going to need a little more than

that."

As he rummages through the packs, I nibble on a piece of dried apple. *I should ask him. Just in case. He might have thought of something. But I hate bringing them up. It just upsets both of us. But if I don't ask now, I'll have to ask later.*

Markus places his hand axe on top of the growing pile by his feet. "I still don't know."

"What?"

"I don't have any idea why my father kidnapped your grandmother, or if he's planning to invade your kingdom. He must have a good reason, although I can't begin to guess what it is. Uncle Garit had to agree. My father never would have done anything that dire without talking to him about it first."

I look at him in astonishment. "How'd you know I was going to ask about him?"

"You make an angry humming sound in the back of your throat when you're thinking about my father."

I do?

"And your nostrils flare."

I chuck a piece of dried fruit at him. He ducks his head with a smirk.

"Do you think he could've changed that much since you knew him? Or mayhap you were too young to really understand what he was like?" We've been having this same conversation for the past week, but I still can't reconcile the loving father Markus remembers with the ruthless kidnapper who took Oma.

Markus shrugs as he rolls up our cloaks. "I thought I knew him."

The flat tone is back. I can't blame him. Nobody wants

to think badly of their father, and Markus has already sacrificed so much for him.

I search for something to lighten the mood. "If your dad is the Wolf King, and your Uncle Garit is the Black Wolf, do you and Fredrik have a fun wolf names? Wait, let me guess. Wolflets?"

"Those are sacred names." He frowns at me. "To earn one, you have to climb to the top of Wolf Mountain during a thunderstorm carrying a wolf on your back while chanting the Wolf Song." A smile cracks through the stern demeanor. "Then you hop on one foot, while spinning around … "

"You rat." I stick my tongue out.

"You're welcome to call me 'Wolf Prince' if it would make you feel better."

"I think I'll stick with Markus. Unless you prefer barbarian?"

"Whatever you want, my heart." He frowns thoughtfully at the supplies he's selected, then adds three pouches before hauling both packs onto his shoulders. "I'll stow these in that big rock pile we passed. You rest. We're not going to get much of it the next couple of days." He puts his hand gently on the back of my neck as he gives me a lingering kiss. "Don't get into trouble while I'm gone."

"I don't find trouble, it finds me." I watch him disappear into the trees with a little tug of guilt. It's hard to admit, but I'm glad I couldn't talk him into leaving. Having Markus at my side makes me feel invincible. I know we'll be able to rescue Oma and get her home safely. After that, this journey has convinced me anything's possible. Never in a million years would I have guessed I'd fall in love with a prince from the Kingdom of the Wolves, but here I am, completely smitten. We'll figure it out together.

I wander to the cliff's edge and settle down to watch the river below. It's odd being without my pack. I feel incomplete without the weight on my shoulders and hips. If only my family could see me now, they'd never recognize me. A little breeze breaks through the stale air. I tilt my head back, enjoying the brief relief from the heat.

A branch snaps.

"Did you forget something?" When the silence stretches on, I shift uneasily. "Markus?" I scramble to my feet as I scan the trees, trying to spot the source of the noise. *Markus said nobody else should be in the area.* "Who's out there?"

"Not to worry. It's only me." A man nearly as big as Markus steps into view. His glassy eyes dart around the small clearing. A thick, ropey scar stretches from his jawline and disappears under the collar of his shirt. "I finally caught up. Kept giving me the slip, staying ahead. But I caught up. Knew they were wrong. Chasing a ghost, they said. I was right. I'll show them. Show them all."

It takes a moment to place him. He's the man we saw in Eelan right before we started this journey. Somehow, he tracked us through the Black Forest, but he's paid a price. The formerly bright green tunic is a dull brown from the mud and dust. His once neatly trimmed hair and beard stick out in odd clumps, and deep scratches on his hands and face throb an angry red. Sweat pours off him and his cheekbones have an unhealthy scarlet flush.

I instinctively take a step back, then jump away from the cliff's edge. "Who are you? What do you want?" My hand drops to the dagger's hilt.

"Not you. Don't need you." His smile is empty, sending chills over my skin. "I knew they were wrong. All of them. Wrong, wrong, wrong. But I'll get the reward."

My hand tightens on the hilt. *He's fever-touched.* My eyes dart between the man and the cliff edge, fighting off the fear creeping in at my precarious position. *I just need to keep him calm and quiet until Markus comes back.* "Sit down and I'll get you some water. What's your name?"

"Can't. Can't lose Von Dien's trail again." His bloodshot eyes rake over me, then widen as they lock onto my hand. "Von Dien's claimed you. The Wolf King will want you too."

Von Dien—Markus's name. My knees threaten to collapse. Ice floods through me. *He's after Markus.* My heartbeat pounds in my ears. "I don't know who you're talking about." *Stay calm. Lead him away so he won't find Markus.* I slide to the side, moving away from him and the cliff.

"Are you trying to trick me, girl? It won't work. Only Von Dien could've given you that bracelet."

How can he know? Never mind. "This?" I hold up the hand with the bracelet to distract him, my other hand half-drawing the blade. "I got this from a woman in Nevenberg." I back up another step.

"Those are Von Dien's colors." He jerks his head side-to-side. "I don't like liars."

The madman roars, lunging at me. I dart away. A blow to my knees sends me crashing to the ground. The man drags me up by my shirt, then wraps an arm around my throat, choking me. The stench of stale sweat and rot pours over me. I gasp, clawing at his arm, but the thick shirt protects him. Kicks and elbows to his body have no effect. I gasp for help, but there's no sound.

Markus's voice growls from the trees, "Stay away from her." Rage shakes the air around him, giving lie to the calm tone.

My heart sinks. *No! Run!* I can't force the words out around the man's arm.

The tracker breaks out into a shrill giggle. "Von Dien, Von Dien. I found you. It's time to see the King. He's been worrying about you. Thought you might still be out here and here you are."

His arm tightens, crushing my windpipe. The edges of my vision dim. My lungs scream for air as stars burst in front of my eyes. My hands are clumsy, feebly plucking at his sleeve. Buzzing fills my ears.

The pressure eases. I cough, tears filling my eyes. My head pounds with every heartbeat. The tracker's arm stays firmly around my throat, trapping me against him. It hurts to swallow and I can't catch my breath.

Markus slowly swims into focus a few feet away. He's glaring at the madman, his eyes promising death. His fists are clenched so tight his muscles are shaking. "I'll go with you. Just leave Lisette alone."

I choke out, "No."

The man slides a knife down my cheek. I shudder as the cold steel scrapes my skin. His arm is a vice, unmoving despite my squirming and efforts to push him away. He shuffles backward, bringing us within inches of the cliff, teetering on the edge, before moving forward again.

Why isn't Markus attacking? His eyes are blazing, darting between me and the man. *He's afraid I'll get hurt.* My mind frantically goes over the self-defense training these past few weeks. *My dagger.* There's a quick flash of relief when my hand finds it still on my hip. My breath quickens. Eager anticipation gives strength to my muscles as my fingers close around it. I've only daydreamed about stabbing an attacker, but I'm happy to do it for real this time.

Markus keeps his eyes on the man, but gives a tiny head shake.

He can't be serious. If anyone deserves to the knifed, it's this guy. I leave the blade sheathed, but keep my hand on the hilt. No matter what Markus thinks, he's not leaving with this madman.

Markus shakes his head again, making a slashing motion with his hand. "We can be at the palace in a few hours if we leave now."

"You can't go with him." My voice shakes. "I won't let you."

Markus keeps his eyes on the tracker. "Do we have a deal?"

The man waves the knife at him. "The King will want you both." He sings, "Time to go to the castle. Time to go to the castle. Sent to find Von Dien, Von Dien, for the King, for the King."

The man's gibberish scratches at my mind, setting my teeth on edge. I yell, "We're not going to see the King." He can't be reasoned with in his feverish state. He's close to losing whatever slim hold he has on reality.

Markus steps closer. "You found me. You don't need her."

"Von Dien claimed her for the Wolf King. I can't leave her now."

Markus drops his gaze to me, his expression twisting. In an instant, his face is blank again, the muscle in his jaw ticking. "She tricked you. She's nobody to me."

"Tricked?" The madman stills. "Are you a trickster, Von Dien? "

His arm tightens again, cutting off my air. The knife

flashes at my eye. A strangled scream fights to escape my crushed throat. My dagger drops to the dirt as I thrash in his arms, trying to avoid the blade.

"No!" Markus lunges forward, then backs up when the man waves the knife.

The tracker strokes the top of my head. His arm loosens enough for me to gasp before tightening again. Markus growls as I shrink away from the man's touch.

"Ah—ah—ah. You're the tricky trickster, Von Dien." My captor sighs. "No, no, no, no. Von Dien is too angry. He won't come."

"I will. If you let Lisette go." Markus holds his hands out to the side. "It's me, or her. I'm the one you want."

The man tilts his head to the side. "You'll come without a fight?"

I gasp out. "Markus, no." I twist, shoving with all my might to break the man's grip, but his arm doesn't budge. Tears streak down my cheeks and my heart clenches. *The big idiot won't listen because I'm in danger. He's insisting on being the hero instead of being smart.*

Markus keeps his eyes locked on the man. "You have my word."

"Good, good." The madman motions with the knife. "Chains, if you please."

Markus keeps his eyes on us as he shuffles to where a pile of chains is halfway hidden behind the cluster of trees. He slowly snaps a manacle around each ankle, then around his wrists. He holds up his shackled hands. "I've done what you asked. Now let Lisette go."

The man dances forward, then back. He yanks on my hair, forcing my head back. The tip of the knife presses into my neck, a bright spot of pain on my skin.

Markus snarls. "Let. Her. Go."

The madman sings, "Girl can't stay, girl can't go." His voice drops and menace creeps into his tone. "It's a shame. So pretty. King Garit will be angry, but one trick deserves another and I can't have her following us. Say goodbye, Von Dien."

My muscles freeze as panic rips through my body. The last thing I see is Markus's terrified face as I plunge over the cliff's edge.

24

The top of the canyon disappears as I plummet through the air. The wind whistling past my ears drowns out my scream. My stomach drops faster than my body. I can't think, can't breathe. All I can do is grab at nothing as the rock flashes past me.

Water slams against my back. I hit the surface with a loud *slap*, the air shoved out of my lungs, before plunging under the river's surface.

There's no room for thought, only pain.

The current tosses me back and over, bouncing my body off rocks and logs. Shapes flash by, too fast for my mind to make sense of them. My body kicks into survival mode, my arms and legs pumping while my brain hangs in a befuddled fog. I break the surface, gulping air before being sucked under again.

It's enough to shake my mind out of its stupor. When I'm slammed against the next rock, my fingers scrabble at the surface, searching for handholds. The stone slips from under my fingertips, the current dragging me along. The next one is rougher, with long cracks. A good handhold lets me drag myself out of the water, and I collapse.

I cling to the stone, my lungs heaving, water roaring around me. My skin feels like it's being burned while frozen. Everything hurts. Every muscle and bone aches. Even my nails hurt. The leathers did a good job of protecting my body from cuts, but my hands and wrists are covered in scratches and nicks. I give a sob of relief when I spot my bracelet still secured on my wrist.

Did Markus try to jump in after me? No, he couldn't have. He'd drown with those chains. I'll tear that madman apart if he's hurt Markus. Why didn't I fight him off? Markus wasted his time trying to teach me anything about fighting. Stupid, stupid, stupid. I'm useless. Worthless. Markus is in trouble, and it's all my fault. What if he's hurt? What if he's—

The shrill keening noise cuts off when I snap my mouth shut. *Markus. He needs me.*

I swipe the wet hair out of my eyes and look around. For a moment, I panic, trying to remember which side of the canyon I fell from. I force my panting to slow, staring at my bracelet until my mind settles. My eyes close and I remember watching the river before the tracker showed up. *The right side.* Focusing on each step keeps my mind from spiraling down the fears and doubts threatening to tear me apart. My rock is in the middle of the water, which stretches out twenty feet on the other side of the canyon walls. No sandbars or dry land to be found.

Looks like I'm going to swim for it.

The thought of going back into the water makes me want to cry. The canyon walls are high. Really high. Something tells me this won't be like climbing out of the mine.

Everywhere looks equally terrifying. My teeth are chattering from fright and cold. Then I spot it: a dangling rope ten feet above water level.

I don't question my luck, just send a thanks to the heavens before plunging into the river. The icy water sucks the restored heat from my skin and turns my muscles sluggish. Arms and legs pump furiously. I break the surface with a gasp. Paddling against the current, I aim for the rope. Something brushes my leg underwater and I redouble my efforts, afraid to look too closely.

My luck holds when I find an underwater ledge on the canyon's wall. Taking a moment to catch my breath, I survey the wall again. *Just as terrifying as it was from the rock.* "What are you going to do, splash in the river all day? Start climbing, you coward. Otherwise, Markus will never let you hear the end of it."

I grasp the rock above me. My wet hands and feet make the going slippery, but the deep cracks and jutting rocks create easy handholds and footholds to make up for it. The hot air quickly turns my leathers from cool to sweltering. Quicker than I thought possible, I've reached the bottom of the dangling rope. A hard tug confirms it's secure. *Better to be sure twenty feet above the water than fifty.* I put both hands on it and yank with all my strength. It holds. I let out a sigh of relief.

My fingers dig into the rope and I risk a glance down. The river spins far below. I cling to the rough strands, swallowing hard, bile leaving a sour taste in my mouth. *Terrible idea. Don't do that again.*

I close my eyes. "It's just like climbing out of my window at home. Easy. Done it a thousand times. Even easier than climbing out of the mine because I have a rope. I didn't have a rope then. A rope makes everything easier." I wrap my leg around the line and brace it between my feet, creating leverage to push myself higher. "Markus better appreciate this. I should win at least fifteen arguments. Although he tried to sacrifice himself for me, so I guess I can consider it even. If he asks nicely."

My hands and feet move automatically while I stare at the canyon wall glowing in the day's dying light. "Height is relative, after all. It doesn't matter if I fall from fifty feet or forty feet, both are going to hurt. A lot." Sweat stings my eyes. "But I already survived one fall. No reason to fall again. Nope. Better to just keep climbing. Don't worry about anything else."

My hand slips. My lungs freeze as I slide down the rope. Fire races across my palms. Fingers dig in, wrenching me to stop. My palms throb in time with my racing heartbeat.

I press my cheek to the rope, letting out a shaky breath. My stomach rolls, my legs shaky. "Perhaps climbing up the rocks would be easier." A hollow chuckle escapes my lips. "If only Maddie was here. She thinks jumping my horse is dangerous. She'd faint dead away if she saw this."

Imagining my sister's horrified face gives my frozen fingers enough energy to move. Every muscle shakes, and my body loudly reminds me of the bruising it's taken. My fingertips are scraped raw from the rocks and weathered rope. Hands and toes cramp, then go numb, but I don't dare look to see how far I have to go. Hours pass. An eternity. I've been climbing since the beginning of time and I'll continue climbing until time ends. My thoughts slow until they stop, leaving only mechanical movements up. Always up.

My hand hits open air. I flail, tilting off balance, my

other hand clinging to the rope. My fingers dig into the dirt. *The top.* My heart remembers to beat as I heave myself over the edge.

I flop on my back and let my shaking limbs go limp. Exhaustion saps the last of my strength and I close my eyes. *I'm never doing that again.* The warmth of satisfaction washes over me. My muscles tense before my mind registers bushes rustling.

Run.

I stumble away, fighting my way through the bushes, listening for attackers over my panting breath.

Five feet. Ten. I break free from the thick bushes lining the cliff's edge. Twenty. I keep pushing farther on, knowing if I stop, I won't be able to get up again. My muscles scream. Thirty feet. My abused body collapses and refuses to move again. I drag myself under one of the thick plants.

Twigs snap. Across from my hiding spot, the leaves on a bush shake. I hold my breath.

A hedgehog waddles out.

It gives a disinterested sniff in my direction, then disappears into the underbrush.

I roll on my back and heave a sigh of disgust. *Great job of avoiding that deadly danger, Lisette. Markus would be so impressed.*

Five minutes. Then I keep moving. The first thing is to find Markus and get him away from that monster.

I have to find them before they make it to the palace. Markus won't go easily. Even chained, he's a force to be reckoned with. That man will have a hard time, especially in his fevered state. At least I know what direction they'll be heading. But it's impossible to know if I'm closer to the palace, or if the river swept me past it. There's also the possibility Markus might escape on his own. If he does, will Markus come back to where we last saw each other? Will he search for me instead? What if he's hurt? *This is all my fault. Markus put himself at the mercy of that madman because of me. He could've avoided the tracker easily. Now he's in danger.*

The tracker said the king was looking for him. Wait—he said King Garit. Markus's father is Wilhelm, I'm sure of it. Garit is his uncle, the Black Wolf. If Garit is the king now, that means ... Markus's father must be dead. His brother, too, since Fredrik was the heir.

My heart aches for Markus. All those years lost they could've had together. His leaving didn't protect his family after all. But it could explain why Oma was taken. Garit must be the one behind all the scheming. If Garit took Oma, I wouldn't put it past him to have used underhanded methods to secure the throne. Including murder. And now he's after Markus. The last legitimate heir to the Wolf King throne.

That imposter king will kill him. I can't let that happen. I may be one girl against a king, but I'm a princess. Kings don't scare me, especially fake ones. He can't have Markus.

Shivers shake me, and I rub my hands up and down my arms. I let my abused body rest for a few minutes while my mind whirls with plans.

A warm, spongy thing slides across my cheek. I splutter, opening my eyes to a pair of enormous amber eyes blinking back at me. The silver wolf is pressed against my side, another one along my back. The large one across my legs grumbles as I force my protesting muscles to sit up.

A sliver of moon is visible above the trees, pinpricks of starlight sprinkled across the midnight blue. Wolves surround me in overlapping piles of paws, muzzles, and tails. They groan sleepily and lift their heads to watch me, tails thumping.

They kept me warm, guarded me. I give the closest wolf a grateful head scratch while cursing myself for falling asleep. *Markus needs me and I'm failing him. He's never let me down, no matter how much I've pushed him away.* The flash of anger gives me enough energy to shove to my feet.

The wolves stretch, then trot off into the darkness. I watch them go with a touch of longing. They came to my rescue again. It would be wonderful if I could give them commands and have them guide me to the palace, if only to have some friendly company. When the last glimpse of silver disappears into the bushes, I follow the canyon's edge in the direction I'm guessing I last saw Markus.

The sleep was necessary, but did little to restore my energy. My boots drag across the ground, each step a test of willpower. My body has turned into one dull ache from the top of my head to the bottom of my feet. There's one blessing. I'm too tired and too numb to be cold. I miss my cloak, not the least because it was a gift from Markus. *That lunatic better not have taken it.*

All the places in the woods look the same to my tired eyes. The shadows of trees, bushes, and rocks blend into a gray-scale landscape until I'm convinced I'm traveling in circles. *Would I even be able to tell if this is where the tracker found Markus and me? Wait, the supplies. Unless the tracker took them, they'll still be there. If only I knew the area better, I could intercept them instead of trying to follow them.*

Voices to the right.

Definitely not a hedgehog. Not stopping to think, I dive under a bush and curl up in a small ball. I press my nose against my sleeve, muffling my breathing.

Silence.

A footstep.

Leaves rustling.

I curl up tighter and curse myself for not covering my footprints. *Is my foot out? Does my hair show through the branches? Why didn't I grab a stone to use as a weapon?* My mind darts from fear to fear. Images of me being dragged to the palace in chains flash through my mind. My hand gropes at the empty sheath, too late remembering I dropped the dagger when I was being choked. I grab the whistle hanging around my neck. *Will the wolves help me if my attackers are palace guards?* Uncertainty holds me frozen.

Shadows appear between the trees, treading softly through the forest. The leader pads by my hiding spot, their foot inches from my hand. Between the darkness and the bush, it's impossible to see any details beyond the vague shapes in the thin moonlight.

The figure pauses. I clench my jaw. Any twitch will give me away. My heart thunders in my chest. My mind screams to bolt. A second shadow joins the first. An itch in the back of my throat grows, scratching and scraping. I swallow hard, but there's no relief.

The two figures silently gesture. Three more people creep by. Then four more.

My eyes water with the effort not to cough. In my mind, I scream at them to leave, but they continue their unspoken conversation. My throat spasms. I gasp, then clamp my teeth on my sleeve. *Go away, go away, go away*. Tears stream down my face.

"... We'll wait until dark."

The woman's voice jolts me out of my frenzy. *Something about her is familiar*. I try to listen, but between the river, my thundering heartbeat, and my wheezing breath, it's hard to pick up anything.

I risk a peek, finding a group of nine men and women gathered in a circle near my hiding place. I dart back, then look again. *That one. He's one of the palace guards. From the Rhonen mountain range. Father sent people. But are they after me, or Oma?*

The woman in charge draws in the dirt with a stick. "We'll enter here and start with the lower levels, working our way up. There's only one chance at this, so we have to make it count. Do whatever it takes to avoid detection. If someone sees you, kill them before they can sound an alarm. Is that clear?"

I gulp at her hard tone as the others nod.

"Once she's retrieved, we'll have to move quickly. Luther, Goethe. You'll be in charge of her safety. Nothing and nobody else matters. We must get the Dowager Queen home. Let's find a place to set up base camp."

They shuffle their feet, then the group moves on. In seconds, they're lost to the darkness.

I stay still as long as I can, the pain building in my throat. A choking cough strangles me. I stuff my fist in my mouth as the coughs keep coming, scraping my throat raw. One last shuddering rasp and the itch finally disappears, leaving me panting. I lay limply on the ground, waiting for shouts and pounding footsteps.

Nothing.

Father came up with a plan to rescue Oma. I wish I'd trusted him enough to believe he would do it. I wish he'd trusted me enough to tell me about it—to convince me he would rescue Oma. I clench my fists. *So much time wasted and so many things we could have done better.*

Enough. No more thinking about what-ifs and mayhaps. It's only wasting time. I have to decide what to do next.

The guards don't know I'm here. I could continue with my plans to find Markus and the tracker before they reach the palace. If I'm too late, then I can sneak into the palace using the secret entrance Markus told me about.

But the Lorrian guards complicate matters. They'll travel in the same direction. It increases the odds we'll bump into each other either on the way to the palace, or once we're inside. I glance down at myself. *Mayhap they won't recognize me. But if they don't, then I'm just another person to kill. Eek.*

Assuming I'm not slain by my own people, and I somehow make it into the palace, I still have to free Oma and Markus. Who are likely under heavy guard. And then we have to get back out again. Without being seen.

I'm doomed.

26

Time to come at this from a different angle.

The guards are here to rescue Oma, but there are too many things that can go wrong to have any real hope of success. The Lorrian guards are bound to be discovered if they're murdering people left and right. Garit will seize on their actions as an excuse to attack Lorria—not that he needs much of one. But it'll be easier to justify to the people and other kingdoms if he frames it as Lorria attacking first. He'll have the casualties to prove it. Garit will play it off as an assassination attempt on him instead of the rescue mission it really is. It'll start the war we're all trying to avoid. And Garit will still have Oma to hold over my parents.

And I'm another liability. Catching a Lorrian princess in the Wolf Palace would give Garit even more power. I thought I was doing the right thing by coming after Oma, but I wasn't. I'm not worried about what will happen to me if I'm captured, but it could be terrible for my kingdom. For my parents. I've distracted them by running after Oma. They should've been focusing on getting her back, not fretting about me.

I could help the Lorrian guards. Tell them about the secret entrance to the palace. It'll significantly increase their odds of rescuing Oma and help limit casualties on both sides. But they don't know about Markus. Nor will they care. A dead Wolf Prince is a good thing from their perspective. If I wait for them to rescue Oma, I can go in after for Markus … *No, burn it. Garit might kill Markus before I can free him. And after Oma escapes, he'll be even more alert and paranoid.*

Father always says he has to worry about the kingdom. I think I understand better now, but is it wrong to want to put Markus ahead of everyone? Lives depend on what I decide, but it's an impossible choice. How can I let a war happen, knowing I can prevent it? How can I sacrifice the person I love most in this world if I can save him?

This could be a potential disaster for both kingdoms. Thousands of lives in danger. Markus needs me, but so does my kingdom. He would say to sacrifice him to keep everyone safe. But that's why I'd make a terrible ruler—I'm not willing to do that. Not for anything.

New plan. Convince the Lorrian guards to rescue Oma and Markus.

And tomorrow it'll rain spiced chocolate and strudel.

There has to be a way. Am I willing to lie to the Lorrians if it means rescuing Markus? Absolutely. But I don't think I'll have to.

If his father and brother are dead, Markus is the rightful Wolf King. That's why Garit's so desperate to find him. Markus is a threat to Garit. I'll have to convince the guards that rescuing Markus will prevent a war between our kingdoms, either because Markus as the legitimate ruler

won't want a war, or the Wolf Kingdom will be too busy
with a civil war to bother with Lorria.

No matter what happens, I'm getting Markus and Oma
out of the palace, and out of danger. Just as soon as I figure
out how to trick the guards into helping me.

*I'll convince them. I have to. Now to find them and talk
them into my insane plan.*

One deep breath. "You're a princess. Now act like one."
I march into the guards' camp.

There're shouts and swords drawn as I stop next to the
campfire centered in the ring of tents. I keep my face calm
and unsmiling. They don't need to know I'm clasping my
hands in front of me to hide the shaking and prevent me
from throwing my arms in the air in surrender. This is a
performance and lives depend on how well I play my part.

*Should I order them to stand down? Will they listen to
me? No, better to start on friendly, but firm, terms. As father
says, never give an order you know will be disobeyed.*

Being small and relatively helpless looking works in my
favor. The guards circle me, uncertain what to do since I'm
not fighting back or threatening them.

A woman pushes through the group and surveys me with
narrowed blue eyes. Her sharp features and short hair
strengthen her natural air of authority. "Who are you?"

Keep them off-balance. You're in control. "I'm not
surprised you don't recognize me. I didn't spend a lot of
time with my father's army. But you." I incline my head to
the man I recognized earlier. "You normally serve in the

palace. Surely you can identify me to your commander.
We've spoken several times about your home in the Rhonen
mountain range and how your family comes from a long line
of hunters. I hope Susanne's ankle has healed."

The man jumps, his Adam's apple bobbing erratically.
He glances from the commander to me. His eyes widen.
"Pr—Princess Lisette?"

I nod coolly as murmurs break out. "Thank you. That
will save a lot of time. Now please make yourselves known
to me."

They didn't choose the commander for her position—or
this mission—because she's a fool. She studies me carefully.
"Princess Lisette? What are you doing here?"

I let some sympathy shine through my mask. "I know
it's hard to comprehend how your princess could walk into
your camp in the middle of the Black Forest hours before
you plan to invade the Wolf Palace. I've been traveling here
for the same purpose as you. To rescue the Dowager Queen.
The heavens have seen fit to bring us together so we can
accomplish our goal, and prevent a war between Lorria and
the Kingdom of the Wolves."

I sense her wavering, but she's not quite ready to believe
me. "How did you navigate the Black Forest alone?"

"I didn't. My guide and I were separated earlier today. I
was making my way back to the last place I saw him when I
found you." Inspiration strikes. "Perhaps you came across
our supplies? Rope, some pouches, and the like. There was
also a red fur-lined cloak, and a dagger with a red stone in
the hilt and engravings on the blade. Those belong to me."

The guards exchange surprised glances. The commander
gestures without taking her eyes off me. One man ducks into
a tent, bringing out my cloak and dagger. I breathe a sigh of

relief as he hands them to me.

I tuck the dagger into the sheath, quickly moving my hands away from the weapon. "Commander, I—"

"General Kier. Let me introduce the rest of my team."

She runs through the names, pointing to each person. I promptly forget them all in my nervousness about what's coming next.

The general rocks back on her heels. "Princess, we're planning on retrieving the Dowager Queen tonight. You can stay here while—"

"It won't work." I keep my voice strong, determined not to let a tremor creep in. "A moat surrounds the palace. I'm sure your scouts saw the drawbridge is up. My source says there's no way to lower it from outside." When the general opens her mouth to respond, I hurry on. "I can get us into the palace without anyone knowing. A secret way that won't be guarded." *At least, I hope it's not.*

She crosses her arms. "It would be good to know how you came by this information."

"My guide. He grew up in the palace. He also told me the best way to get to the dungeon undetected. And other areas in the palace they might hold Om—the Dowager Queen." I look around the circle of faces. "The king's brother, the Black Wolf, has taken control of the throne. He's the one responsible for my grandmother's kidnapping. He wants a war with Lorria. But we won't give him that opportunity."

The guards nod, but the general is harder to impress.

"Our orders are to rescue the Dowager Queen and that's what we'll do. If you'll tell me what you know about the palace, I'll take it under advisement."

This is it. I lift my chin and meet her eyes. "I'm going

with you."

The general presses her lips together. "With all due respect, Princess Lisette, this is a dangerous situation. We can't risk taking you with us. The King and Queen would never allow it."

I stand as tall as my short frame will allow. "General, I've been traveling through the Black Forest for weeks. I can take care of myself. You need my help. We're stronger when we're together." My heart gives a painful thump, remembering when Markus said those words to me. "And there are some other things you need to know before we leave."

The small garden is enchanting in the moonlight. Two white marble wolf statues twice the height of a man guard the entrance. The feeling of entering a hidden world intensifies as I step inside. Instead of a wide-open space, there's a curtain of greenery with twisting, turning paths. Statues peek between waterfalls of ivy and moonflower blooms. A gentle tinkling promises fountains hidden somewhere in the depths. It breaks my heart a little knowing I'll never get to explore the garden, but time is running out.

The palace entrance is tricky to locate in the dark. Markus's fuzzy childhood memories sketched out the basics, but the years have marked the landscape. Goethe finally locates the crouching wolf statue behind layers of ivy. Even with the marker, it takes several minutes of hunting and hacking through the greenery to find the stone covering the entrance. The guards wrangle it to the side, revealing a tunnel leading into the hillside. It's so small, even I'll have to crouch to fit.

General Kier holds the torch inside, sword drawn. "Close quarters. No room for fighting, but it won't give anyone a chance to overwhelm us with numbers. A few of us can easily block the route while the others retreat. Spread out and watch the person in front of you for signals."

She takes the lead, subtly indicating to Luther to guard me, which I choose not to protest. The General's been pushed to her limits tonight. It's better to let her have some semblance of control if I want to keep their cooperation. I don't know if the general objected more to bringing me along or helping Markus. Both seemed equally repugnant. It took all my persuasion, plus a little bit of cajoling and threatening, to get her to agree to help him.

Markus failed to mention the rough going and spiderwebs we encounter as we proceed up the small tunnel. Probably not something a child would notice, but I still plan to give him an earful after I rescue him. It keeps my mind off the hopefully imaginary insects crawling across my neck and in my hair.

More than cold air chills my skin. Markus is still out there. He needs help. I can only pray to the heavens he isn't hurt and we'll find him soon. Time is hard to track as we creep along the tunnel. We've covered at least a mile when the air becomes noticeably thick.

Something hits my neck. I swallow a scream, frantically slapping at it until I realize it's water. At Luther's panicked look, I wave him down, not bothering to explain. *We must be under the moat.* I press forward. More water drips, making the torches hiss and creating little streams on the tunnel's floor.

Abruptly the ground slopes up, the angle so steep it feels like my nose is inches from the dirt. After thirty paces, it levels out, ending against a thick wood door. General Kier flashes her hands and the guards all nod. She flips the catch at the top. The wall silently swings ajar a few inches. I hold my breath as the General presses her eye to the crack. She waves her hand again, then pushes the door open. One by one, the guards extinguish the torches and slip through.

The king's closet reminds me of my father's at home. Racks and racks of the formal robes and other clothes, with a small section dedicated to personal favorites for his private time. The sight makes my fists clench. Before Luther can stop me, I grab my dagger and slash a particularly fine velvet tunic near me. I give the startled guard a cool nod as I slip the knife back into the sheath and stalk out of the small room. *Good thing the general didn't see that.*

The king's suite is surprisingly sparse, with simple dark furniture set against pale walls. It reminds me of Markus with its efficiency and elegance, which only feeds my anger. I don't want any part of the king to lay claim to Markus. His family forfeited that right a long time ago.

General Kier leads our group through the rooms and out of the suite. We go unchallenged down the dark hallway and descend the servant's staircase at the back. The plastered walls give way to bare black stone walls, floors, and ceilings.

There should be guards outside the king's rooms and in the hallways. Not to mention the normal army of servants buzzing around the palace attending to the thousands of endless duties. *Why is it empty? Where is everyone?*

My puzzlement grows the farther we travel. The guards break their training to send nervous glances at the passing doorways and hallways.

When the first Wolf Guards appear, it's almost a relief. General Kier and another guard dispatch them quickly, injuring but not killing the men. As they tie up the guards and stow them in a side room, I send a silent thank you to the heavens they listened to me.

She whispers, "A patrol unit. The dungeons are next and should be heavily guarded. Princess—"

"I'm not leaving." I keep my tone level and my gaze steady. "But I'll stay out of your way. And I expect each and every one of you to walk out of here with me before the night is over."

She gives a grudging nod, a hint of respect in her eyes. "Avoid killing if you can. Your priority is protecting the Princess and the Dowager Queen. *Primo Proelio.*"

The Lorrian guards kiss their fists, then put them on their chests. The general returns the gesture. I sense the energy binding them together, knowing I'm outside it. It's something only a soldier can know, something that ties you to your comrades when you place your life in their hands and vow to protect theirs.

The guards move forward down the passageway, their movements fluid and coordinated. Keeping to my word, I hang back, letting them move ahead before creeping after them.

More undecorated black rock. No windows. A small slit above the thick iron doors lets light into the cells. Mounted torches along the walls are mostly unlit. Except for the color, this is like the dungeons I used to sneak down to and gawk at in our castle. Now I deeply regret terrorizing Maddie with stories of how invaders would lock us up in the cells, leaving the rats to nibble on our fingers and toes while we slept. I shudder and hope Oma never experienced anything that horrible while trapped here.

Yells and clashing metal explode in the corridor. I clutch my dagger, crouching against the wall. Shadows and steel flash in the flickering torchlight. The Lorrian guards have the advantage of surprise, but the Wolf Guards outnumber us. More Wolf Guards swarm from the back room to join the fight. If not for the narrow space, they would overrun us in moments. But the Lorrians use the layout to their advantage, crowding the Wolf Guards, so they trip over each other and don't have room to maneuver or surround us.

One man does a flying tackle, pinning Goethe to the ground near me. Goethe struggles under the man's weight, trying to push the enemy soldier off him. When the Wolf Guard raises his sword, I dart forward and slash his arm, distracting him long enough for Goethe to deliver a ringing blow to his head. The Lorrian nods in thanks, then runs back to the line with a yell.

I stare at the downed man in shock. *I didn't even think, I just acted.* My shaking hands fumble the dagger as I cut strips from the man's shirt to bind him. *I attacked him. With a knife.* The knots are clumsy, but should hold long enough. *I'm not even sorry. Shouldn't I be sorry? But I'm not, and I can't pretend to be.* My thoughts bounce around, trying to make sense of who I've become.

A sword clatters on the stones next to me, breaking me out of my daze. One of the Lorrians collapses against the wall with a groan, his arm hanging limp at his side. I cut another strip from the unconscious man's shirt, then hurry over to help the guard dress his wound. His face is a blur as I wrap the strip around his shoulder and tie it off.

I scoop up the unconscious man's sword and watch the battle, darting forward to wildly stab when a hole opens in our line. I don't think, I just let my instincts guide me and try to stay out of the way as much as possible. Impossibly, we're winning. The remaining Wolf Guards barricade themselves in the room at the back of the corridor as the stragglers fight or surrender. The last enemy finally yields.

Our small group has two arm wounds that look nasty, but otherwise they escaped with minor cuts and bruises. General Kier secures the defeated Wolf Guards in empty cells, then the search begins.

The general is thoroughly organized—and too slow. The doors use old-fashioned wooden bars in iron brackets instead of keys. Instead of having the group check several cells at once, the general searches them one-by-one. After the third empty cell, I lose my patience and yank open the door closest to me.

A huge man close to Maddie's age sits on the bench. The flickering gives his hair a golden tint, his eyes dark shadows. Purple bruises highlight his cheek and chin. The tattered red tunic and black pants are well tailored to his broad, tall frame, and made of quality material.

His eyes narrow. "Who are you?"

I slam the door shut. "She's not in this one." Ignoring the man banging on the door, I move to the next one and fling it open.

Oma blinks in the torchlight. "Lisette? Heavens. What are you doing here, child?" She stands up from the bench, her white hair pinned back in a disheveled bun.

"Oma." I throw myself into her arms with a sob. "Are you all right? Did they hurt you?"

"I'm fine." She pats my back as my tears leave stains on the front of her midnight blue dress. "No need for such a fuss. I'm perfectly unharmed. That fool had no idea who he was dealing with. All he did was bore me and remind me how annoying nobles can be."

Her frame feels frailer, her skin thinner. I pull back far enough to see her face. A few more wrinkles around the eyes and mouth, skin pale from being hidden from the sun. But her eyes still have the same fire, her lips that twist of mischief I've known all my life.

General Kier bows in the doorway. "Your Majesty. We need to leave before the Wolf Guards regroup."

"Nonsense." Oma smooths back the white hairs escaping from her bun. "The Wolf King needs our help."

My jaw drops open. "Oma, did you bump your head? Are you feverish?"

She swats away my hand. "Don't look at me like that. I'm old, not daft. I've been listening to the guards and servants gossip. The Wolf King is in one of these cells awaiting execution. His brother betrayed him." She grimaces. "That imposter is a bloodthirsty tyrant. He's gathering up the nobles to make them witness the king's execution and crush any resistance."

King Wilhelm's not dead. My mind flashes to the large blond man in the cell. *Too young to be Markus's father. But it could be—No. It doesn't matter. We're going to get Markus, leave the palace, and I'll never waste another thought on the Wolf King or the Black Forest again.*

But the little voice inside me insists that's not what Markus would want. He'd want us to help his father and brother. Markus always sacrifices himself for the people he loves. *And he's not here to say it himself because that big, dumb barbarian got himself captured to save me.*

The general's frown deepens. "The Wolf King is no concern of ours. We're leaving before they raise the alarm."

I shake my head. *I'm letting anger cloud my thoughts instead of doing what's needed.* "My grandmother is right. We have to help the Wolf King."

The general turns her sharp scowl on me. "Princess, there isn't—"

I cut her off, matching her glare for glare. "The Dowager Queen and I are in agreement. If the Wolf King is here, we must assist him. It's our duty." I let my face soften and step closer to her. "General. A man who's willing to kidnap my grandmother and risk a war is a danger to everyone. He won't hesitate to abuse the people here, and then he'll turn his sights on Lorria. This kingdom needs our help. There's no one else. It's up to us to render aid. And I'm not leaving here without Markus. I owe him my life several times over."

My stomach twists in the heavy silence, the general weighing my words. When she finally nods, I want to cheer, but contain myself to a dignified nod—ruined by my broad grin.

General Kier says, "We'll search the cells. Queen Emera, do you know what the Wolf King looks like?"

I clear my throat. "I think I know someone who can help with that."

General Kier and a Lorrian guard enter the cell first, taking up stances on either side of the doorway as Oma and I step inside. The prisoner glowers at us from the bench.

Oma inclines her head. "Good evening."

"Lorrians?" His tone is full of disgust. "Uncle really has gone mad."

My grandmother signals our two guards to loosen their grips on their swords. "Impressive. Is it the accent?"

I bristle. "We don't have accents."

The man barks a short laugh. "Only a Lorrian would think they don't have an accent."

Oma steps between us before I can snap at him. "You may call me Emera. Are you Prince Fredrik?"

"My name is no concern of yours."

Only a prince would be this arrogant. "It's not polite to insult your rescuers. Unless you'd like us to leave you in your cell." Impatience demands to slam the door and find the king without this man. *This is taking too long. He'll be perfectly fine in the dungeon while we rescue Markus and deal with his usurper uncle. We don't need him.*

"Rescuers? You look like—where did you get that?" His eyes widen. The man leaps forward, stopping short when the guards draw their swords and press him back against the wall.

The prisoner holds up his hands. "My apologies. I didn't mean to startle you. It's just—please." He gestures to my waist.

Reluctantly, I hold up my dagger so he can see the engraving on the blade. The guards watch him warily, but he doesn't move.

"I thought it was destroyed. That night." He swallows hard. "Do you know what it says?"

A smile tugs at my lips. "Something cryptic that takes too long to figure out."

"It's a binding. The gifter vows in life and death to protect the person it's gifted to."

I narrow my eyes. "He said it was a blessing for protection." I don't know what game this man is playing, but

I don't like it.

"You know Markus." His expression doesn't change, but the air vibrates with tension.

He's practically begging to be left here. "Is it a family trait to be annoying before answering any questions?"

A hint of a smile breaks through. "Yah, I'm Prince Fredrik."

"See. Was that so hard?" When I slide the dagger back into the sheath, my bracelet catches on the edge of the leather. I gently tug it away, then check it for damage. Still in perfect condition, thank the heavens.

The prince draws in a sharp breath. "Did Markus give you that too?" It seems to have him mesmerized. He looks from it, to me, and back again.

Ignoring his question, I cross my arms. "Do you want help taking back your kingdom, or would you rather rot in a cell?"

His eyes lock onto my wrist, then he nods. "I'll help you."

27

Fredrik is brimming with impatience, but I keep silent about Markus as we check the rest of the cells. My heart sinks when the search confirms he's not in the dungeon. The Wolf King and the guards loyal to him are quickly identified and freed with Fredrik's help. The Wolf King is shorter than his sons, though no less broad of shoulder despite the recent weight loss. Beneath the bruises on his face are the deep lines that come from the weight of the crown.

Oma greets the king with a courtly nod of her head. "King Wilhelm, I'm Queen Emera. It'll save us time if we can skip the suspicious interrogation stage and determine whether to remove your brother from the throne now, or retreat and regroup."

He strokes his graying beard, surveying our group with a raised eyebrow. "The Lorrians are going to help us? Why?"

I mutter, "Here we go."

Fredrik puts his hand on his father's shoulder and whispers in his ear. The king's eyes widen and he shoots me a surprised look.

With impressive self-control, I manage not to stick my tongue out at them. *Markus is going to owe me a big explanation when all this is over. I'm tired of everyone looking at me like I have a second head just because he gave me a fancy dagger and a bracelet.*

The king returns my grandmother's nod. "My apologies. Please, call me Wilhelm. I don't stand on formality between allies."

Oma beams. "Thank you, Wilhelm. Call me Emera. Now, are we running or making a stand?"

General Kier steps forward. "I advise we leave. We've already lingered too long. There's only three dozen of us against the usurper's forces. Our luck won't hold much longer."

Fredrik nods. "Better to get you to safety, then regroup with our supporters."

"No!" The word bursts out before I can stop it. I don't want to betray Markus, but this is my one chance to rescue him. We can't leave him in his uncle's hands. "Markus is in the palace."

Fredrik and Wilhelm both roar, "What?"

"Why didn't you tell me—"

"Why should we trust you after—"

Oma claps her hands sharply. "I seem to be behind. Who is Markus?"

The king keeps his eyes locked on me. "My son."

"Ah. In that case, the answer is clear. General, arrange for the injured guards to get outside the palace. The rest of us will continue with a rescue operation."

"Oma, no. You have to leave, too. I won't let you put yourself in danger."

My grandmother gives a light laugh. "You sound just

like your father."

"I do no—don't distract me. You are not coming with us. I didn't come all this way to rescue you just to have you get into trouble again."

Oma pats my cheek. "Now you sound like your mother."

I clench my fists. *Gahhhh.*

Fredrik holds up his hands. "I don't want to get in the middle of your family, err, discussion. But Captain Hiller says the escaped soldiers were regrouping at the farmhouse by the crossroads. If my father and Emera go with the wounded, they can bring the reinforcements back to the palace while we search for Markus."

Oma folds her arms. "Captain Hiller can take care of that on his own."

"Please, Oma?" I put my hand on her arm. "If we're captured, someone has to warn Lorria about what's happening and spread the word to the rest of the Wolf Kingdom. It's my turn for an adventure."

She sighs. "I think you've already had one. I guess I better let you finish it." She pulls me into a tight hug, then smooths my hair back before turning to the prince. "You watch out for my granddaughter."

He nods solemnly as I glare at him behind Oma's back.

We quickly outline a plan, making our best guesses about where they're holding Markus and the strength of the usurper's forces. Fredrik and the Wolf King have a hard time hiding their anger anytime Garit is mentioned. Family or no family, I can't imagine Garit will get any leniency if we can wrestle the crown from him.

Our group leaves the dungeons, creeping up the stairs. Once we reach the main floor, the king, Oma, and fifteen guards break off for a hidden stairway that will bring them close to the king's chambers and the secret passageway. Oma and I exchange determined looks as she leaves, my heart sighing in relief that she'll soon be out of danger.

Besides Fredrik and myself, there's a mix of twenty men and women from our kingdoms to search for Markus. Fredrik and Captain Hiller take the lead, directing us down side passages and narrow hallways toward the tower they think Markus may be held in. I keep my stolen sword in the scabbard, concerned about stabbing someone accidentally as we silently walk in a tight group. Now that Oma's safe, all my thoughts turn to Markus. *He must be in the palace. He has to be. We have to find him. And I owe that tracker payback for tossing me over the cliff.*

The door at the base of the tower is wide open. The prince and the captain exchange a look, then hold a hurried whispered conversation. The captain and the general slip through the door to scout it while the rest of us wait at the bottom.

Fredrik edges over to me. "Tell me about Markus. How is he? Where has he been all these years?"

My lips press together and I stare straight ahead. Irrational anger at Fredrik fills my mind. Now that they know Markus is alive, there's no harm in telling Fredrik something about his brother. But I don't want to. There's a petty part of me—a part I don't want to examine too closely—that refuses to give Fredrik any piece of Markus. That thinks he doesn't have the right to know anything about Markus, even now.

"If I'd known he was alive, if—he should've come home. Why didn't he come home? "

I check my dagger, then tug my shirt straight.

He shakes his head. "Taking up with a Lorrian. If father

wasn't so happy, I think he'd throttle him."

Grrr. "He won't have the chance." I go nose to chest with the prince, glaring up at him. "Nobody is going to lay a hand on Markus. Not now, not ever. He's under my protection."

His eyes flash. "Father would never actually hurt him. What do you take us for, a bunch of barbarians? Father never wanted to believe Markus died in that fire. He searched for years for any clue he survived, chased down every rumor. He always held out hope Markus was alive, even when I didn't. What I don't understand is why Markus wanted us to think he was dead."

I poke his chest. "Don't play dumb with me. All this drama over some silly superstitions and meaningless accidents. And now you'll never leave him alone, and he'll spend the rest of his life terrified he's going to hurt you." *And it's all my fault.*

The prince frowns, his eyebrows slamming together. "I have no idea what you're talking about."

"Ask your father."

I'm saved from more questions by the reappearance of the captain and general. They signal to move down the corridor. Fredrik keeps shooting me curious looks that I ignore. We creep through the eerily silent palace. Every step increases my uneasiness. *It's too quiet.*

We get to a long stretch of corridor that spurs a whispered consultation between the captain and the general. I peer into the shadows, trying to see what has them on edge, but there are only doors and walls. I look at Fredrik, but he seems just as bewildered as I am. The commanders have grim looks as they signal everyone to be at the ready. Unnecessary, as everyone's nerves are already stretched to the limits.

Four members of the group lead the way, slowly inching forward. We don't have long to wait. Before the guards are halfway down the corridor, doors burst open on both sides and enemy guards pour out to attack.

28

Yells and screams mix with steel clashing. More of the group runs forward to fight, but it's obvious even to my untrained eyes we're outnumbered and will be surrounded in minutes. My knees shake and I clench my jaw to keep my teeth from chattering.

Fredrik draws his sword, but the captain shakes his head.

"We're outnumbered." He looks back, then turns to the prince. "You have to warn the others."

Fredrik puts his hand on the man's shoulder. "Surrender if you can."

I gasp. "We can't leave them."

"We have to."

Coldness spreads through my chest, but I lift my chin and stare him down. "Then you go."

General Kier grabs my arm. "This is our duty. Yours is to escape and carry word. Stop wasting time." She runs toward the melee, shouting over her shoulder, "We'll hold them off as long as we can. Find your grandmother and warn Lorria."

"Go." Captain Hiller shoves Fredrik, then sprints after the general.

I give a last anguished look at the battling soldiers as the prince grabs my hand and drags me away. Shouts and screams fill the air. Fredrik roars as soldiers burst into the hallway in front of us. I yank his arm, crashing through the nearest doorway.

He slams the door closed and presses his back against it. "Quick, find something to block it."

We've landed in a sparsely decorated room with a few dusty pieces of furniture. I push a heavy armchair over, then join him in bracing the door. It shudders as the soldiers pound the other side, muffled yells coming through the wood.

I scan the room. "Is there a secret passage or another way out of here?"

Fredrik grunts as the door gives a violent shudder. "No."

"It's your castle. How are we going to escape?"

"I wasn't the one who dragged us in here. You come up with something."

"I saved you from getting skewered by those guards. It's your turn."

Fredrik grins. "No wonder he likes you." He nods to the window. "Can you swim? "

"Why—" I groan. *Not again.* "You must be joking."

"Do you have a better idea?"

Burn it. "If I die, I'm going to kill you." I sprint across the room and push the window open. Blackness looms below. *Burn it, burn it, burn it, burn it. Markus, you better not be dead.* I take a deep breath and fling myself into space before I can talk myself out of it.

29

It's worse than being thrown off the cliff. I can't see anything. Blackness surrounds me. I plunge into the icy moat. Scum and stagnant water flood my mouth. My momentum shoves me to the muddy bottom. A loud boom of something hitting the water near me is followed by waves knocking me sideways. I push off the soft ground and resurface, gagging against the foul taste. Fredrik pops up a few feet away.

He treads water, using one hand to wipe his face. "I guess you can swim."

I shove the damp blond curls out of my face. "We need a plan."

"You go warn my father and your grandmother. If there's enough troops, you can mount a rescue. Otherwise, smuggle them back to Lorria. I'm assuming since you got here, you can get yourself home."

"I'm not leaving Markus."

"Neither am I."

We glare at each other.

266

"Great. We're in agreement." I spit, trying to clear the swampy taste. "What now, genius?"

"I got us out. It's your turn."

I roll my eyes, then study the palace. "There."

"There, where?"

Obviously Markus got the brains in the family. "We can climb up to that open window."

"Why don't we use the side entrance instead?" Fredrik grins.

The resemblance to Markus is so strong, my breath catches. "Fine," I squeeze out. Then I splash him for being an insufferable idiot.

We swim around the corner to where a small door is tucked in the shadows, blending in perfectly with the stonework. Fredrik hauls himself up the side of wall, then yanks on carved handle.

Nothing.

He gives it another tug.

I raise my eyebrow. "You should try knocking."

"Helpful. Give me your dagger."

"What? No. Use your own."

"I lost it." He looks down to where I'm treading water. "Or we could stay out here until the eels find us."

"Gah." I scramble up the wall, kicking at the shadows below me. "What's wrong with you? Why didn't you tell me there are eels in there?"

"If they're not biting you then you don't need to worry about them. Dagger?"

I shoot him a murderous look as I hand over my blade. He slides it in the crack, then jiggles it. The door swings open into a narrow tunnel.

He looks over his shoulder at me, his wide frame filling

the tiny space. "This will take us to the inner courtyard."

"Great. Now give me back my dagger." I hold out my hand.

He tucks it into his belt and walks away. "Family heirloom. Thanks for returning it."

If I hadn't lost the sword in the moat plunge, I'd stab him. I settle for kicking him in the back of the knee. "Give it back."

He stumbles, then keeps walking. "We should check the other tower. It's still the most likely place he's being held."

"That's my dagger."

He dodges my next kick. "Or mayhap we should wait and try to free the guards first. We'll need help."

It's just a dagger. We have more important things to worry about, like saving Markus. I need his help. I shouldn't make a big deal out of it. Let it go, Lys. "Markus will pound you into pulp when he finds out what you did. He gave it me."

He stops short. Mutters. Then hands the knife back to me with a glower.

I clutch it to my chest, a knot loosening in my stomach. It may be just a dagger, but it's another tie to Markus. Something to remember him by after tonight. A lump in my throat forms, choking me. *He won't be coming to Lorria with me.* Markus loves his family. He needs them. That's why he never left, even if he can't admit it to himself. He always hoped to come home to them.

At the end of the small hallway, Fredrik signals to stop. He peeks his head around the corner, then backs up. "There should be at least a few guards stationed at the entrance to the receiving room and the barracks, but it's empty."

"Your uncle must have his forces spread too thin."

"That means we don't have much time, but we have a chance. The tower is this way."

I grab his arm before he can move. "No. We have to stop your uncle. Now." I narrow my eyes, my mind racing. "He's weak. Once he finds out you and your father have escaped, he'll be on the lookout for an attack. Surround himself with guards. If we strike now, we have a chance."

He presses his lips together, then nods. "Fine."

"*Fine?*" I put my hands on my hips. "Markus would tell me it's a stupid plan and come up with something that actually stands a chance of succeeding."

He shrugs. "He's the smart one in the family."

"Stupid plan it is."

# 30

Fredrik guides me through the palace. Unlike the faery tales I loved growing up, there are no magic swords waiting in the hallways for me to grab along the way. Facing the throne room door with nothing but my dagger has me rethinking my planning skills.

Too late now.

Fredrik puts a finger to his lips and crouches. I huddle behind him as he silently inches the door open.

It's constructed of the same black stone from the dungeons, shrouding the room in shadows despite the plentiful lit torches. Blood-red banners hang on the walls. The room is empty of furniture except for the black and silver throne on the dais at the far end. Howling wolves decorate each arm of the throne, the back covered with silver phases of the moon that match the design on my dagger.

The man sitting there is easy to overlook on the first pass. Garit doesn't have much resemblance to his brother or nephews, with his average frame and height. There's no trace of the bear-like features evident in the rest of the family. His black and silver coat blend into the chair, his black hair and trim beard completing the look. I'm not sure I would give him a second look if I passed him on the street. Garit rests comfortably on the throne, a silver crown dangling on his fingertips as he glances at the man kneeling in front of him.

Markus is nowhere to be found. My heart sinks even as a thread of relief trickles through me. I don't want him anywhere near his traitorous uncle. A low rumble builds in Fredrik's chest. I smack his arm. We need to wait until the man leaves. The heavens know I'm going to be useless in a fight, and Fredrik can't risk taking them both on.

Garit places the crown on his head and leans forward, addressing the man. "You claim to bring me a prize."

"Aye, aye. You'll be most pleased."

Every muscle tenses as anger takes hold. A growl escapes my lips and Fredrik clamps a hand over my mouth. *It's the tracker.* Fredrik yanks me back as I lunge toward the door, every rational thought smashed out of my mind. I struggle against his hold, pounding my fist against his arms and chest. I can't feel anything except the need to grab the tracker and shake him until he tells me everything. *Where's Markus? He must be here. I have to get to him.*

Fredrik crouches down to my eye level. He mouths, "Markus?"

I nod frantically, my hands tearing at his fingers.

He disappears, racing into the throne room with a war cry. I follow, hot on his heels. Fredrik charges at the throne, but I look desperately around, trying to spot Markus.

He must be here. Where is he?

There's nobody else in the throne room, not even a guard. A small set of doors off to the left side is the only other exit. I burst through them into the receiving chamber.

Markus is kneeling on the floor between two guards. His hair is matted with blood and mud, his leathers ripped and filthy. One eye is swollen shut and his cheekbone is covered in a deep purple bruise. A small pool of blood has formed on the floor beneath him.

I can't think, can't breathe. Red fills my vision as rage takes over. I scream, launching myself at the nearest man, the dagger already in my fist. The man doesn't blink. Markus's head jerks up as my weight carries the guard to the floor. Everything is a blur of arms and legs and blood and heat. My body takes blows, but it doesn't interrupt my shrieking attack on the guard. I'm dimly aware of Markus roaring as he bodily tackles the other man to the ground. The dagger grows slippery in my grip.

"Lisette." Markus's soft voice breaks through the frenzy a moment before he grabs me, crushing me to his chest. "You're alive."

I stand frozen, arms hanging by my side. My throat works, words fighting to get out past the lump. My heart pounds furiously, trying to escape my chest.

"I—I thought … I didn't …" He squeezes me, then pulls back enough to look me in the face. "Are you hurt?" His face is a mass of cuts and bruises, concern shining from the one eye not swollen shut.

I burst into tears and throw my arms around his neck. "Markus. I'm sorry. I'm sorry, I'm sorry, I'm sorry." I bury my face in his shoulder, clinging to him as hard as I can, breathing in his scent.

His arms tighten around me, making it hard to breathe, but I don't care. My poor Markus has been beaten and abused, but he's not broken. His fingers gently tilt my face up. He kisses me as if he would die without me, as if I'm a lifeline thrown to a drowning man. My insides feel light. There's nothing except his mouth on mine, his arms around me.

He jerks away. "What are you doing here? You could be killed." He gives my shoulders a shake, then crushes his lips against mine again before yanking away with a gasp. "We have to leave."

"No, Fredrik. He's inside," I pant, pointing to the throne room.

Markus utters a curse. He presses a hard kiss to my forehead, then grabs a sword from one of the fallen guards. "Get out of the palace. I'll find you."

"Go." I shove him toward the door.

With one last look, he races into the throne room.

I quickly confirm both men are dead, carefully keeping my eyes averted as much as possible. My stomach rolls as flashes from my feverish attack play through my mind. My foot slips in blood. I close my eyes and clamp my lips together as bile rushes up my throat. The cuts on my arms and hands should hurt, but I feel nothing.

A sword is next to my foot. I could do what Markus asked. Escape the palace, find Oma and the King Wilhelm, and bring reinforcements back to the palace. It's the same thing Fredrik tried to convince me to do. It didn't work then, and it's not going to work now. I can't leave Markus again, not when I just found him.

Love makes you stupid.

I grab the sword and race after Markus.

Markus has already joined the fight.

Garit trades blows with Fredrik in front of the throne while Markus and the tracker face off near the middle of the room. The tracker's illness lends his muscles a fevered strength, his movements unpredictable and wild. Markus is already dragging, his abused body lumbering instead of moving with its usual graceful efficiency. He's purely on the defensive, giving ground to the tracker with every block.

My heart leaps into my throat as I sprint toward them. *Hang on, Markus.* Running with the sword is awkward, throwing off my balance, dragging me down. Every step is too slow, every breath too long when Markus is in danger.

Markus stumbles, dropping to one knee. He barely gets his sword up to deflect the tracker's swing at his head. The tracker doesn't pause, raining blow after blow at Markus while he's trapped on the ground. Markus clumsily blocks the weapon, gaining cuts on his arms and shoulders.

"Stop!" I yell, trying to distract them. I'm moments away, but it's still too far.

The tracker cackles. "Little girly came back. Double prize for me." The man easily evades Markus's swing, dancing to the side, then back.

Markus grunts as their swords meet. "Lisette, go."

I don't try to stop as I reach the men. Letting my momentum pull me, I drag the sword through the air, aiming for the madman's side. He sidesteps the strike, easily moving his sword to crash into mine. The blade spins out of my hands. I back away, sweat breaking out over my skin.

Markus uses the distraction to lunge to his feet, swinging at the man's legs. Too quick, it's blocked, and Markus is on the defensive again. I pull out my dagger and jab the tracker in the side. Then again. The tracker ignores me. He twists Markus's sword out of his hand. The man raises his blade to deliver a killing blow.

With an inarticulate scream, I jump on the man's back, clawing at his face with hands and steel. The tracker bellows. He lashes out, his fist connecting with my cheek. Stars explode. Tears flood my eyes as ice, then fire, race across my skin. Markus roars. Metal clashing cuts through the buzzing in my ears. I wrap my fingers around the tracker's neck and squeeze.

The man's throat muscles work beneath my fingers, but I keep my hands locked in place. His body jerks. We tumble to the floor, my shoulder slamming into the ground, bouncing me across the stones.

Markus yanks the sword out of the tracker's chest. He pulls me to my feet. "Will you ever listen to me when I ask you to do something?"

"I always listen, I just don't always agree with you." I gingerly touch my face, wincing at the heat coming off my skin. "Mother's going to kill me."

"That's what you're worried about?" He shakes his head. "Lorrians are crazy." He presses a quick kiss to my lips. "Please. Stay here while I help Fredrik."

"No promises." I press my dagger into his hand. "I expect that back when you're done."

Markus salutes, then hurries toward where Fredrik and his uncle are battling near the throne. Both men are drenched in sweat, but their movements are quick. The blades whirl through the air almost too fast to see. Markus doesn't jump into the fray. Instead, he quietly circles his uncle, forcing the man to jump onto the dais to fend off both his nephews.

I pick up my fallen sword and follow. I'm not about to let Markus get himself into trouble again while I sit by and watch. There's no point in joining the fight since I'm clearly outmatched, but I can't stand by and do nothing.

My legs tremble as I creep closer. Garit must know he'll eventually lose now that he's fighting both brothers. The dais isn't large, and the wall at his back offers no retreat, but he refuses to yield.

Fredrik steps back, holding his sword at the ready. "End this now, while you still have your life."

Garit sneers. "It's you who should be surrendering. Your brother is crippled, and you're barely able to hold on to your sword." He looks around the room before refocusing on his nephews.

"Don't be a fool. You're only alive now because we once called you family. But after everything you've done, Father won't shed any tears over your death."

Markus holds out one hand to his uncle in a pleading gesture. "Why are you doing this?"

"You, of all people, should understand, Markus. We've grown weak under your father's rule. Cowering behind our borders because we fear Lorria. We've licked our wounds long enough. Forgotten our past. It's time to show the world the strength of the Kingdom of the Wolves."

Fredrik shakes his head. "You want to put everyone in danger. Bring war to our land instead of the peace we've fought so hard for. The world has changed. We need to change with it."

Their uncle glances across the room, then flourishes his sword. "Changing doesn't mean bowing and scraping. We have pride. You think I'm putting the kingdom in danger? I'm saving us. The only way to gain respect from the world is to show we aren't afraid to fight. We've been too quiet. Your father doesn't know what's going on outside our borders because he hides in the palace and expects the rest of the world to forget us. They haven't. They're starting to question whether we're as formidable as they think. Whether our reputation as warriors is earned or only rumors. If they see as us as easy prey, they won't hesitate to swarm our borders and swallow us whole."

"The people won't support you. They'll rebel when they find out what you've done. They'll never accept you as king."

"How would they know? Outside the palace, one king is the same as another. They won't notice any difference. They'll go on with their miserable little lives, unaware and uncaring about who rules over them." Garit looks at the throne room doors before snapping his attention back to the princes. "All I have to do is convince the nobles there's no use resisting. That's easy enough. They're even weaker and more cowardly than your father. They've grown complacent without a war to keep them sharp. If I kill one or two of them, they'll stay in line."

He's stalling. I look around wildly. *Reinforcements must be coming, or he thinks they are. It might be two against one now, but if Garit's soldiers find us, we'll be outnumbered.*

I sprint across the throne room. Pausing, I give Markus one last look, then duck through the doors into the huge hallway. Nobody in sight in the long corridor. *Where would they be, where would they be, where would they be? And what am I going to do if I find them?*

Remembering Markus's advice in the forest, I stop, take a deep breath, and close my eyes. Snatches of voices off to the left. Coming this way.

I step into the center of the hallway, making myself as conspicuous as possible. Holding the sword up, I swallow hard, steeling myself. The voices get louder. My heart thunders in my chest, my mouth going dry. It's a group—at least four or five people. I clench my jaw and narrow my eyes. *Distract them. Save Markus. And Fredrik too, I guess.*

It takes a moment for the men to spot me when they turn the corner. I can only imagine how they see me. A short, blond woman dressed in filthy leathers and holding a sword is probably not very intimidating to trained guards.

One bellows, "Oi! Who are you?"

Get their attention and keep it on me. I yell, "For Lorria!"

That does it. With curses and shouts, they charge down the hallway. I hold my position—then turn and run. Their footsteps thunder behind me, their cries echoing off the walls as I dart away. *They're getting closer.* As I round the corner, I toss the heavy sword aside. My feet stumble, tripping me, losing me precious seconds and distance. A knife flies past me, hitting the wall ahead with a loud *clank*.

I slide around another corner to find the large entrance

hall. There's no time to appreciate the paintings and tapestries brightening the black walls, or the polished furniture around the room. My eyes zero in on the large double doors. *Get outside the palace. Hide in the woods.*

Another knife flies by, the blade slicing my sleeve. I crash into the door, shoving with my shoulder. It springs open into a courtyard. I spin, desperately looking for a way out. No exit. *Burning moat. Burning castle with stupid burning moats and stupid hallways and burning moa— drawbridge. Get the drawbridge down.*

I race across the courtyard. There has to be a way to lower it. *Where's the mechanism?* The guards tumble into the courtyard. Their swords gleam wickedly in the moonlight.

"There she is."

"Get that Lorrian scum!"

The hatred in their voices sends a spike of fear through my chest. I fling myself into the closest doorway and slam it closed, throwing the wooden slider to lock the door. It won't hold long against an assault.

The small room has a tiny table and chair across from a large wheel wrapped with thick chains. No windows or other doorways. The wheel has a lever on one side, a winch on the other, the chains going up and out a hole in the ceiling. *It must be for the drawbridge.* I jump over to the small arrow slit and peer at out.

The moonlight shines on the far edge of the moat and the forest. Between the trees, shadows flicker and move. *More guards? Oma and the King Wilhelm with reinforcements? My imagination?* If I can get the drawbridge down, whoever's out there can get inside the castle. And anything that distracts from me is good.

Bam. The door shudders. I hurl myself at it, bracing it from the inside. *Bam. Bam.* Each hit rattles my teeth. The door won't hold much longer.

The wheel's mechanism looks simple enough. Pull the lever, lower the drawbridge. I flinch as the door takes another hit, wood snapping. Whoever is in the forest won't be able to help me, but they can help Markus and his brother—if they're on our side. But there might already be more guards heading toward the throne room.

It's their only chance. I dive at the lever. It doesn't move. The door smashes open as I spot the small wedge at the base of the wheel, locking it in place. The first guard through the door lunges at me as I kick the block away.

The wheel groans, then spins as the man grabs me. He shoves me against the wall, banging my head on the black stone. Chains clank as the wheel turns faster, freed from its restraints.

"Stop that thing," he spits, as two more men crowd into the small gatehouse.

One grabs the wheel's lever, stiffening as he pulls back, trying to slow the wheel's movement. The other tries to grab the whirling winch handle, getting his hands bruised by the spinning wood for his efforts.

The guard holding me presses the sword against my neck. "Thought you could give us the slip, eh?" He steps closer. His thick beard is tangled, his rough skin pockmarked and greasy.

My fingers brush against his belt. "You're a traitor to your king and kingdom. You all deserve to rot." I spit in his face.

The man wipes his cheek with one hand, his eyes burning with rage. He bares his teeth, the sword's edge biting into my skin. Fire races across my neck. "You're going to pay for that."

The two men behind him squawk as the wheel slams to a stop. He looks over his shoulder, the sword's pressure on my neck relaxing for a fraction of a second. I yank the knife out of his belt and plunge it into his stomach. He groans and slides to the floor. The two other men stare at me. I crouch against the wall, the bloody dagger in my hand.

The guards crowding the doorway turn away, their attention caught by something in the courtyard. Thumping feet on the drawbridge. A lot of them. Their comrades shout and clashes sound outside. The younger of the two men runs through the door and out to the courtyard.

The remaining man in the room looks from me to the empty doorway.

I lock my shaking knees and bare my teeth. *Goawayggoawaygoaway.*

The yells from the courtyard get louder. He races through the door.

I drop my arm.

Burning.

Tearing.

I gape at the sword piercing my side. The guard on the floor sneers, then his eyes roll up into his head. He goes limp, his blade sliding out my body and clattering to the floor. I fall to my knees, pressing my hand against the wound, gasping at the white-hot pain ripping through me. Blood seeps between my fingers. *Running out of time.* I sit back against the wall. Tears stream down my face and I grit my teeth as I try to stop the bleeding. My fingers are cold and clumsy. *I wish Markus was here.*

A man's silhouette appears in the doorway. "There's a

girl in here."

"Lisette? What happened, child?" Oma pushes past him, kneeling next to me. She shouts, "Get the doctor!"

"Oma?" My voice sounds thin. "He stabbed me."

She gently strokes my hair, pushing the limp strands off my face. "You're going to be fine. Stay still and conserve your strength."

My sluggish thoughts struggle to surface. *Oma's here. She'll take care of everything. She'll take me home. All of us. Markus has his family now, but he's mine, too. If I don't make it, he can still come home.*

I grip her hand. "He has a home with us. If he wants it. Tell him."

"I will. Shush now." She looks at the men hovering in the doorway. "Where's the doctor? Get them in here now."

A woman with short hair and an oversized pack shoves into the room. She quickly cuts the shirt away from my stab wound, her face impassive while Oma pelts her with questions. The woman thrusts a thick pad against my side, making me cry out.

The healer presses a vial against my lips. "Drink this."

I gulp down the bitter contents, pressing my lips together to keep from gagging. A numbness spreads through my body, taking the edge off the blinding pain.

She partially peels back the bandage. "It's going to need stitches."

Oma clutches my hand. "You have to help my granddaughter. Shouldn't you take her to the hospital ward? She's badly hurt."

"Markus's grandmother was a healer," I murmur. "She taught him." I close my eyes, my mind slowly drifting away.

A sharp smack against my bruised cheek makes my eyes

fly open. My grandmother gives an outraged gasp.

The healer grabs my chin and shakes it. "Don't go to sleep."

"I'm tired," I complain, my words slurring. Unconsciousness beckons, promising a release from the pain and exhaustion.

The lingering guards scatter, and King Wilhelm steps inside the crowded room. "Where are they? Where are my sons?" The sword in his hand is coated in blood.

Markus. I force my eyes open. "Throne room," I gasp. "Hurry."

He takes off running, the soldiers following. Oma mutters something I can't catch as the doctor holds a sharp needle in a flame, then threads it with silk.

She holds another vial against my lips. "Try not to cough."

When I wince, Oma glares at her. "You could be a little kinder."

"I don't have time. I'm trying to save her life." She pinches the inner muscles together, sewing the wound with brisk efficiency.

"Oma." I give her hand a feeble tug. "Tell Father and Mother I'm sorry."

"You'll tell them yourself."

The healer wipes her hands on a cloth, then slathers something cool and green smelling on the wound.

"Well?" Oma demands. "Is she going to live?"

"She's young, healthy. But her body's been through a lot of abuse. She lost a lot of blood. It's up to the goddess now. Keep her awake as long as you can."

The healer leaves to attend to the other wounded. I'm carried through the Wolf Palace on a stretcher, Oma fussing and fretting over me. I'm relieved to glimpse some of the Lorrian guards in the halls. Others are in the healing ward getting treatment for cuts and broken bones. General Kier is talking with a healer, a bandage wrapped around her head. She gives me a sharp salute, then turns back to her conversation.

I'm taken into a small side room and given a more thorough inspection. Scrapes and cuts are cleaned, then they spread salve and ointments over almost every inch of my body. After bundling me into a soft, clean nightshift, they finally let me rest in one of the many beds against the walls with another warning not to fall asleep.

Oma commandeers a chair to sit next to me. I drowse in the bed, trying to pay attention to Oma's chatter, but all I want to do is close my eyes and sleep. I try to scan the room for Markus, but my eyes refuse to focus on anything farther than the next bed. From the bits of conversation I pick up, King Wilhelm's reinforcements easily overcame the traitors holding the palace. Garit had surrendered by the time they arrived in the throne room. Guards are scouring the place for hidden enemies. All the traitors are being held in the dungeon until the king decides what to do with them.

My heart starts to race, and my skin tingles. Like a magnet, my gaze is drawn to the doorway. Markus hobbles into the room, Fredrik supporting him. Markus's eyes lock on mine immediately, relief rushing over his face. He looks at me like I'm the most beautiful woman in the world.

"Lisette."

I gaze hungrily at him, my eyes running over him, trying to determine how badly he's hurt. One of the healers must have already seen him because there's an ointment on his swollen eye and his cuts look cleaned. The rocks in my chest dissolve and my muscles go limp. *He'll be all right.*

Markus pushes away from his brother and limps over, gently taking my outstretched hand. "How badly are you hurt?" He kneels next to the bed.

I lift one shoulder, flinching when the motion pulls at the stitches in my side. The medication has walled off the pain for the moment, but it doesn't numb the odd sensation of thread in my skin. "I needed a few stitches, but I'm fine."

I give Oma a warning look. She presses her lips together, her face tense, but eyes lit with curiosity. Fredrik watches the interchange, but says nothing.

Markus runs his thumb lightly over the bruise on my cheek. "What happened?"

"There were guards coming toward the throne room. I led them away, then hid in the gatehouse." I hate not telling him everything, but now's not the time. We're both exhausted and surrounded by eager ears. There's nothing he can do now but worry. If the heavens allow it, I'll tell him everything tomorrow when we find a moment alone.

Oma puts a hand on my arm. "She lowered the drawbridge so your father and his troops could get into the castle. She handed him the victory."

Markus blinks, looking surprised to find someone else on the other side of my bed.

I suppress a smile. "Markus. This is Oma. I mean, Queen Emera."

His bruised face breaks out into a grin as he nods his head to her. "A pleasure. I've heard a lot about you."

"All good, I'm sure. And I look forward to hearing more about you." Oma glances at our linked hands. "You and my granddaughter must have a lot of stories to share."

"She saved my life."

I put my other hand over his. "We saved each other."

Fredrik looks sad for a moment, but the expression disappears too quickly for me to be sure.

An attendant with spiky brown hair and a reddish beard walks over. "Prince Markus? I can show you to your room if you're ready."

Markus glares at the poor man, causing him to stumble back a step. "I'm staying with Lisette."

I squeeze his hand. "Whatever they gave me is already putting me to sleep. I can barely keep my eyes open. Go, you'll see me in the morning."

His face softens as he looks down at me. "I'm not leaving you. Not after everything."

My heart skips a beat, knowing exactly what he means. Selfishly, I'm glad he wants to stay. His presence lends me strength and makes me feel protected. It would hurt to be parted from him again after all the dangers we've faced. Seeing him and knowing he's safe sets my fears at ease.

Fredrik sets a soothing hand on his shoulder. "Nobody is saying you have to." He points to the bed beside mine. "You can stay right there. You're not doing anything until the healers clear you, anyway."

Markus grumbles, but climbs between the sheets, then reaches across to take my hand again, setting my heart fluttering. His hand is warm and solid in mine. Heat floods my cheeks—I'm not used to such open affection in front of other people. An edge of shyness creeps over me and a blush spreads across my skin.

Fredrik grins. "You've gotten less stubborn in your old age." He glances at me with a speculative look, then looks back to Markus

"It's been a long day." Markus leans back against the

bed. The attendant hands Markus a cup filled with a dark wine which he drains quickly. He yawns, rubbing a hand over his face. "They must have mixed whatever they gave you in that wine."

The urgency and danger that kept me going has disappeared, leaving me an exhausted shell. I manage a smile. "It's strong stuff. My compliments to your healers."

"Wake me if you need anything. Or want to talk." He squeezes my hand again. "I'm glad you're safe." His eyes slide closed, black lashes fanned against his cheek. A content smile is on his lips as his breathing deepens into a steady rhythm.

Oma looks between me and Markus, then shakes her head. "This can wait. I'm going to check with the healer and see if you can eat something. We need to keep your strength up." She kisses my forehead, then sets off purposefully across the room.

Fredrik tugs the blanket over Markus's chest. "Rest well, brother mine. Father and I will be back shortly. We have a lot to talk about." The prince gives me a respectful nod before walking away. He stops the red-bearded attendant near the door. "Please send a runner to my father and me every half hour with any updates on my brother and his betrothed."

My stomach jumps as all the blood drains from my face. *His WHAT?*

32

The night is rough. Healers and attendants drop by every few hours to look me over and pour tonics down my throat. I suspect their checks are mostly to give them a chance to see the newly returned prince and his intended. Markus sleeps through the visits. The powerful remedies of the Kingdom of the Wolves show their power once again as his cuts heal and the bruises fade as the hours pass.

Even with Fredrik's revelation to occupy my mind, my exhausted body longs for sleep. Oma chatters, nags, and threatens to keep me awake when all I want is oblivion. I thank the heavens she didn't hear about my betrothal status, otherwise I would be subject to constant interrogation and wheedling to get the information out of me. But I don't have any, not really.

It must be the bracelet. I knew it was special, and I've had a growing suspicion it was more than it seemed. But surely Markus doesn't think we're engaged? Not that I'm against it. On the contrary, I can't imagine anything better. But a girl likes to be asked this kind of thing. One doesn't get engaged without realizing it. I know Markus will explain everything once we have a chance to talk, but it doesn't stop my mind from circling through the what-ifs.

The wound in my side continues to draw pinched looks and furrowed brows as day dawns. Markus wakes and immediately looks over at me. Despite the fantastical healing properties of their medications and my drugged state keeping the pain locked away from my mind, his shocked face confirms the sleepless night and injuries have taken their toll.

He utters a string of curses, yanking the closest healer over and demanding to know what's going on. His face goes gray as the healer carefully explains my injury and how it's being treated. That I survived the night is viewed as significant progress, but I'm not out of danger.

Markus holds off on his explosion until the healer walks away—not that it matters. The healing ward isn't that large and sounds carry easily in the stone room.

"How could you not tell me you were stabbed? Do you realize how serious that is? Don't you think I deserved to know?" He tears at his hair, pacing back and forth next to my bed. "You made me think everything was all right. You let me sleep—*sleep*—while you were in pain, when anything could've—" His voice chokes off.

My grandmother leaps up from her chair. "Don't you dare yell at my granddaughter, young man. I don't care who you are. Lisette needs rest. I won't sit here and let you abuse her. If you can't control yourself, you need to leave."

Markus blanches, but I jump in before he can respond.

"Oma, it's all right." I feebly gesture her back to the chair, then look at him. "I should've told you last night, but I didn't want you to worry. I'm sorry. Truce?"

Marks shakes his head. "That won't work this time. You could've—" He shakes his head again. "It's my right to worry about you. You don't get to choose for me. You're not protecting me by pushing me away."

I wasn't—no, he's right. I was making it easy on me because I don't want to hurt him. But if the situation was reversed, I'd kill him for doing that. I blink back tears. "I really am sorry. Truly."

"Good. I'm claiming three argument wins as payment."

"Two."

"Deal." Markus drops a kiss on the top of my head.

Oma plops into her chair, her eyes appraising me as though she's never seen me before. "I see we have a lot to discuss."

Markus and Oma stay by my bed, standing watch and keeping me awake with stories. As the sun climbs the sky, my prognosis worsens. Now that enough time has passed, the healers urge me to rest, but all I can manage is dazing nightmares where invisible monsters chase me until my eyes snap open. A metallic taste fills my mouth that no amount of water will wash away. Shadows appear and disappear from the foot of the bed. Fredrik and King Wilhelm may be among the visitors, but I'm too hazy to be sure. Fevers and chills attack me, leaving me soaked and freezing in turn. I should be terrified, but between the medications and being on the edge of collapsing, I'm too numb to feel anything. I experience everything with detached disinterest, observing changes as though I'm a stranger to my own body. The only thing that breaks through my apathy is Markus's pain. Knowing I'm the cause of his unhappiness is a knife to my heart, and it keeps me fighting when all I want to do is give up.

The stab wound turns an angry red and is hot to the touch. Three healers, including my original healer with the short hair, hold a whispered conversation out of range, before returning with a recommendation they reopen the wound to drain it. Markus insists on coming with me into the small side room, seeming to sense I might slip away if he gives me the opportunity. He strokes my cheek and tells me his favorite moments from our travels and all the adventures he wants to take me on next. I want to cry and curse him and beg him to let me go. But I don't. Because I would do the same thing for him. It's hard, so hard, but I won't give up. He'd never forgive me, and I'd never forgive myself.

Time wanders on. Oma and Markus have hushed conversations across my bed as they try to tempt me with broths and teas. I obligingly sip the offerings though I don't have an appetite.

It's late evening when my mind finally emerges from the dense fog. The medications drag at my thoughts and trip them up, but for the first time since I was carried in here, there's a stirring of strength in my muscles. It's only enough to reach over and touch Markus's hand, but it's something. "Hi, barbarian."

His eyes snap down to mine. "Hi there, flatlander." He rests his hand on my forehead. "You feel cooler. Good. Do you need anything?"

"A new body would be nice."

"I'm rather fond of this one, if you don't mind." He kisses the back of my hand. "Can you eat something?"

I sigh. "If I must."

He gestures to one of the attendants in the room. "I finally convinced your grandmother to get some sleep. She's been watching over you all night. You always seem to end up in a healer's care around me." There's deep pain behind the smile.

"None of this is your fault." I tug weakly on his fingers until he takes my hand. "Believe me, I'd tell you if it was. You know I never miss an opportunity to gloat." That gets a small smile. "Unfortunately, it was my mistake. I forgot one of the first rules you taught me. Make sure they're dead." I grimace. "I'll never do that again."

A growl rumbles in his chest. "If he was still alive, I'd tear him limb from limb."

"I'd help." I wince as I try to sit up.

"Careful. Don't tear your stitches. Here, let me." Markus carefully lifts my upper body, then tucks pillows behind my back to prop me up.

I settle back into the fluffy softness with a groan. "Don't get used to this. I'm only letting you pamper me because I don't want to be a rude guest."

"Don't worry. I plan to put you to work as soon as you can get out of bed." He tucks a strand of hair behind my ear, his hand lingering. "You scared me."

I press his hand to my cheek and close my eyes. "I'm a little bit sorry about that."

"We'll have a proper argument about it when you're feeling better."

"Do we need to argue about this, too?" I touch the bracelet on my wrist.

His fingers trace the beads. "I don't think so, but you can decide after I explain."

The attendant brings a covered mug over, a healer close on his heels.

The healer strikes me as one of those perpetually happy people, always smiling no matter how dire the circumstances. He checks my stitches, declaring the wound is healing well and there's no sign of infection now. He smears more of the green-smelling goop on it before applying a fresh bandage.

He nods to the mug in Markus's hand. "Once you finish that, I'll send over a sleeping dram. The best thing you can do now is rest."

Sleep sounds heavenly. Markus thanks the healer, the tension lifting from his body.

My hands shake as I try to lift the mug, sloshing the liquid over the side. Markus wraps his hand around mine, helping me hold the cup as I sip. I make a face, the bland broth not doing much to excite my tastebuds. "It's not the best food I've had on this trip. But I guess it's not the worst, either."

He chuckles. "I promise I'll have the kitchen make you gallons of spiced chocolate as soon as the healers say you can have it. In the meanwhile, drink up."

My eyes are fighting to stay open as I finish the last few swallows of broth. The attendant brings a cup filled with a dark wine like they gave Markus that first night. I gulp it down, then Markus helps me lay back down on the bed.

He settles back in the chair as I slip into sleep. "Dream something beautiful."

After I wake up from two days of solid sleep, I'm moved to a bedroom suite in another part of the palace. Over the next few days, I quickly turn from invalid to cranky patient. The healers stuck me with bedrest for at least a week so I can't explore the palace. Reading for more than a few minutes gives me a pounding headache. Being bored and trapped in bed with nothing to do does not improve my mood. Thankfully, while I was asleep, Oma and General Kier smoothed out why Lorrian guards were so close to the palace. My grandmother being held hostage and then helping King Wilhelm regain the throne earned us a lot of leeway.

Plenty of people stop by to chat. Besides the novelty of my being a Lorrian princess, Oma and Markus spread the word of my help in overthrowing Garit. There was a very awkward and heavily supervised hour with King Wilhelm, Fredrik, and Markus. At least Markus provided some entertainment for the visit, alternating between squirming with the effort not to interfere, and then bursts of conversation where it was painfully obvious he wanted us all to get along. He's adorable when he's tongue-tied. Both the Wolf Guards and Lorrian guards stop by in small groups. General Kier and Captain Hiller make a point of visiting together; I suspect Oma had her hand in that.

After weeks of traveling with Markus, the polite chitchat feels forced and contrived. Surface smiles and conversations have their place, but now I crave more. Even having my grandmother here doesn't help. The visits with Oma were welcome at first, but she subtly and then not-so-subtly probes about my relationship with Markus. Instead of enjoying my time with her, I have to brace myself to face the onslaught. I've shared everything I'm comfortable telling her, which is more than most people, but not everything. There are some things I want to keep for myself and not share with the world.

Worst of all, Markus and I barely have any moments to ourselves. His father and brother are keeping him understandably busy, catching up and getting to know each other again. But whenever he has a moment to come by my suite, someone else always pops in. I considered locking the doors and pretending nobody is home when he's here, but I suspect they'd knock the doors down. After all our time alone, it's difficult to adjust to the dynamic another person brings to our conversations. It takes considerable effort to avoid our verbal shorthand and inside jokes so the other person doesn't feel left out. Fredrik proves to be especially sensitive to our relationship, lapsing into silence or clumsily changing the topic when we slip.

Today, Markus surprises me by arriving with my breakfast tray. He calls out from the sitting room, "I thought we could get an early start to our day together."

"Day?" I start to scramble out of bed, then roll my eyes

when he gives me a warning look. "I'm fine. Getting myself out of bed won't hurt me."

"I still have two days to spoil you, and I'm taking full advantage of it." He comes into the bedroom and sweeps me into his arms. "Which means no walking when I'm here."

Pretending I don't love every moment, I cross my arms and frown. "When you're not here, I run around the bedroom and jump on the bed."

"Then I'll have to make sure I'm here more often, so you don't have an excuse to do it."

He gives me a lingering kiss, his Markus-smell washing over me as I melt against his chest.

He smiles down at me. "Good morning."

I kiss the tip of his nose. "That's a much nicer way to start my day."

He sets me on the couch, then pulls the table closer so I don't have to reach for the tray. Fruit, griddle cakes soaked in honey, fried dough balls dusted in sugar, and spiced chocolate for two.

"Yum." I grab my fork and dig into the griddle cakes. "What are you going to eat?"

He slides one plate out of my reach. "I'll figure out something."

While I snag one of his griddle cakes off his plate, he filches melon off mine. Exchanging grins, we continue our pilfering, snatching bites between thefts.

I lean back and take a sip of the chocolate, savoring the warmth. "You never explained about the bracelet." I give him a pointed look.

He rubs the back of his neck. "There hasn't been a moment to."

"And you've been skillfully avoiding the topic for

almost a week."

"There's no skill required when we barely have a moment alone."

"We're alone now."

There's a loud knock on the door. Fredrik calls out, "Good morning. Can I join you?"

Markus snorts. "See what I mean? I promise, I'm not avoiding the topic—much. And we're not betrothed."

I figured, but it doesn't stop my heart from sinking the tiniest bit. "Your brother thought we were."

"He was mistaken." Markus takes my hand. "I'd like to ask you to marry me, but there's a lot we need to figure out first."

And just like that, my heart is soaring through the clouds as sunshine floods the room. A silly smile spreads across my face, but I don't care. "I understand it's complicated. But just so you know, I'd like you to ask me."

He gets a sappy grin on his face, his eyes shining. "I'm really glad to know that."

I wrap my arms around his neck as he pulls me into his lap, his lips crashing down on mine. Goosebumps break out over my skin, and I shiver despite the heat blasting between us, sizzling the air.

There's another knock. "Hello? Can I come in?"

Markus breaks away, groaning. "I'm going to kill him."

I try to catch my breath, my hands still clutching his shirt. "Get in line."

The knocking gets louder. "Markus? Lisette?"

I wave my hand at the door. "Better let him in before he calls the guards on us."

Markus yells, "Just a moment." He grabs my robe off the dressing table and holds it out for me. When I lift my eyebrows, he shrugs. "Old fashioned family. You don't want Fredrik fainting from the sight of you in your nightgown."

"Is that all it takes? If I'd known, I would've worn it the first day and scared him away." I grudgingly put it on, then plop back on the couch.

Fredrik beams when Markus opens the door. "Ah, you are here. Good."

Markus sighs. "Did you need something?"

"Is that anyway to greet your brother on a fine day like today?" Fredrik eases past him into the room. "Lisette, good morning. Are you having breakfast? Wonderful, I'm starving."

Our uninvited visitor settles on the couch, crowding me over to one side. Markus shakes his head and takes an armchair, since there's not enough space for the three of us on the tiny couch.

Fredrik pops a strawberry into his mouth. "Father wants us to meet him at the top of the hour. He's taking us on a tour of the west farmland."

Markus's brow furrows. "He doesn't need me for that. I was planning to spend the day with Lisette."

"He's insisting. After everything with Garit, he's obsessed with checking every inch of the kingdom. He'll probably have us visiting towns and inspecting roadways next."

"We don't need to do everything immediately. I'll go talk to him."

When Markus leans down to kiss me on the cheek, I mutter, "Are you sure you're the younger brother?"

"Sometimes I wonder." He straightens. "I'll be back shortly."

A moment after the door closes, Fredrik jumps up. "I

should go too.”

“Wait a moment, if you please.” I fold my hands in my lap, tilting my head to the side as he reluctantly sinks down in his seat. “You don’t have to do this.”

He gives a light laugh. “Do what? What are you talking about?” He looks at me, then to Markus’s empty chair, then the dishes sitting on the table, then back to Markus’s chair.

“I should be well enough to travel in a few days.” A stone settles in my stomach at the reminder. “Oma and I will go home. And Markus will stay here.”

“He’s not going with you?”

The raw hope on his face makes me forgive him a little for all his interference these past few days. A little—but not completely. I’m not a saint, after all.

“You could have asked him. He’s missed you and your father. Why do you think he never went farther than the border? He wanted to come home.”

Fredrik stares at his hands. “He should have. It was his choice to leave. To stay away.”

“You all lost a lot of time. Nothing can change that, but you can do better from now on. Forgive him. And forgive yourselves.”

“We’re working on it. Having him home has been a dream come true.” He looks up at me. “But he loves you.”

“We have a lot to figure out.” I grin. “You haven’t seen the last of me. But these few days will be the last I see of Markus for a long time. It would be nice if I could actually spend time with him before I go home.”

He nods slowly. “I’ll talk to Father.” He smiles. “I’m not the only one who’s been worried about Markus leaving.” Fredrik stands and kisses my hand. “I look forward to getting to know you better on your next visit. For now, I’ll send

Markus back. And see if I can distract your grandmother.”

I clasp my hands to my chest and beam. “You are my new favorite person.”

“Remember that the next time I interrupt you and Markus.”

“Absolutely not. I have a terrible memory when something doesn’t benefit me. Markus should’ve warned you about that.”

“I am thus educated.” He chuckles as he opens the door. “You’re going to be fun to have around.”

By the time Markus returns to my suite, I’ve changed into my leathers and red cloak. They’re totally impractical for the palace, but it’s comforting wearing them, like I’ve gotten a piece of myself back.

I grab his hand and drag him back to the hallway. “Come on, we’re making a break for it.”

He stops. “You’re still on bedrest.”

“A couple of days won’t make a difference. Besides, I only want to go as far as the gardens.” I lean back, putting my full weight behind it, but he’s immovable.

“Only if you promise to take it easy and tell me if you get tired.”

“You’re highly annoying. Most men would jump at the chance to steal a few kisses in the garden with their sweetheart.”

“I’ll only be annoying today and tomorrow. After that, if the healers clear you, I’ll help you if want to climb the castle walls or jump from the towers into the moat again."

"We're going to have to work on this rule-following tendency of yours. It's definitely going to get in the way of our adventures." I blow a curl away from my face. "Fine. I promise. Now will you come?"

"One more thing." He scoops me up into his arms as I squeal. "Now I'm ready."

I laugh as I shake my head. "You're really taking this whole thing too seriously."

"I just want an excuse to have you in my arms." He sets off at a brisk stride down the hall. "Are you sure you want to go to the gardens? It's going to rain soon."

"That's perfect. Less chance we'll run into someone there."

"Worried we'll be interrupted again?"

I nuzzle his neck, feeling his heart skip a beat. "Perhaps."

We draw some curious stares and a lot of amused ones as Markus carries me through the castle and out into the gardens. The sky is filled with gray clouds, the air heavy with the promised rain. But the summer heat makes it comfortable to walk through the rosebushes and trees. The gardens are wilder than the ones at home; the plants growing across the paths and spilling on top of each other. I settle against Markus's chest and enjoy the rhythmic beating of his heart as we wind our way down the paths. We end up at a small gazebo at the end of one of the side paths. Braziers set around the edges fill the space with warmth, and a stone bench with cushions makes for a comfortable spot to lounge.

Markus leans back and closes his eyes with a sigh. "I have to admit, it's nice to have a moment's peace. I love my father, but he's so stubborn."

"So that's where you get it." I nudge him. "After you left, Fredrik said he was going to talk to him."

"That would be a major change in attitude. Did you threaten him?"

"I told him I would show him my nightgown if he didn't help you." I snicker. "He's just excited to have you back. I can understand it. I want you all to myself, too."

He takes my hand and holds it against his cheek. "I hate that you're leaving. I wish I could go with you."

I press against his side and lean my head against his shoulder. "So do I. It'll be so strange traveling out in the open like a normal person. No sneaking around or being terrified of being discovered at any moment. Nobody trying to hunt us down. It would be wonderful to have you there so we could find out what being normal for a few weeks feels like. But we'll write. And you'll visit soon. It won't be too long."

We both know any time is too long, but leave it unsaid. Our upcoming separation is hard enough without lingering on it. If I wasn't worried about Father starting a war if I didn't come home, they wouldn't be able to drag me away. And I do miss my family. It'll be good to see everyone again. I just wish Markus could come with me, but his family needs him, too. They haven't seen him in years. It would be cruel for him to leave again so soon. And once we get everything sorted, we'll never have to leave each other again.

At least, that's what I tell myself. If I don't have hope to cling to, I'll go mad. But after everything Markus and I have gone through, we'll make it work. We always do.

Markus says, "I owe you an explanation about the bracelet."

My heart speeds up. "You've certainly kept me in suspense."

"We use our jewelry to express our relationships to each other. A father will give his daughter a necklace, a mother gives her a ring. Sons get daggers and rings."

I purse my lips. "Girls can't like daggers?"

The corner of his mouth twitches. "It's outdated, I know. Sometimes we stick to traditions even when they need to change."

I harrumph, but let him continue.

"We use bracelets for friendships and romance. What I said before is true. The beads and stones describe the relationship between the wearer and the giver. The different colors and engravings are for different events and milestones between the people. Some are traditional, and some are personal to the people."

He holds my hand out in front of us and runs his fingers over the bracelet, sending shivers across my skin. It's still as lovely as the day he gave it to me, not a scratch or mark on it. The braided silver wires shine even in the dim light. The blood-red stone sits between two thin metal beads engraved with coriander flowers, then a clear stone on both sides, capped off on either end with two more metal beads engraved with the phases of the moon.

"The moon beads at each end are traditional. It's a promise we'll be together, no matter how life changes." He kisses my fingertips. "The two clear stones are quartz, also traditional. They're a symbol of balance, unity. The two stones are separate, yet perfectly matched. They also show a willingness to be open and truthful."

I grin. "It's a good thing we already know how to bicker."

"Are you implying that being honest means we'll disagree all the time?"

"More that it's hard for you to accept that I'm right and you're wrong. But if we're supposed to be truthful" —I shrug— "I guess I'll have to keep arguing until you agree. It's my duty, after all."

He chuckles. "The flowers on the beads, as you know, are coriander." His lips brush the inside of my wrist and I shiver. "In that moment, when I was terrified I would lose you, I knew I loved you. That I would do anything— sacrifice anything—if it would keep you alive."

He moves to my neck, his lips feather light. "The red stone is my favorite."

"It's not for my signature color?" I ask faintly, surprise distracting me from the delicious tingling spreading through me at his every touch.

"It is your color … "

His breath tickles my skin, his lips touching a particularly sensitive spot behind my ear, my toes curling in my boots.

"Because of what you are. Your courage. Your passion. Willingness to give into trouble without thinking twice. The stubbornness that won't yield just because it's easy. You're the fire that ignites in my heart. The reason it beats."

Love and warmth mingle with just a touch of fear. These feelings are so big. I've never felt anything like it before. I don't know if I can hold them all without shattering. I swallow hard, tears stinging my eyes. "You know I hate to cry."

"You're beautiful when you cry." He kisses my closed eyes. "I wanted to tell you this sooner, but I didn't want to scare you. You were already going through so much."

"It's a good thing you didn't. I would've had a hard time being mad at you if I knew all the sweet things you were thinking. But, Markus" —I put my hand on his chest— "that wouldn't scare me. I love you. Knowing you feel the same way, that you love me too, is the most wonderful thing in the world."

The tips of his ears go red. "There's a bit more to it. I said we use bracelets for friendships and romance. The different arrangements mean different things. There's a lot of complicated rules. Most of them are cryptic and take too long to figure out."

I grin and nudge him in the side, impatient for him to get on to it. "But not all of them." My heart speeds up.

"The arrangement I gave you means I've bound myself to you. In my culture, it would mean we're betrothed." Markus's eyes soften. "I knew you didn't understand the customs or what the bracelet meant, so you weren't constrained by it. But I also know there will never be anyone else for me. I said the bracelet was my promise to you and I meant it."

My breath catches. "Oh, Markus."

Now I do shatter, everything hitting me all at once. Like a wave swelling and rising to unimaginable heights before crashing on the shore. There's no pain; I'm instantly reformed into myself, but new. Someone who can hold these infinite feelings and not lose herself.

"Smart, assertive, and used to giving orders. It was impossible not to fall in love with you." His eyes twinkle, full of mischief and laughter.

Is that how he sees me? I bite my lip. "I'm not the girl you imagine. I don't know what I'm doing half the time, and I'm usually causing a disaster the rest of it."

"Do you think I really don't know you?" He tips my chin up and stares deep into my eyes. "I fell in love with the girl who yelled at the forest. The one willing to risk her life for the grandmother she loved, and the strangers who needed her help. It broke my heart to see how scared you were after Lutach. Yah, I was happy when you looked to me for comfort because it meant you trusted me. But I was even happier when your wounds healed and you didn't need to." His hand caresses my cheek. "I don't want to be with someone who needs me. I want to be with someone who wants to be with me. That can stand on her own, but knows we're stronger when we stand together. That I'm always here for her those times when she needs me."

I shake my head. "You're wrong. I always need you. When you leave, you take my heart with you. I wasn't looking for love, but it found me, and now it's everything."

The heat in his eyes blazes and he cradles my face in his hands. Markus touches me so tenderly my body turns to fire. I can't speak, can barely breathe. He whispers my name before capturing my mouth in a searing kiss. Fire and energy and passion all wrapped into one. He kisses me like a man who's been starved. A shudder ripples through his body. I lose myself in a blaze of heat and love.

When he breaks away with a gasp, I whimper, desperate for more. He presses his forehead to mine and we both let out a shaky breath. It started raining without either of us noticing, the pattering of drops a gentle background symphony.

I whisper, "I know there's a lot to figure out between us. But just for today, can we pretend I'm not leaving in a few days? You're Markus, and I'm Lisette, and the biggest thing we have to decide is whether we should stargaze in the gardens or from the tower."

He presses a kiss to my forehead. "I'd like that."

Markus tucks the edges of my cloak around me, then wraps his arm around me. I snuggle into his side, resting my head on his shoulder as we watch the storm.

Oma breezes into my room. "Good afternoon, darling."
She's unsurprised to find me lying on the sitting room floor.

She's already made herself at home in the Wolf Palace.
Her white hair is tucked up in a neat twist, her fringed shawl
embroidered with animals, and her bright yellow and green
dress brings spring into the room with her. Her nose and
cheeks have a healthy pink from her walks outside the castle
walls.

I twist my head to the side. "Hi, Oma. What's the latest
news from the outside world?"

"The Lorrian guards are dicing with the Wolf Guards in
the evenings."

*Mayhap there's hope for our kingdoms to get along after
all.* "I hope we're winning."

"I'd be ashamed to show my face otherwise." Oma
moves a plate off the couch and takes a seat. "General Kier
and Captain Hiller are pretending they don't know it's going
on, but they're planning on stumbling across the game
tonight. The general doesn't want the men up late since

we're leaving tomorrow."

A weight settles in my chest. I roll my eyes upward. "Have you ever noticed the cracks in the ceiling look just like a rabbit?"

"I can't say that I have. You should point it out to Wilhelm when he arrives. I'm sure he'll find it as fascinating as you appear to."

I bolt up. "King Wilhelm? Markus's dad? The Wolf King, King Wilhelm?"

She tilts her head to the side. "Yes, that Wilhelm."

"He's coming here?"

"He'll be here any moment. He said something about wanting to talk to you."

"Why didn't you tell me?" I grab a discarded towel off the back of the armchair and stuff it behind one of the couch cushions. The tray of leftover tea things on the sitting-room table gets shoved under the bed. "I wasn't expecting visitors. Why is he coming here? He already thanked me. What else could he want?"

Oma pats her hair. "Who knows, darling. The man always looks so serious, it's impossible to tell what he's thinking. He'd get along well with your father."

Why is he coming? Why did he wait until now? Does Markus know his father wants to see me? Should I try to find him? No—there's no time. Oma can find him. Or it might be better if he's not here. Does he want to warn me away from Markus?

"Calm down, Lisette. I'm sure everything is perfectly fine." She raises an eyebrow. "But if you want to make a good impression, see if there's something in your closet that doesn't look like you've slept in it."

Burn it, burn it, burn it. I dive into the closet and find a day dress one of the court ladies loaned me for my stay. The blush rose garment hangs loose on my shoulders, but it's a vast improvement over the wrinkled mess I had on before.

Oma is helping me tie up the back when there's a knock on the door. She gives my arm a reassuring squeeze, then opens the door for King Wilhelm.

His appearance has gone through a drastic change in the days since I last saw him. He's transformed from the malnourished prisoner to the picture of kingly vigor. The hollows in his cheeks have filled out and the bruises have disappeared. There's the feeling of barely restrained energy as he walks across the room, his black fur robe rustling against the carpet.

The Wolf King inclines his head to my grandmother. "Queen Emera."

"Emera, please. As you said, we don't need to stand on formality. Won't you please join us?"

My grandmother gracefully gets us seated in the sitting room, nudging an abandoned book on the floor under the armchair without calling attention to it. She draws the Wolf King into a discussion on the weather we should expect during our trip home while I sit silently, my heart hammering. I swallow, trying to relieve the dryness in my throat as wild speculations fly around my mind.

Too soon, Oma shakes out her shawl and wraps it around her shoulders. "I imagine you two have a lot to talk about and I want to speak with General Kier about our arrangements for tomorrow."

I send her a pleading look, but she just smiles and kisses me on the cheek.

She whispers, "You trekked through the Black Forest and saved a kingdom. You're braver than you think."

Oma slips out of the room, leaving me alone with the Wolf King. I try to believe her words, but brave is the last thing I feel right now. All my life, the Wolf King has been the dark shadow that threatened the border of our kingdom. A boogie man in the night my sister and I used to scare each other after dark. It was easy to forget that when he was a prisoner in his own dungeon, but this man is every inch the Wolf King. I don't know how he feels about me, or me and Markus. Especially since he hasn't seen his son in years. Not to mention the little thing about me being Lorrian. Our kingdoms haven't spoken in generations. Everything's changing, but that doesn't mean feelings can change overnight.

He clears his throat. "The healers tell me your recovery is going well."

"Yes." *Say something else, fluff brains.* "Your kingdom has amazing healing. I mean, the healers are amazing. And the medicines." *Never mind, keep your mouth closed.*

"You're welcome to stay longer. If you need more time to recover from your, ah, injury."

"Thank you, but I've fully healed. I'm sure my parents are worried about me and Oma—err, my grandmother."

"General Kier sent word so they know you're safe. They're sending a contingent to meet you at the border." At my confused look, he adds, "We have courier birds. They can carry brief messages to your palace in a day."

It would've been nice if someone had told me that. "Ah. I'm glad. They won't worry now."

"Parents always worry. It's what we do."

What does that mean? Is he trying to tell me something? He's worried about Markus? I'm worried about Markus, too. Does he think I don't know Markus has a lot of changes happening in his life right now? So do I. Or mayhap he's trying to tell me he's worried about me. Is it a good worry or a bad worry?

He leans back, then frowns. He pulls the towel from behind the cushion and sets it on the floor, his brow furrowed.

Heats floods my cheeks. *The heavens should strike me down now and put me out of my misery.*

"My son had a talk with me."

I twist my hands in my lap, trying to remember all the decorum Mother tried to shove in my head and I promptly shoved out. "Which one?"

A smile bursts across his face, lessening the harsh lines. "Fredrik. I'll have to get used to that again. It's a good thing to have to get used to."

I give him a tentative smile.

"All those years, wondering what happened, thinking Markus was dead." His face grows haggard as he looks into the past. "Cursing myself for not protecting him." He shakes his head. "We lost too much time we'll never get back, and that's my fault. Having him home now, I can't describe the joy it brings me. And I have you to thank for it."

A knot loosens in my stomach. "I can't accept thanks for something I didn't do. Markus brought himself back. He knew what taking me to the palace would mean." I look down. "He never gave up hope he would be reunited with you and Fredrik one day. He was always trying to find his way home. I just gave him the excuse."

"Be that as it may, you brought him here. And you rescued me and Fredrik from the dungeon when you could have left us. You've proven yourself to be more than a friend to my family, and we are eternally in your debt. So." King

Wilhelm claps his hands together. "I've come to offer you a boon. Anything you ask for within my power to grant, it's yours."

I try to keep the shock off my face. Of all the ways I expected this conversation to go, this was not it. *Mayhap I need to work on my optimism.*

My thoughts immediately jump to Markus. I could ask the king to let him live in Lorria with me. But that would tear Markus away from his family. I can't do that to him. I can't sacrifice his happiness for mine. Knowing I'm the reason he's miserable would smother us. Even asking him to visit after he's just returned home would be cruel to all of them. I can't make Markus choose between me and his family. That's a losing scenario for all of us. Markus and I will figure something out eventually. It doesn't have to be decided today.

His blessing for Markus and I to get married would be wonderful, but I don't want it to be forced. I want the king to give his blessing because he's happy for us, not because he's paying a debt.

There's nothing else I can think of. I don't need gold or jewels. Markus is happy to let Fredrik have the throne and so am I. A second son marrying a second daughter will raise a lot less opposition from councils and other busybodies trying to make it their business.

The king's looking at me expectantly. *What do I say?*

"My dagger," I blurt out. "Or rather, your dagger. I'd like to keep it. Please." When I couldn't find it in my room, I asked Markus where it was. He told me regretfully, with Fredrik hanging on every word, they locked it in the treasury since it really is a family heirloom, passed down from father to son.

His eyebrows go up. "That's the only thing you want?"

I nod firmly. "Yes." It's an heirloom to them, but it's precious to me.

"I'll have it brought to you this afternoon." He studies me, then nods at my wrist. "Did my son explain what that means?"

After a lot of prodding. "He did." I bury my fists in my skirt. "He also said I'm not bound by it since I'm not part of your kingdom."

His eyes narrow. "But you love him. You want to marry him."

I gulp, forcing my fingers to relax. "I do. More than anything."

"And yet, you didn't request my permission when I gave you the perfect opportunity. I wonder why that is."

Time to leap. "I will marry Markus. He loves me, and I love him. It's that simple." I sit up straight, my fear disappearing. "I'd marry him today, but the world presents difficulties. Our kingdoms have been enemies for hundreds of years. I've come to respect and like your kingdom, but will Lorria? They believe you kidnapped my grandmother and it will take a lot of convincing otherwise. Can it put aside the old fears after all the hostility? Can you? You've been very gracious and welcoming these past two weeks. Will it last, or does it disappear at the first misstep? If Markus and I were anybody else, we wouldn't have to worry about these things. But being who we are, we can't escape these concerns without leaving our families behind. And we're not willing to do that. We will marry, but our kingdoms need peace first." I collapse back in the chair, my forehead damp.

King Wilhelm's expression doesn't change. "A heavy

weight for young love. Are you sure it is? Love? Perhaps the extreme circumstances have fooled you into believing it is, but normal life will reveal your true feelings."

Since I've asked myself the same thing, I don't take offense at his question. "I can't imagine life with Markus will ever be normal, but I hope we can treasure those moments. I love him and I always will."

"And if I forbid Markus from ever seeing you again?" The king's face is unreadable.

I swallow the sharp pain at the thought and answer honestly. "I'd ask myself why you'd do that if you love him. I would never make him choose between me and his family. But if you force him to, I won't choose for him, even though I think it would be a kindness." I square my shoulders and meet his eyes without flinching. "I took his choice away before. I was wrong. I won't make that mistake again." A smirk steals over my lips. "Also, my father taught me long ago to never give an order you know will be disobeyed."

That earns me a smile. "I can see why he likes you." He nods to himself. "You've given me a lot to think about. It's time for the hatred between our kingdoms to end. A sign of good faith from my kingdom to yours is in order."

The Wolf King leaves my room with a promise he'll have an answer tomorrow. Hope fills me. He seems committed. This could be a major step forward in improving relations between the kingdoms—and a major step forward for Markus and I getting married. I have no idea what he has in mind, but it's going to have to be considerable if he wants to impress my father with his intentions of friendship.

I can't wait to find out what it is.

35

Home.

The Lorrian palace has never been more beautiful. The golden stone is a beacon of sunshine calling me to it. Rolling green fields are broken up with gardens and roads. We're too far away, but I swear I can see people hurrying in and out of the doors to make ready for our arrival. And yet … everything is a little smaller than I remember. The overgrown meadows are tamer after seeing the true wilderness of the Black Forest. A thread of uneasiness goes through me as I look at everything anew. I thought when I was home everything would feel exactly as I remember it, but something is different. Everything is the same, but I've changed.

Normal jitters, nothing to worry about. I look over at the Wolf King's gesture of goodwill. "Are you ready for this?"

Markus tugs at his collar. "I'm fine. It's Fredrik you should keep an eye on."

His brother looks green around the edges. "I think the general poisoned the eggs."

The Wolf King sending both his sons—and one of them heir to the throne—without an entourage certainly makes a statement. Messengers have been appearing with increasing frequency as our party gets closer to the palace. After the first three messages resulted in longer and longer lists of questions, General Kier rode ahead to brief the council and my family on everything that transpired in the Black Forest. Or at least, most of it. We agreed she'd downplay my injury, knowing some things are better told when I'm standing there in front of them, healthy and whole. I'd prefer the two Wolves in our party not be met with swords at the palace.

General Kier trots up on her horse. "We'll arrive in two hours."

I shift my weight from side to side. "My parents are going to greet us?"

The general says in an overly patient tone, "And your sister. Then our guests will be shown to their rooms and given a chance to freshen up while you have tea with your family. Dinner will be a small reception tonight, followed by a larger banquet tomorrow night."

The itinerary hasn't changed in weeks, but hearing it again doesn't soothe the butterflies in my stomach. "We should continue on, then. You know how Mother hates it when I'm late."

The general clears her throat. "Would you like to check in with your grandmother first?" She looks pointedly at my outfit.

Heat rushes into my cheeks. I've been wearing my leathers for so long I'd forgotten about them. My parents will be on edge enough without seeing me in trousers. "Of course, thank you."

She cracks a smile before wheeling her horse around.

I sigh. "That's my cue, gentleman. Time to be a princess again."

Markus takes my hand, giving it a light squeeze. "Everything will be fine." He looks over at his brother. "We should change too."

"Finally, some good news." Fredrik yanks on the hem of his leather shirt. "I don't know how you two can stand this stuff."

I snicker as Markus slaps his brother on the back. "It's better than those fussy court outfits."

"If you like sweating and itching. I'm wearing my normal clothes on the way home."

I roll my eyes. "If you're going to insist on being the pampered little prince, you might as well ride in the carriage."

Fredrik gives an exaggerated sniff. "I would have, but as a manly prince, it's my duty to protect you."

I raise my eyebrow. "Is that what you were doing when that tiny snake crossed the path and you ran away shrieking for help?"

Markus turns his laugh into a cough.

His brother lifts his nose in the air. "I was scouting the perimeter for threats. You and Markus were too busy making eyes at each other to notice anything."

"I can't help it if your brother has beautiful eyes." I grab Markus's shirt and tug him forward. "I'm helpless against them."

Fredrik groans as I kiss Markus, letting my lips linger.

Markus nuzzles my ear. "You're the one with beautiful eyes. I could spend hours gazing into them."

He kisses me again as Fredrik groans louder.

"This is what I'm talking about. The two of you could

ride off a cliff and not notice because you're too busy ogling each other."

I smirk. "Don't worry, Fredrik. One day you'll find a woman to gawk at. Of course, you won't know what to do with her, but Markus can give you some pointers."

Markus nods seriously. "Insults worked really well with Lisette. And poisoning her, that was a big hit."

I eye Fredrik doubtfully. "Perhaps he should stick with bribery. I'm not sure he can manage a proper insult."

Markus wrinkles his forehead, then nods. "True. Mayhap if he practiced, he could get better at it."

Fredrik shakes his head. "I'd rather not put my beloved in peril to convince her I love her. I'll stick with the normal courting rituals. Insults and poison can be my backup plan if she proves to be as odd as Lisette."

I look at Markus. "I've just been insulted."

He nods. "That's what it sounded like."

It's my turn to slap Fredrik on the back. "You're getting the hang of this."

Fredrik shrugs, trying to hide his smile. "Don't you have a frilly dress to change into?"

"Right. We all know it's bad form to keep the king and queen waiting." I put my hand on the back of Markus's neck and pull him in for one more kiss, tasting his lips, craving more, but knowing now's not the time. "Don't worry, everyone will love you."

"Are you telling me, or yourself?" Markus presses his forehead against mine, his hands gently running up and down my arms. "Everything will be fine. We'll figure it out. We always do."

The words are confident, but the tightness in his jaw and shoulders betrays his worries. Even so, he's right. We will figure it out.

"See you at the castle." I wink at the boys. "Prepare yourselves for battle."

Oma pats my knee. "Stop fussing, Lisette. You look beautiful." My grandmother could make a burlap sack look elegant, but today's ensemble makes it easy. Her blue and lavender patterned dress falls in graceful folds, her hair braided into a crown around her head, with small touches of gold jewelry for accents.

The pale yellow dress is beautiful—my favorite among the clothes Mother sent with the messenger. I must have lost weight since I left home because the shoulders and waist are too loose, but the sleeves are annoyingly tight. It's impossible to get comfortable. I left my blond curls loosely tied back, nervous that any attempt at something more complicated would be a mess by the time I made it to the palace.

The carriage rocks gently as it rolls toward the entrance. Everyone's gathered on the stairs, ready for our arrival. Despite our astonishing guests, it's a small group of my family and a few staff. I'm not sure how to interpret the lack of pomp. My already-stretched nerves are ready to break. Mother and Father stand together, beautiful and elegant as always. Maddie and the rest of the people watch our approaching carriage with eager faces.

Ice water trickles into my stomach. "Do you think they'll be nice to Markus? I—I don't want them to blame him for anything I did. What should I tell them?"

"I find in situations like these, the truth is usually the best option."

I chew on my thumbnail. "All of it?" I can't imagine Markus accidentally poisoning me will go over well with my parents.

My grandmother frowns. "Perhaps not all of it. At least, not right away."

The carriage rolls to a stop.

Here we go.

I step out, careful to keep my head up and my skirts clear just as Mother taught me. I spare a quick glance at Markus and Fredrik dismounting from their horses. Both look handsome in their matching red and silver tunics, their silver crowns glinting in the sunlight.

Up close, the dark circles under my parents' eyes are obvious, their skin pale. My gut twists. *Were the signs of exhaustion always there and I didn't notice? Or am I the cause of their recent worries?*

Before I can curtsy, Mother throws her arms around me. "Lisette."

She gives a small sob as she buries her face in my hair. Tears fill my eyes as I embrace her, the pain in my chest disappearing. Father wraps his arms around both of us, and Maddie joins the crushing hug. We're all crying and talking over each other. Eventually we disentangle ourselves, remembering we have guests.

My father nods to Fredrik and Markus. "My apologies for the delay." He looks them over. "Which one of you do I have to thank for bringing my daughter and mother safely home?"

I draw Markus forward. "May I introduce Prince Markus Von Dein of the Kingdom of the Wolves? He guided me through the Black Forest and helped rescue Oma."

Markus gives my father a formal court bow, clicking his heels together as he sweeps his hand back. "King Stefan. It's my pleasure to meet you."

Father offers his hand. "Thank you for looking out for Lisette. I don't yet know what dangers you two faced, but that she's standing here today speaks well of you."

Markus smiles at me as they clasp hands. "She's quite capable of taking care of herself, but I was happy to assist."

My father lifts an eyebrow, then turns to Fredrik. "And you must be Prince Fredrik. Welcome to Lorria."

Fredrik repeats the bow. "Thank you, King Stefan. We're looking forward to spending time at your beautiful home. My father, King Wilhelm, wishes to convey his deepest apologies for the distress caused to you and your family because of our uncle's actions. We hope our kingdoms can turn this into a chance for a new beginning."

"Hmm, yes. We have much to discuss. But I'm sure you both would like to get settled first. Will you join us for a late supper?" Considering today's events have been reviewed and approved over and over again, my father manages to make it sound like a genuine invitation instead of a scheduled event.

Fredrik and Markus of course agree, and then there's a flurry of servants descending on the baggage while others escort the princes to their rooms. Fredrik gives me a confident smile and a wink. Markus touches his hand to his heart before turning to follow his brother.

I bury my fingers in my skirt as they leave. It strikes me how alone they are here with no one from their kingdom. The Wolf King didn't even send guards with them. Whether that was a good decision remains to be seen, but he's committed to showing his trust and desire to strike up a friendship with Lorria. I'm regretting his faith in my kingdom. While I'd like to think nobody from Lorria would harm guests under our protection, old hatreds are not easily forgotten.

General Kier pauses next to me. "The guards who went to the Kingdom of the Wolves have all volunteered to help the princes while they're visiting. They're going to take rotating shifts outside their quarters."

I throw my arms around her. "Thank you."

She stiffens. "Yes, um." The general steps out of my embrace, straightening her shirt, trying to repair her wounded dignity. "If you need anything, Princess, let myself or one of the guards know."

I beam after her retreating back. *I knew she liked me.*

My father offers me his arm. "Lisette, walk with us."

Mother loops her arm through my other one. They guide me through the entryway and up the stairs. Feeling a bit like a prisoner being led off to the gallows, I glance over my shoulder. It doesn't help my fears that Maddie looks a bit worried. Oma is the only one who is unperturbed, ushering my sister off in the other direction.

When we turn toward Father's study, my mouth goes dry. The room is strictly off limits to us until we're in trouble. Serious trouble. The bookshelves and dark wood paneling are only interrupted by the wall of windows behind his large black desk. The rest of the room is devoid of furniture, forcing the condemned to stand in front of the desk and squint into the light.

Except today. A small settee and two armchairs are crowded into the previously vacant corner. Mother sits next to me on the settee, while Father takes an armchair across from us. He pulls it so close that our knees are almost touching.

Mother takes my hand between hers. I swallow hard, burying my other hand underneath my leg, bracing for the upcoming interrogation.

Father leans forward, setting his elbows on his knees, hands folded in front of him. "Lisette, are you all right? Do you want to talk after you've rested?"

His concern catches me off guard. "I'm fine. General Kier was very careful not to set too strenuous a pace on the way home." We were practically crawling for the first part of the journey until I convinced her I was fully mended and could handle a normal pace. I want to get this over with. If we don't talk now, I'll spend every minute waiting for the summons.

Mother squeezes my hand. "Are you truly? Your letters and the reports were very … circumspect about what happened in the Wolf Palace. We know you were hurt. Do you need to see the doctor? Is there anything we can do? What happened? How did you get hurt?"

"I'm completely healed now, I promise. Their kingdom has incredible medicines. They can fix a small cut in a few hours." I debate how much to tell them, weighing Oma's advice to parse out the details over time. *No—better to be honest.* "One of the enemy guards stabbed me in the side with a sword." I rub the spot, remembering the pain and surprise when the sword slid through my skin.

Mother gasps, her hands clamping onto mine. My father rears back in his seat, his face pale.

I hurry on. "I'm fine now, really. It was bad, but the healers at the palace stitched me up right away and put me on bedrest. A lot of bedrest. Much, much more than was needed.”

Mother says, “Stitches,” like it’s a curse.

Father looks me over as though trying to spot blood on my dress. “The doctor needs to check you. I’ll send for him.”

As he rises, I grab his hand with my free one and tug him back to his seat.

“I’m really fine. If it’ll make you feel better, he can check the scar, but there’s no hurry. Their medicines work so well, they’re practically magic.”

He sinks slowly into his chair, watching me. “It would put my mind at ease for the doctor to see you. But if you say it can wait, then it can wait.”

Another surprise. “Truly, I’m fine.”

Mother puts her arm around my shoulder and hugs me. “I’m so sorry you had to go through that, and so thankful you’re healthy and here now. I’ll send a letter to the Wolf King and his healers to thank them for caring for you.”

“Oma can tell you their names. I think she made friends with everyone in the palace before we left.” When my father scowls, I put my hand on his arm. “Don’t blame Oma or General Kier for not telling you. I asked them not to. I wanted to be here, so you could see me safe and not worry needlessly.”

“Worry?” Mother gives a strangled sob. “We’ve been frantic since the night you left. We’re your parents and we love you. Of course we’re going to worry when you run away to sneak through an enemy kingdom with a reputation of brutality and murder.”

“But they’re not like that at all! They’re just like us. All they want is peace.” I twist to face her. “Their people tell stories about us the same way we do about them. They think we’re monsters that want to hurt them. The border towns blame every misfortune on Wolf mischief, but they do the same to us. When was the last time there was an actual attack by the Kingdom of the Wolves? We have no reason to be afraid of each other."

Mother shakes her head. "It's hard to believe."

"That's why the King Wilhelm sent Markus and Fredrik here. Alone. Completely unguarded. You'd have to be crazy to send your only sons to your enemy if you weren't trying to prove your goodwill, right?"

Father's eyes narrow. "To lose his crown to a traitor, and then send his heirs unguarded." His fingers drum on his knee. "He's very foolish."

"But he's not." I struggle for the words, trying to capture the Wolf King in a way my parents can understand. "To them, family is everything. It creates blind spots. He couldn't conceive of his brother trying to wrestle the crown away from him because it would be like—like me trying to take Maddie's place as heir. It's laughable. And that's why his sons are here. Because he's showing he trusts us with the most precious thing in the world. That he trusts me when I said Markus and Fredrik would be safely returned home after their visit."

"And they will be. We'd never harm a guest, you know that. But whether we can trust the Kingdom of the Wolves is another matter entirely."

I stiffen, my jaw clenching. *Because he always has to think of the good of the kingdom first.* "Isn't it better for Lorria to make peace with an enemy and gain an ally?"

"Certainly, but that's not what I'm worried about. If my daughter is going to marry a Wolf Prince, I need to know he's worthy of her." He smiles, a hint of sadness in it. "After all, you deserve someone who loves you and will always put you first.”

Tears prick my eyes. “I didn’t say anything about marriage.”

“I wouldn’t be a very good king—or a good father—if I couldn’t spot the obvious.” He moves to my other side on the settee, then puts his arm around my shoulders. “Markus seems like a fine young man. I look forward to getting to know him. If it takes a treaty with our enemy to guarantee your happiness, then that’s what we’ll do.”

It’s like I’m seeing him for the first time. While I was in the Kingdom of the Wolves, I’d gained a better appreciation of what Father goes through ruling the kingdom and the hard choices he has to make. But even then, I’d never thought of him as an ally. He’s my father, and he loves me, of course. But I thought he always put the kingdom first and always would. Then he goes and shows me how much he loves me, that my happiness means everything to him.

“Thank you.” I wrap my arms around him, sniffing as tears stream down my face. “I love you both so much.”

“I love you, too.” He kisses the top of my head.

Mother brushes the tears from my cheeks. “The heavens know we’re not perfect, but we would do anything for you. You have to know that, darling.”

I’m starting to realize that. My father passes me a clean handkerchief and I dab at my face.

Mother touches the bracelet on my wrist. “That’s lovely. Did Markus give it to you?”

A smile tugs at my lips. “Yes. It’s a traditional gift in their kingdom. They use the beads and stones to represent different events in a person’s life.” It’s an opening for them to ask me about everything that happened in the Kingdom of the Wolves—but they don’t take it.

Mother says, "What a beautiful tradition. So sentimental and meaningful. It's a shame we never developed a similar custom."

Father chuckles. "I'm sure once the nobility learns about it, it'll become the newest fashion craze."

"Too true. They seize on any excuse to buy more jewelry."

What are they waiting for? I twist my fingers in my skirt. "You haven't asked about my journey through the Black Forest."

Mother says, "When you're ready, we'd like to know the full story. Until then, it's enough to know you're safe and home."

It would be easy to lie. Nobody but Markus and I know what happened until I found the Lorrian guards by the palace. But I tell them. Not just because they deserve to know, but because I want them to. I want them to understand what I saw and learned while I was in the Kingdom of the Wolves, so they can see it through my eyes instead of the nightmarish falsehoods built up over the years. They don't interrupt as I pour everything out, ending with the Wolf King's visit.

"Um, I want to say … To tell you … Both of you …" I take a deep breath. "I'm sorry. For leaving. And not trusting you to save Oma, or waiting for you to come up with a plan. I know you have to look out for the good of the kingdom, but I also know you love us and will always protect us." I sniff, my voice cracking. "I'm sorry. I wasn't thinking. I was being selfish."

Father squeezes my shoulder. "I'm sorry, too. You were upset and frightened, and I didn't respect your feelings enough. I should've explained myself so that you wouldn't have felt the need to rescue your grandmother on your own. I didn't realize how much my secrecy was hurting you. I should have trusted you, too."

Mother says, "We're both sorry, dear. We all made mistakes. I'm just so thankful you and Emera are all right."

"We wouldn't have been without Markus."

She smiles, patting my hand. "And I'm sure your father will remember that when we speak to him."

Father grumbles, pretending to frown. "You're acting like I'm going to scare him."

Her eyes twinkle. "You can be a bit overprotective when it comes to your little girls."

"When have I ever?"

"There was that Schneider boy you chased out of the palace last summer when he kissed Maddie on the cheek."

He crosses his arms. "He deserved it. Maddie is too innocent to know how to deal with boys like that."

Mother and I exchange amused looks.

"Then there was Prince Ryker who asked permission to court Maddie."

"He was too old for her," he grumbles.

"They're the same age, darling. And before that—"

"Enough, enough." He waves down my mother's next point. "I promise I'll be on my best behavior."

I kiss him on the cheek. "Just give him a fair chance. He loves me as much as I love him. You'll see."

Mother sniffs and touches a finger to the corner of her eye, while Father blinks rapidly.

He says, "We'll see if the boy can live up to the legend."

Instead of going to my room to freshen up for tea, I slip down to the hallway where we house visiting dignitaries. Just as General Kier promised, two of the Lorrian guards that helped the Wolf King regain his throne are stationed outside two rooms. Nicko and Terel snap to attention as I walk up to them.

They both bow. "Princess."

I smile at the two young men. "I think we've been through too much to stand on formality."

Terel chuckles. "Not if General Kier catches us. That woman will have us on latrine duty for the rest of our lives."

Nicko nods vigorously, his eyes wide.

I wrinkle my nose. "There's latrine duty?"

"Usually only when we're traveling. But the general will make an exception and have us digging latrines every day if she thinks we're not taking our duties seriously."

"Ah." *Hmm, that complicates my plan.* "Well, I wouldn't want to do anything that gets you into trouble. I guess, um, I should go." I look longingly at the doorways, trying to guess which one Markus is behind.

Terel looks at Nicko. "I think it's time to patrol the hallway, don't you?"

Nicko wrinkles his forehead. "What do you mean? We're supposed to stand guard."

"Yes. And part of that is patrolling the hallway." Terel raises his eyebrows.

"Wha—oh, yes. Patrol. Yes, time to patrol." Nicko snaps to attention, then turns smartly on his heel and marches away, his back to me.

Terel shakes his head with a small laugh. He inclines his head to the nearest door, then turns and walks the opposite direction from Nicko, whistling a soft tune.

I slip into the room and press my back against the door. "Markus? Are you here?"

"Lisette?" His head pops out from the bathing chamber. "What are you doing here? Did something happen?" He wipes his face clean with a towel.

He looks so handsome freshly scrubbed, his dark hair damp and curling at the ends. My mind goes completely blank and I blurt out this first thing I can think of. "You shaved again. But you shaved this morning."

His ears turn red. "Um, I thought it would be appropriate since we're having supper with your family." He tosses the towel back into the bathing room and then crosses to me. "Did something happen?"

I take a deep breath, letting the spicy scent of his soap wash over me. Unfortunately, it doesn't help my brain power. "No, I mean, yes. I mean, everything is fine. I wanted to see you. I missed you."

"It's only been an hour, and you'll see me at supper. That's not a lot of time to miss me. Are you sure that's it?" His lips twitch.

I poke him in the chest. "You just want me to say it again."

He grins. "I do like hearing it."

Markus brushes a soft kiss against my lips, leaving them tingling. I pull him down for a deeper kiss as he slides his fingers into my hair. My heart stutters, then kicks into a full gallop.

I pull away with a gasp. "Come on." I grab his hand and inch open the door.

Terel looks over his shoulder, then claps Nicko on the shoulder. "Time for another patrol."

I mouth 'thank you' as the two men walk down the

hallway together. Markus and I dash the other direction, then I lead him through a maze of hallways to a small side door. We tumble out of the palace onto a small dirt path. After a few minutes of walking, we're in my favorite meadow. A breeze stirs the warm air, the tall grasses waving. A bird lands on the stone wall, tilting its head at the odd creatures visiting its hunting ground. Markus indulges my antics, holding off his questions until we're sitting behind the low wall and hidden from view.

Once we're settled on the ground, he takes my hand. "You're worrying me. Did it go that badly with your parents?"

"The opposite of bad. I can hardly believe it." I quickly fill him in on the conversation. "Assuming you don't completely mess up, my parents are prepared to give their blessing."

"So you're saying I can still get out of marrying you?" Markus winks at me. "After all, you promised me an introduction to Maddie for taking you to the Wolf Palace. She's the firstborn."

Laughter bubbles up in my chest as I smack his arm. "Maddie's much too smart to fall for you. Besides, we both know you're getting the better deal here. I'm a sophisticated princess from a wealthy kingdom. You're a barbarian prince. Clearly, I should be the one rethinking my choices."

"Hmm, good point. But my father has his heart set on you joining our family. You don't want to anger a barbarian."

I pretend to think it over. "There are two of you. Mayhap I should reconsider which brother I chose. Fredrik will sit on the throne someday."

He tugs on my curl. "Don't you dare. This barbarian

prince is very much in love with you and I would hate to have to fight him.”

“I would never.” I wrap my arms around his neck. “Besides, he’s terrible at bickering. I would be bored within a day.”

“Then I have nothing to worry about.”

“You never did.” I softly nuzzle his cheek. “When do you grow the beard back? “

“Miss it?” His breath catches as I trail my fingers along his skin. “After we’re married. Unless you prefer me clean shaven.”

“It has its advantages.” I kiss the corner of his jaw, enjoying the way his heart stutters at my touch. “But I like the beard too.”

“Are you trying to drive me crazy?”

“Yes. Is it working?”

“Definitely.” With a growl, he pulls me into his lap. The fire in his eyes blazes.

His kiss steals my breath. I can taste the sweet saltiness lingering on his lips. A heat coils in my belly. His body is warm and solid against mine. Softness and desire and passion mix, leaving me desperate for more. He’s flames and energy and passion all wrapped into one. My body melts into fire.

When I’m sure I’ll explode, a shudder ripples through him and he pulls gently away. I let out a shaky breath as he presses his forehead to mine.

He takes a deep breath. “Anytime you want to sneak me away to do that, just know I’m willing to go. But only because it makes you happy.”

“That’s one of the things I like best about you. You’re always thinking of me.” I giggle as I snuggle against his chest, laying my head on his shoulder.

"I got used to spoiling you while you were recovering. It's a hard habit to break."

"I'm not complaining. But you'll probably feel differently after we've been married for ten years and I remind you it's your turn to feed our pet wolf, or you lose another argument because we both know I'm always right."

"No, I don't think I will." Markus kisses my fingertips, sending delicious shivers across my skin.

"You're only saying that because we're not officially betrothed yet," I tease him. "Once we are, you'll realize what a brat I am."

"I'm already well aware. The only reason we're not betrothed is because I want to do this properly. According to your customs, I need to speak with your father first." A slow, tender smiles spreads across his face.

I would die for that smile. "Who told you that?"

His ears go red again. "Your grandmother."

"You asked Oma about our betrothal customs?" He's adorably traditional.

"I wanted to do it right." He shrugs, the blush spreading to his cheeks. "I didn't have a lot of options since nobody in our kingdom knows Lorrian royal customs, and General Kier might've stabbed me."

I look up at him from under my lashes. "Is that all that's stopping you? He's already said he approves."

He traces my lips with his fingers. "He hasn't officially."

"Since when do we play by the rules?"

"You make a very persuasive argument. But if we don't follow your kingdom's customs, then we'll have to do something else." His pleased tone clues me in he's already come up with something.

It's just like Markus to think about these things. "And what are your customs?"

"We'd be betrothed when you accepted the bracelet, and then there's a simple ceremony that can be performed privately or in front of family and friends. But since we're from different kingdoms, I thought we could do something that's unique to us." He reaches inside his shirt and pulls out a small satchel. Inside is a large carved ruby ring with a silver band.

He takes my hand. "It was my mother's. My father gave it to her on their wedding day. He gave it to me for the day I could finally ask you to marry me." His eyes, so intent, makes my stomach jump. "Lisette, my love. I told you before the bracelet was my promise to you there would never be anyone else for me. That I was bound to you. With this ring, I'm asking you to bind yourself to me, too. You found me when I was lost. You showed me how to be brave and leap without looking. I want us to always walk beside each other and have adventures, no matter where the path leads. Nobody will ever love you as much as I do. I promise to quarrel with you, and make you laugh, and buy you a cup of spiced chocolate in every village we visit. I will always be myself with you, and I want you to always be true to yourself. If you fall, I will catch you." He slides the ring on my finger. "Will you marry me?"

I can't do anything but stare helplessly into his beautiful eyes. My heart knows—this one, he's for me. If anything can last forever, I'll always love Markus. Our love may change over the years, but it will always be there, strong, binding us together.

"Lisette?" His hand cups my cheek. "You don't have to answer now. I know this is sooner than you expected and

I—"

I fling myself into his arms, holding on with all of my being, kissing him desperately. I didn't realize how gray the world was until he walked in, bringing all the colors with him. He won my heart. Touched it, changed it. Changed me. Love found me, and I'll never let it go.

Trying to pull him even closer, I lose myself in the kiss, pouring all my love and happiness into it. The sounds escaping my throat seem to drive Markus wild. His hands hold me, tracing my shape, the line of my spine, the curve of my hips. My name tangles on his lips.

We finally break apart, both gasping. I clutch his shirt, trying to keep from attacking him again. If I kiss him now, I'll burst into flames on the spot.

He brushes a strand of my hair back, his hands lingering on my skin. "Is that a yes?"

"I have to think about it." I nip his neck with a laugh. "Of course, it's a yes. I love you."

A blissful smile bursts out, the joy on his face making my heart flutter. He cradles my face in his hands. "I love you. Don't ever doubt it, not for a moment."

"You'll have to keep reminding me. You know how forgetful I can be."

"I think I can manage that."

"And let me win all the arguments."

He chuckles and shakes his head. "Never. You'd get bored with me."

I press my hand against his heart. "I could never be bored with you. Who else will let me have pet wolves or teach me to throw a hand axe?"

He lifts an eyebrow. "I don't recall promising you that."

"You will. You can't say no to me." I give him a sassy

grin.

"You must be confusing me with someone else."

I tug him closer. "Let's find out."

***

Note from the Author: Word of mouth is crucial for any new author. If you enjoyed the book, please leave a review on Amazon, Goodreads, or your favorite review site. Even a few words make a huge difference and are greatly appreciated!

Thank You!

Amanda Kaye

Want more Lisette and Markus? Sign up to my newsletter to get an exclusive BONUS EPILOGUE for more flirting and steamy kisses:

https://www.amandakayebooks.com/wolves-blades-subscribe/

ALSO BY AMANDA KAYE

To hear about the next exciting release from Amanda Kaye,
sign up for her newsletter at:
AmandaKayeBooks.com/subscribe-now/

<u>Blades Series</u>

Cinders & Blades (short story)

Briars & Blades

Wolves & Blades

Beasts & Blades

Sirens & Blades

Trails & Blades

<u>Other Short Stories</u>

An Oath of Fire

Slithers & Swords

Restless Tides

ABOUT THE AUTHOR

Amanda Kaye loves plotting new ways to torture her characters and throw them into danger. Nothing makes her happier than reading an amazing book with an awesome character arc; her favorite authors include Mercedes Lackey, Robin McKinley, and Patricia Briggs. She can always find an excuse to buy sparkly nail polishes and chocolate chip cupcakes. Amanda lives in sunny California with her two mini-monsters masquerading as kittens.

Her stories remind you that there's always a silver lining no matter how dark the night. She'd love to chat with you about your favorite books at:

https://www.amandakayebooks.com/subscribe-now/